## Praise for Rachel Rowlands

'I absolutely loved my visit to the cat café . . . For anyone that loves cats, coffee and romance.'

READER REVIEW ✭✭✭✭✭

'As cosy and heartwarming as a lap full of kittens!'

M.A. KUZNIAR

'Oh I loved this so much. What a heartwarming and cosy read.'

READER REVIEW ✭✭✭✭✭

'The purrrfect, feel-good romance. I absolutely loved it!'

DONNA ASHCROFT

'You need to read this. It will warm you from the inside, like a soothing mug of hot chocolate.'

READER REVIEW ✭✭✭✭✭

'A really heartwarming book that just makes you feel all warm and fuzzy.'

READER REVIEW ✭✭✭✭✭

'Located in a beautiful setting with great characters. Beautifully written and you can feel the love for cats that this author has.'

READER REVIEW ✭✭✭✭✭

'I devoured this book, and couldn't get enough of it and read it in a few short hours.'

READER REVIEW ✭✭✭✭✭

'Cat lovers everywhere will love this warming tail!! Highly recommended!'

READER REVIEW ✭✭✭✭✭

T0385173

Rachel Rowlands lives in Manchester, England, with her husband and two cats. She grew up devouring any book she could get her hands on, and after earning her degree in English and Creative Writing, she built a career as a freelance editor while working on her own stories in her spare time. When she's not writing or editing, she enjoys playing video games and crying over romance Kdramas.

You can find her on Instagram @racheljrowlands and at racheljrowlands.com.

Also by Rachel Rowlands

*Snowed In at the Cat Café*

# Rachel Rowlands

# Cake Off
## at the
# Cat Café

HODDER &
STOUGHTON

First published in Great Britain in 2025 by Hodder & Stoughton Limited
An Hachette UK company

The authorised representative in the EEA is Hachette Ireland, 8 Castlecourt
Centre, Dublin 15, D15 XTP3, Ireland (email: info@hbgi.ie)

1

Copyright © Rachel Rowlands 2025

The right of Rachel Rowlands to be identified as the Author of the Work
has been asserted by her in accordance with the Copyright,
Designs and Patents Act 1988.

All rights reserved. No part of this publication may be reproduced,
stored in a retrieval system, or transmitted, in any form or by any means
without the prior written permission of the publisher, nor be otherwise
circulated in any form of binding or cover other than that in which it is
published and without a similar condition being imposed on the
subsequent purchaser.

All characters in this publication are fictitious and any resemblance to real
persons, living or dead, is purely coincidental.

A CIP catalogue record for this title is available from the British Library

Paperback ISBN 978 1 399 73804 0
ebook ISBN 978 1 399 73803 3

Typeset in Plantin Light by Manipal Technologies Limited

Printed and bound in Great Britain by Clays Ltd, Elcograf S.p.A.

Hodder & Stoughton policy is to use papers that are natural, renewable
and recyclable products and made from wood grown in sustainable forests.
The logging and manufacturing processes are expected to conform to the
environmental regulations of the country of origin.

Hodder & Stoughton Limited
Carmelite House
50 Victoria Embankment
London EC4Y 0DZ

www.hodder.co.uk

*For my husband, who makes life sweeter —*
*and richer in the only ways that matter*

# Catpurrcino Cat Café Rules

1. If a seat is occupied by a cat, do not move the cat.
2. Please do not pick up the cats, pull them away from equipment, or corner them. But feel free to make a fuss of them and pet them gently.
3. Sanitise your hands before and after touching the cats.
4. Photos welcome – but no flash!
5. No feeding. Cover your food with the covers provided to prevent grabbing paws.
6. Don't carry your hot drinks around. We will bring them to your table.
7. Walk, don't run! We don't want any trampled tails or paws!
8. Only children over the age of eleven are permitted. Supervise children closely, and don't let them play on or climb the cats' equipment.
9. No smoking, vaping, or laser pens.
10. No disturbing a napping cat. (We all like our sleep.)
11. You may fall in love with a cat.
12. Falling in love with a human is optional.

# Chapter 1

Clem stood over the cake, her hands gripping the steel table either side so tightly her knuckles paled. She was *nervous*, although a faint smile ghosted her lips in spite of that. The cake had turned out well: two tiers of pale turquoise icing, a ball of fake yarn and edible string spinning around the middle tier. She'd made miniature versions of the cat café's cats to decorate it; they danced around the edges of the tiers and curled, slept, and played along the icing. Emmie's name was written in silver letters on top, and 'happy birthday' swerved around the rim. The cake was finished off with an iced white bow.

When they cut into it, they'd find a rich and decadent chocolate centre with mint frosting, perfectly fluffy and creamy. Emmie had a fondness for mint chocolate, so Clem had been determined to use it in her cake. She'd taste-tested everything herself, and it would taste like mint chocolate ice cream, the frosting melting onto the tongue. Perfect for summer, which was just around the corner. But would Emmie like it? Would the others, when they presented it to her? Clem clutched the steel table harder. They were going out to a restaurant – Clem, and her colleagues at Catpurrcino, the cat café where she worked as a baker. Clem rarely went to work social events – her nerves always held her back, like a pair of reins being clutched by a nervous rider – but she couldn't exactly say no to this one, when she'd made the birthday cake.

Sylvie, the owner of Catpurrcino, bustled into the kitchen, her heels clack-clacking on the tiled floor and announcing her presence.

'Can I see it now, Clem?' she asked.

When Clem turned, Sylvie was standing on tiptoe to try to see her creation, her auburn hair shining in the overhead lighting. Instead of her trademark Catpurrcino apron decorated with chubby cats, Sylvie was wearing a long black dress and shiny Mary Jane heels, her throat adorned with a silver necklace, and her hair scooped up in an elaborate bun.

'I promise I won't look if you aren't ready yet!' Sylvie continued, pretending to hide her eyes but peeking. 'But we should get going soon—'

Clem laughed. 'No need to peek. You can look properly. It's done now.'

Sylvie shifted her hands, and Clem moved to one side so she could see the cake.

Sylvie gasped, her hands flying to her mouth. 'Oh, Clem! It's amazing!' She hurried over to the cake to observe it from every angle. She pointed at a tiny re-creation of a black cat sitting proudly on the second tier with his tail curled around him. 'You've even added Salem's little diamond shape on his forehead!'

'Of course. It's what makes him unique.'

'It's perfect! Adorable, and so beautifully done. She'll love it.'

'I hope so.'

'You didn't have to go to all this trouble, love.' Sylvie tilted her head to the side. 'You bake all the time here for work!'

'I don't mind. I love baking. And Emmie did a lot to make me feel welcome here when I first started, so . . .' Clem smiled hesitantly. Emmie was Sylvie's niece; she worked at Catpurrcino as a barista and lived above the café in one of Sylvie's flats.

Sylvie reached out and hugged Clem unexpectedly, and Clem squeezed her back after a beat of hesitation. She was glad Sylvie liked the cake as much as she did. But the sweet scent of Sylvie's perfume had her stomach tangling, setting off her nerves again. She drew back from Sylvie and looked down at her apron, patterned with cartoonish cats.

'I should get changed,' said Clem. 'We're leaving soon?'

'Yes, go ahead. There's no one in the staffroom.'

'Let me box up the cake first.'

Once Sylvie had helped her successfully navigate the cake into a box, and a bag large enough to hold it, Clem hurried from the kitchen and weaved her way into the staffroom, closing the door behind her.

It was bright and fun in here, like a kid's nursery room, Clem had always thought: a table set with colourful plastic chairs, a duck-egg-blue fridge covered in magnets shaped like cat paws, and framed photos of the cats adorning the walls. Once, as a joke, Sylvie had added an 'employee of the week' section with a photograph of Binx, his big green eyes looking up at the camera and his soot-grey body in the loaf position. It had remained there ever since because everyone found it so funny.

Tugging off her apron and hairnet, Clem quickly dressed in the clothes she'd brought for Emmie's birthday meal: one of her favourite brown dresses patterned with little orange foxes and a pair of flat shoes. She ran a brush through her hair and fringe and checked her appearance in the mirror by the kitchenette. A dash of nude lipstick and she was done, hooking her bag over her shoulder.

Clem paused by the doorway, pulling in a deep breath to gather herself.

*Just be yourself*, her mum had said, when she'd started working here a couple of years ago. Clem was trying, but it was hard to do sometimes, even now, when her head was filled with buzzing static at the mere thought of stepping outside of her comfort zone.

She met Sylvie in the main café room. Sunshine was spilling through the wide front windows of Catpurrcino, buttery yellow, splashing itself over the cat towers pushed up against the walls and the wooden tables scattered around. Thomas and Lilian were snoozing on a squashy cream armchair, Thomas's huge ginger bulk almost pushing Lilian off the edge, though she didn't seem to mind – her head was tipped sideways as she slept, exposing a fuzzy white chin. This room was large, with a drinks station, counter, and chalkboard menu. Rows of glass cake displays were set up on the countertop, filled with some of Clem's cat-shaped, pastel-coloured biscuits. A door off to the side led into a cosier room, the Cat Lounge, and there were steps leading up to the second café floor.

'Emmie's on her way to the restaurant with Jared,' Sylvie told Clem, tapping away on her phone before shoving it back into her purse. 'You grab the cake and I'll hold all the gates and doors open.'

'Okay,' said Clem, carefully lifting the bag that contained the cake. 'Thanks.'

'Shoo, mischief!' Sylvie said. She waved Salem away, who had made a beeline for Clem's ankles, and he retreated to a nearby chair to watch them, black tail swishing.

The café had a triple-door system to make sure no cats escaped – Sylvie held open the latched gate for Clem. They navigated their way through, and through another door, and into the small gift shop and reception area, which was quiet and empty since the café was closed. When they finally passed the huge poster of the café's rules and stepped out into the street, Clem felt that swimming sensation again. It was Friday evening, and so the restaurant was bound to be busy. She imagined the eyes on their table when they sang Emmie happy birthday, the attention her cake might get, and she wished, stupidly, that she had a reason to go home. To curl up with her cat, Misha, and a Netflix show and a cup of tea, where she felt safe.

It was April, not long after Easter, and the cherry tree outside the café was in full, glorious bloom, its petals spilling a pink dusting onto the road and pavements like the frosting of a cake.

*Everything is going to be fine,* she told herself, trying to turn her worried thoughts around, like she'd been taught. *No one is going to judge me.* She tried to focus on the rustling of the cherry blossom tree, the soft petals whispering, like it was comforting her.

Their taxi was pulling up across the road, slowing to a crawl by the kerb.

'Come on, love,' Sylvie called, already glancing both ways to cross the street, some loose pink petals falling onto her shoulders. She dusted them off. 'You'll have to be careful with the cake in your lap so it doesn't tip sideways!'

★

The restaurant was, as Clem had been expecting, extremely busy. There were only a few restaurants in Oakside that weren't pubs, and so this place was a popular spot for both locals and the tourists and hikers who visited Cumbria year-round. It was large enough for big groups – and there were more than a few of those this evening. The noise when they stepped over the threshold was like a jolt to the eardrums. Nearby tables were filled with people eating and drinking, waitstaff hurrying to and fro with plates and trays of cold drinks. Clem clenched onto the cake bag, following Sylvie as one of the staff escorted them to their table. She kept repeating her mantra, though her body had already tensed, inching towards a fight-or-flight response. *Everything is going to be fine.*

They were taken through an archway into a wide space, where a table sat beneath an array of foliage, fake flowers and paper lanterns set off by a vibrant green light. Emmie was already there with her boyfriend Jared, and she leaped to her feet to greet them, enveloping Sylvie in a hug. Emmie had her light-brown hair curled into ringlets, and Jared had pulled his back into a smart ponytail. He waved at Clem and she returned the gesture.

Clem scanned the room; the tables either side of them were full to bursting, and it was a squeeze in here. A waiter rushed by, nearly knocking into Clem's bag and dashing off an apology before hurrying away to the kitchens. She set the cake bag down on their table and squeezed into a high-backed seat, feeling a tightness in her chest that she tried to ignore.

'What's that? It's big,' Emmie said, leaning over to squeeze Clem's shoulder because she couldn't get through the chairs to hug her.

Clem opened her mouth to reply, but Sylvie spoke first: 'When everyone's here, we'll show you, won't we, Clem?'

Sylvie beamed down at Clem and took the seat opposite Emmie.

Clem nodded, grateful for the distraction – maybe if she talked, she wouldn't think so hard, wouldn't notice the roaring of laughter coming from a nearby table and the way it made her jaw clench. 'Have you had a nice birthday, Emmie?' she asked her.

'Oh, lovely, thanks!' Emmie shot Jared a smile. 'Jared made me breakfast in bed – poached eggs. I'm terrible at them, but his are always perfect. Perks of being with a former chef.' She gave an affectionate eye-roll, and Jared squeezed her hand across the table.

'Did you get any nice presents?' said Clem. Talking was good; talking helped take her mind off the nerves.

'Ooh yes, a new sticker machine, some nice pens for my illustrations—'

The table behind them roared with laughter, making Clem jump, one man pounding the table with his fist.

*Relax*, she told herself. *They're only laughing.* Something she seriously needed to do more of, if her brain would only let her. *They're not laughing at you. Relax. Enjoy yourself. Have fun.* That was what she was here for. She painted on a smile, did some deep breathing, keeping her hands gripped together in her lap.

The rest of the staff filtered into the restaurant: Faye, who worked part-time at the café while attending university here in Cumbria, and another recently hired barista Clem didn't know very well yet, Matt – who was so tall his head almost touched the fake foliage hanging over their heads. He grinned at Clem as he took a seat next to her. Kaitlyn had arrived too; she looked after the reception and gift shop. She waved at Clem and sat on the other side of the table. The only people who were missing were Miles and Sophie, their cat caretakers – both of them had plans and couldn't make it.

Clem fidgeted with her napkin as she watched everyone exchanging greetings and small talk. When a waitress came to take their orders, she asked for a glass of white wine with lemonade and went for the least messy food item on the menu.

Before the waitress could leave, Sylvie beckoned to her, cupping her hands around her mouth. When the waitress leaned down, Sylvie whispered something in her ear. The woman nodded, whipped the cake bag from the table and took it away.

When the food eventually came, it was delicious. Clem focused on the taste of each bite, feeling comforted now her belly was being filled with rice and vegetable spring rolls. Matt was chattering away to her about the café book club that he helped run with Sylvie.

'We're doing a book about a homeless man who befriended a cat next,' Matt was saying enthusiastically. 'Sylvie told me about it and I read it so quickly – she never did it for book club so we thought we'd get everyone to read it. It really shows how animals can help us through tough times . . .'

Now, cats, Clem could talk about. It was probably why the cat café had been the one job she'd been able to stick at. Tuning out the rest of the room, she nodded. 'There was one about a cat and dog with a special bond, too – a true story. I can't remember the title. I'd have to look it up . . .'

Clem took a swig of her wine and lemonade, the sharp twang hitting the back of her throat. They were quiet, both sipping at their drinks, the rest of the group talking around them.

'You didn't have anyone to come with tonight?' Matt asked her, and glanced across the table at Emmie and Jared, who were sharing another affectionate hand-squeeze atop the table. 'Or do you have someone to go home to?'

Clem shook her head. 'No, it's just me.'

She absolutely *wasn't* going to add that the 'someone' she had to go home to was her mother, because she still lived at home in her mum's cottage in her mid-twenties. So far, she had avoided her colleagues knowing anything about her living situation – and she intended to keep it that way, if she could, though word might get around on the Oakside grapevine soon enough.

'Same here.' Matt sighed, lifting his beer and swirling the remaining liquid in the bottom. 'Just cats and books for now. Probably more trouble than it's worth anyway, eh?' He drained the glass in one gulp and winked at her. 'Cats are better than people.'

'I'll drink to that,' said Clem, clinking her glass against his.

His words remained with Clem like a persistent echo. Faye hadn't brought anyone with her either, but Clem knew she was seeing someone at uni.

If Clem *did* meet someone, what would they think of her, living with her mum at twenty-five? Would they look down on her? When she was younger, twenty-five had seemed so *mature*, a whole lifetime into the future. She'd had this image of herself being married with a child by this age, which was laughable to her now. She still felt like a child herself, and not ready to cope with those kinds of responsibilities.

Her thoughts were interrupted by singing breaking out around the table, quiet at first and growing louder as everyone else joined in. *Happy birthday to you* . . . Clem caught on and joined in the song, her voice catching when she saw her cake had been brought out by the wait-staff, a few lit candles stuck carefully in the top.

They cheered and clapped, and Emmie squealed with delight when the cake was placed in front of her. When she blew out the candles and the laughter and singing subsided, she turned to them all, her eyes shining.

'This cake – it's *amazing*,' she said. 'Clem! Did you . . . ?'

Sylvie turned to Clem, a wide smile on her face. 'Yes, it was our very own Clem! She made it for you. I was going to hire someone – I figured she'd be sick of baking and not want to work in her free time, but she insisted.'

Clem smiled, a pinprick glow of pride in her chest spreading as everyone looked at her in awe. 'I never get sick of baking,' she said honestly. 'I enjoyed making it. And you deserve it; you work so hard.'

'Clem, *thank you*,' said Emmie. 'It's almost too pretty to eat.'

'Right?' said Jared. 'And look how accurate the cats are!' He pointed at the iced figure of Salem and the white diamond shape on his forehead.

'Well, you don't have to eat it straight away,' said Clem, 'but if you want to taste the mint chocolate filling . . .'

'*Mint chocolate?*' Emmie stared at her, and examined the cake, as if looking for evidence of the minty-ness. 'Clem, seriously, it's a dream – thank you.'

'You could start a cake business with this level of talent,' Kaitlyn agreed. 'My kids would kill for one of these on their birthdays.'

'I'd like to someday,' said Clem, her cheeks warm. Her whole body now enveloped in a happy glow, the pinprick having spread to a wave, washing over her. *This* was why she baked. Not only to see the creation come to life – the puzzle of getting everything right, the ingredients coming together – but to see other people experience what she'd made, the joy it brought to them.

'Speaking of talent,' said Sylvie. 'I'd been meaning to ask you something, Clem.'

'What is it?'

'Have you heard of *Whisked Away*?'

'The online baking show?'

Clem had seen the clips and watched a couple of episodes – she posted short videos of her own creations online too, and there was plenty of talk about *Whisked Away* in her circles there. It was set up by a man who made his living online as a baking influencer. The baking competition pitted small businesses against each other for prize money. She hadn't known Sylvie was aware of it.

'That's the one. It's coming here, to the Lake District,' Sylvie explained.

'You're kidding.'

'We've been getting tagged in the announcement for days – people suggesting we enter. And I thought . . . well, you have so much talent, love. I think you'd do well and could represent Catpurrcino as part of the contest.'

'You want *me* to enter?' Clem said, her breath hitching.

'Yes. There's a £100,000 reward. Half goes to the winning baker and half to the small business. The contest is done in pairs, with you doing the baking and me super-vising on behalf of the business – I'm sure you already know if you've seen it. We could make some upgrades to make Catpurrcino more accessible. You could use your portion for whatever you like.'

Equal parts excitement and dread seized Clem. A whirling excitement because . . . what an opportunity. It could change her life. She could plan a baking business, like she'd always dreamed of, maybe study again, pay for some business courses to learn the ropes. And . . . *move out* of her mum's cottage.

But . . . going to a restaurant with her colleagues had been a monumental effort. How could she go on a baking show that would be put online for hundreds of thousands of people to see? That would be filmed? *What if I got into the contest and messed it all up?* She tried to turn the thought around again, spinning it the other way, revers-ing the anxiety-led thinking. *What if I didn't mess it up? What if I did well?* But the thought didn't feel as authentic as the anxious one.

'I mean . . . it's popular. There are loads more talented bakers than me so I doubt I'd be picked . . .' Clem fum-bled, because Sylvie was waiting for her to say something. And she didn't want to share her real feelings in front of everyone.

'You need to give yourself more credit,' Sylvie said. 'You *are* incredibly talented!'

Before Clem could say anything else, the rowdy table from before were getting up to leave, having ordered more drinks after their main meal and dessert. The tightness of the space between tables meant Clem had to tuck her chair in slightly to let a particularly large man pass.

'Thanks, love,' he grunted. He paused mid-way through squeezing past her chair, glancing down. 'Nice dress! Foxes! They're vermin, but at least they kill the rats, eh?'

He roared with laughter, clapping her shoulder with a horribly warm hand, making Clem's neck feel hot. As he went by, his foot caught on Matt's chair leg as he attempted to manoeuvre it out of the way. The man stumbled, struggling to straighten himself in the small gap.

And somehow, the leftover beer in the man's glass ended up all over Clem's front, wetness pooling over the foxes on her dress. His laughter was still echoing in her ears. *Ha, ha, ha*, like water dripping from the roof of a cave.

The sudden, sticky coating and wetness made the anxiety rise inside her like a dragon ready to belch flames. It clawed at her throat, made it tighten until she couldn't find oxygen.

She needed out of this tight space – and fast.

# Chapter 2

The man was apologising profusely as he squeezed away past Clem's seat. The smell of the beer was overpowering, climbing her nostrils. Matt was trying to help her mop up the mess, throwing napkins at her and shouting down the table for more. 'Don't worry, Clem, we'll sort you out!' he was saying. The noise, the activity, the attention, the overwhelming curveball Sylvie had thrown her way – she had become like a particularly crumbly cake, ready to disintegrate beneath someone's fingers.

When the other group had finally gone, and she'd held it together long enough to let them pass, Clem scraped her chair back and mumbled, 'Bathroom.'

She snatched up her bag and jacket from her chair, and darted away from the table so quickly she nearly barrelled into a waitress carrying two plates of hot, steaming noodles. The toilets were through the other room, and up a set of wooden stairs. She hurried past more rows of filled tables, keeping her head down, trying to breathe even though the air felt cloying and thick.

When she burst inside, the toilets were mercifully empty – and clean. She splashed water on her dress with shaking hands, hoping to erase the smell of booze, rubbing over one of the little orange foxes. All that did was remind her of the booming, sarcastic laughter and the man's comments, grating against her eardrums. *Nice dress! Foxes! They're vermin, but at least they kill the rats, eh?*

*He was joking,* she tried to tell herself. But it was only bringing her back to that time, with her friend Genie, the laughter ringing in her ears at her expense. It was like someone was holding her in a tight fist.

Positioning her dress under the hand dryer only made her feel hotter and sicklier, and she suddenly wished she hadn't eaten as much as she had. *Oh no, please don't be sick, please.* All she could think about was home, and her cat Misha, and her cosy, comfortable bedroom.

The door to the toilets burst open, and Clem kept her back to it, not wanting a stranger to see her trembling hands, her lack of composure. The cacophony from the restaurant flooded in: noisy conversation, children crying, the clatter of knives and forks on plates, drinks being set down. It set her teeth on edge.

As the heat and roar of the hand dryer petered out, a tentative voice said, 'Clem? Are you okay?'

She knew that voice. And she *really* didn't want to turn around – this was so embarrassing – but she drew back her shoulders and tried to paste on a normal expression, even if it did come out as more of a grimace. Clem turned to find Emmie standing behind her, a worried frown on her face.

'I'm okay,' she said. Her voice was an empty shell, giving her away, and a clamp was fastened around her chest, trapping in her breath.

'You sure? I saw what happened.'

'Just . . . the smell . . .' Clem gestured down, at the damp patch where the beer had spilled on her dress, still visible. She attempted a deep breath but she could still smell it, as if it were trying to claw its way into her nose. A lump rose, hard and painful, in her throat. She didn't want to fall apart here in front of Emmie, least of all on her birthday. This was meant to be a celebration.

'Here,' said Emmie. Clem hadn't noticed it right away, but she'd brought her little star-shaped handbag with her, hooked into the crook of her arm. Emmie pulled open the zipper and dug around inside, holding out a small packet of wet wipes. And in true Emmie fashion, the packet was decorated with little pink bows and a cartoon cat. 'Use these. They're scented so they might help?'

'T-Thank you . . .' Clem took them, clenching her hands around them, hoping Emmie hadn't noticed the shaking.

'Keep them. Freshen yourself up.' Emmie zipped her handbag up again and smiled, tucking her light brown hair behind her ear. 'I better get back. Matt wanted me to cut the cake so we could all have some, but I thought I'd make sure you were okay first. Take your time – I'll save you a piece.'

'Okay . . . thanks, Emmie.'

Emmie left, the door banging shut behind her, and Clem's shoulders sagged. She didn't feel any calmer, even as she rubbed a scented wet wipe across her dress, because her brain was ringing with alarm that Emmie had seen her, acting like this over something so normal. Could she face them all, after that? She didn't know if she could. Her throat was burning.

She pulled out her mobile, cycling through her gallery for videos of Misha. Back pressed against one of the walls, she watched a video – on mute – of Misha leaping excitedly around Clem's bedspread, chasing the crinkles in the bedsheets. She swiped to the next one: Misha sitting in her lap, blinking up at her lovingly, her long white whiskers pronounced, Clem's fingers rubbing her stripy head. She tried to imagine she was at home in that spot right now, Misha's silky fur under the pads of her fingers.

The videos calmed her somewhat. Enough for her to feel ready to leave the toilets.

She ordered a taxi first – she hadn't brought her car so she could have some wine – and was soon heading back downstairs, through the throngs of tables, and outside, grateful Sylvie and the others couldn't see her from their position in the restaurant. When she was in the taxi, she would text Sylvie and say she was sorry but she'd gone home early. She was sure Emmie would understand. Clem didn't doubt she'd picked up on how off-kilter she was feeling. And Clem had stayed for the main meal – that meant something, didn't it? If she tried to go back now, after that bump in the evening . . . She couldn't do it.

She stood outside, away from the door and on the corner, beneath the eaves. The whiff of alcohol on her clothes was still making her uneasy, though the orange citrusy scent from the wet wipes had masked most of it. The spring air was mild but not too stifling yet, and she was glad of the breeze rustling the trees across the street, bringing with it fresh air.

She could still smell the beer and her hands were shaking, every loud and rowdy voice inside setting her teeth on edge. She glanced at her lock screen, and Misha's striped face, but it didn't have the same soothing effect as it had earlier. Clem fumbled in her bag, searching for the raspberry gum she often carried with her.

'Where is it?' she muttered under her breath. The tremors in her hands made her clumsy, and her mini hairbrush and lipstick clattered to the pavement.

She was about to bend to pick them up, but someone beat her to it, holding them out to her. When she looked up, there was a man standing before her. He was flooded by the sinking sunlight, and Clem wasn't sure if the hitch in her chest was the anxiety, or those piercing green eyes framed by thick, dark lashes.

He was older than her, though perhaps not by much, with pale skin cast slightly warm-toned in the light of the setting sun. He had messy dark brown hair – artfully messy, as though done with purpose – thick brows and a scattering of shadowy stubble to match. To say he was downright gorgeous was an understatement.

'Easy there, don't want to lose the essentials,' he said smoothly, holding the items out to her.

'Th-Thanks,' she said, taking her things from him and doing her best not to drop them as she shoved them in her bag, her phone wedged under her armpit.

'Are you okay?' he asked gently, and glanced back towards the restaurant, tracking the route she'd taken.

Had he seen her rushing outside? The idea that strangers had probably witnessed her idiocy as well made her feel light-headed. But the way he'd picked up her things, casually asked if she was okay . . . It was almost calming to her, putting her at ease, his tones soothing. The expression on his face was one of concern, not mockery. She let out a shaky laugh, glad he wasn't the type to laugh at someone for being so vulnerable.

'I'm fine. Thanks.'

She finally picked out the gum she'd been searching for and unwrapped it, popping a piece into her mouth, focusing on the burst of gooey flavour as her teeth broke the shell. Even though she felt a fraction calmer, she couldn't still her quaking fingers as she straightened up, phone in her hand again, almost dropping it. It wouldn't be long before her taxi got here and she could escape this evening altogether, although she couldn't help but feel as though it would be a shame to escape this gorgeous man. A part of her wanted to stay, drawn to those forest-green eyes of his.

He half-turned to the restaurant and hesitated. 'Did you come here with someone?' he asked. 'It looks like you're not feeling well. Do you need—'

'Oh! N-No, I just ordered a taxi, so I'm going home anyway . . . But thank you.'

Her taxi was already here, rolling up to the kerb. Turning from the stranger, she hurried to clamber inside. When she looked out of the window as they pulled away, the man was gone, disappearing inside the restaurant. Probably going back to a girlfriend – with good looks like that, there wasn't a single doubt in her mind that he was taken.

Clem focused again on the chewing of her gum and the raspberry flavour rushing over her tongue, unable to get the image of him out of her mind.

★

'You're home early!' Clem's mum called as soon as Clem stepped over the threshold of their tiny cottage. That was the only problem with a home where the front door led directly into the living room: you couldn't exactly sneak inside or get to your room without being spotted. 'I didn't expect you for another hour or two at least. Did it go okay?' she asked.

Clem hung her bag and jacket on the hooks behind the door, and manoeuvred around the umbrella stand to drop into an armchair to the left of the sofa. Her mum was sitting in the centre of the settee, with a cup of tea and a worried frown line across her forehead. The TV by the brick fireplace was playing a David Attenborough documentary, his smooth, calming tones filling the room, underscored by the sound of birds chittering. Her mum reached for the remote and turned the volume down.

'Don't turn down Attenborough on my account,' said Clem, sinking back into the chair. 'It's the new one you wanted to see, isn't it?'

'Never mind that. How did tonight go?'

Clem picked at a loose thread on the cushion sandwiched beside her. She'd come home with the window open in the taxi, which had eased the sickliness she'd been feeling. By the time the cottage came into view, she felt better. 'I came back early. After dessert. They brought the cake out, and a guy spilled his drink on me. He was laughing, and . . .' She trailed off. It sounded so silly now, in hindsight, and in the cosy warmth of the cottage.

'But you stayed through dessert!' said her mum. 'That's good. And you went – even though you didn't want to.'

'I *did* want to,' she clarified. 'Even if my brain was trying to tell me I didn't. I feel bad for not staying.' She'd also texted Sylvie in the taxi on the way home, apologising for leaving so soon, claiming a headache. She felt bad about that, too.

'Well, maybe next time you will. Small steps. Gradual, remember?'

'I just wonder how long I'll be stuck on *gradual*.'

Her mum drained her tea and set it on the table, beside a stack of magazines. She'd been subscribed to the same nature magazine since Clem was a child; the space under her bed was filled with them and she often had to recycle some for lack of space. Clem was surprised the magazine still existed.

'You should be proud,' said her mum. 'It wasn't easy for you.'

'I know,' said Clem, watching David Attenborough talk quietly on the screen as he wandered through a light-dappled forest. 'It's just . . . well . . . Sylvie . . . She asked me to enter a baking contest. To represent the café. *Whisked Away*, it's called.'

'That's wonderful!'

'I know, but . . . It'll be posted online.' She quickly explained about *Whisked Away*.

'But, Clem, this could be an amazing opportunity for you! I know you love the café, but it's not what you truly want to do, is it? Not forever.'

That was true. She'd once wanted to work in conservation, with animals, before that was ruined for her. She'd turned to baking as a means of relaxing and easing her anxiety; turned out, she actually loved it and could see herself doing it for a long time. Her dreams lay outside of Catpurrcino, in the prospect of starting her own cake business.

'I . . . don't know if I can,' she managed. 'Look what happened tonight. I came home early because people were laughing and someone spilled a drink on me.' Her throat ached at the admission – she was so stupid.

Her mum shook her head, a gentle smile playing around the edges of her mouth. 'You need more self-belief. That's how you'll reach your dreams. Not by putting yourself down. Sometimes, dreams take a path you don't expect.'

Clem smiled tentatively. Her mum was a photographer – originally, landscapes and wildlife. But when she decided she wanted to do it for a living, she shifted, swapping kestrels, red deer, and sheep for weddings and family portraits out in nature instead. That was the more profitable path and she'd ended up doing well, and enjoying the work just as much.

'This could be that for you, Clem,' said her mum. 'The path you don't expect.'

'Have you been talking to Jared's mum?' Clem joked. Clem had never met her, but she'd heard about her tarot reading from Emmie. 'Want another?' she asked, motioning at the mug her mum had emptied of tea.

'Sure. Thanks.'

Clem headed into the little kitchen. It was small in here, too, with a hodgepodge of weighed-down wooden shelves, and appliances, including Clem's electric whisk, crammed the worktops. The window ledge was lined with her mum's plants, the walls decorated with wildlife photography in wooden frames, some of them crooked. Clem had baked more things in here than she could remember but she longed for a space that was entirely her own.

She boiled the kettle and set to work making tea for them both. When she was done and had given her mum her fresh cup of tea, she retreated to her room. Misha was there, curled on Clem's pillow by the wooden headboard, sleeping. When she heard Clem come inside, the cat yawned widely, and hopped down to greet her, threading her tail and her stripy body around Clem's ankles.

Whatever remaining tension Clem had been carrying in her shoulders slid away.

'Hi, little one,' said Clem, setting her tea down and scratching the cat on the chin. Misha pushed her face into Clem's hands, exposing her teeth, as if grinning happily at her touch.

Clem's chest gave a squeeze. She was glad to be back here. But this feeling of needing to move on – she couldn't shake it. Most of the people she knew who were her age had moved out – or moved away entirely, trading the Cumbrian fells for cities like London, Edinburgh and Manchester.

She needed to grow up but here she was, standing in her childhood bedroom: with the hedgehog-print bedspread on the single bed pushed against the wall; the stacks of wildlife and baking books in the slightly leaning bookshelf; her corkboard filled with ideas for cakes and cat cookies; the wooden desk she'd been sitting at since high school, scratched and worn. University books from a conservation course she'd never finished were shoved under the bed.

Clem knew things needed to change. She just didn't know how, or if she could do it.

# Chapter 3

From the little alcove inside the restaurant, Lucas watched the taxi pull away and disappear down the street. He hoped the woman in the fox dress was okay – she'd been shaking so badly, those pretty eyes full of fear, as if a bear had cornered her in the middle of the street.

'What are you looking at?' said Dwayne, craning his neck to see out of the restaurant window, too. Splatters of rain were falling on the glass, April living up to its reputation for showers.

Dwayne was Lucas's friend from university – a big, broad-shouldered man with dark skin, a bald head, and a thick fuzzy beard he kept long. He could always be found in a brightly coloured shirt: today's choice was a blue shirt with mini alligators all over it. Lucas didn't know how he managed to look so effortlessly cool, even with some very questionable shirt choices.

'Nothing,' said Lucas quickly.

'Wait, was it a woman? Where?' Dwayne continued to lean to the side, trying to see.

The man cottoned on far too quickly, but he supposed that was a result of knowing one another since their first week of university. 'No,' he lied.

'I always know when you're lying.' Dwayne broke out into a grin. 'Come on. Did you ask for her number?'

The woman's face popped back into Lucas's mind – why was it he could remember every line of her face? But she had been striking: shiny black hair hanging a little above her shoulders, eyes the colour of creamy coffee, and a peachy tint applied to her lips. He wondered what her mouth would look like when she smiled; instead, she'd looked troubled and nervous. Why was that?

'She was a random stranger,' he said. 'Why would I ask for her number?'

'Because that's what people *do* when they like someone?' Dwayne laughed, knocking down the last of his beer and wiping the foam from his beard.

'When did I say I liked her?' he said, rolling his eyes.

'It's obvious from the way you're pining at the window. You should have talked to her.'

'I'm not looking for a relationship, Dwayne.' But the woman's face was imprinted onto his mind like a footprint; she had been beautiful. He couldn't remember the last time he'd sensed that little tug of attraction inside him.

Dwayne lifted his thick eyebrows questioningly. 'You don't want a relationship and yet you have a dog, which is a big commitment—'

'*Exactly*. A dog is more than enough commitment for me, thanks.'

Dwayne groaned. Lucas pushed the image of the woman far from his mind – it didn't matter. Lucas and Dwayne didn't live here in Oakside; they lived in Windermere, where they ran Muddy Paws Café. They'd come for a meeting with a local coffee supplier, since it was a good in-between location to meet – the meeting had just finished, the plates cleared.

'I have too many responsibilities,' Lucas pointed out. 'And I'm not talking about having a dog. Running our business, paying stupid amounts of rent, trying to save up – and I want to help my parents sort themselves out. You know family comes first. They always have. Dating is never worth it.'

It still made him feel low-key irritated when he thought of his last girlfriend. In spite of knowing about his dad, she'd hated him having his phone on him at all times, or sitting with it on the table if they were at a restaurant. And if he didn't reply to her messages within thirty minutes, she took it as some personal affront, rather than realising he was a grown-up with a busy life. She also didn't understand his commitment to Muddy Paws Café; she'd said he was *wasting his time* and his film degree by continuing to work in catering. More than that, she'd screamed at him one day because he cancelled their date – his dad was in pain and his mum too busy at work to pick up painkillers or help him.

If a girlfriend meant neglecting the family who needed him – and the career he was building himself – well, he didn't want one.

'You're missing out,' said Dwayne, shaking his head. 'You'll realise it at some point.'

Lucas shook his head, because he didn't feel he was sorely missing out in life by not diving back into the dating pool. It was full of sharks anyway.

★

'Morning,' Lucas called across Muddy Paws Café. A damp breeze whipped inside along with a new customer.

The skittering of dog's paws on wood was almost louder than the din of conversation coming from the nearby hikers seated around a table, loading up on strong Colombian coffee and thick, iced cinnamon buns before tackling the Brant Fell walking route. An older woman approached the counter in a light rain jacket, her greying hair scooped into a ponytail, with a younger woman at her side. Two dogs were straining at their leads, tails wagging fiercely, tongues lolling out in excitement – one shadow-black, the other like a caramel toffee. The younger woman was trying to keep them restrained.

'What can I get you?' Lucas asked them.

'A flat white for me,' said the older woman, turning to the glass display counter to her left, where baked and sweet treats were set out alongside little handwritten labels. 'And a tea. Go on, I'll have a garlic and tomato flatbread too – looks delicious. Want any snacks?' she added to her friend – or daughter? – who shook her head.

'Sure thing. Baked that flatbread fresh this morning,' said Lucas, offering them a winning smile.

He went to grab a plate, picking up the flatbread with a pair of tongs. As he did so, he couldn't help but overhear a part of their conversation. He glanced up briefly. The older woman was talking rapidly out of the corner of her mouth.

'. . . she's so young though, she can't possibly have "chronic pain".' The woman rolled her eyes heavenwards. She said the phrase with quotation marks, as if she were talking about the existence of a unicorn or the Loch Ness monster. 'Goodness, everyone thinks they have *something* these days! She's exaggerating.'

'I don't think she—'

'Trust me, she is. I've met her type before. Work-shy, lazy. Can't be bothered to work hard like the rest of us.'

Lucas dropped the flatbread – and the plate quickly followed, smashing into dozens of pieces around his feet. The women looked up, startled, and the café quieted in the wake of the breakage. The two of them said something to him, but the conversation was muffled now, like someone had clamped their hands over his ears. Someone cheered jokingly across the café at his blunder, and noise and chit-chat broke out once again.

Dwayne came hurrying out of the back and assessed the situation in a fraction of a second. 'Here, I'll sweep up. You sort out the order—'

'God, what kind of service is this?' the woman muttered, though it was loud enough that Lucas heard, as if she wasn't trying to keep her voice down at all. 'We should have gone to the other place, like I told you.'

Forcing himself to unstick his feet, Lucas gave a shaky half-laugh and moved off to make the drinks. He did it mechanically, though the hissing of the milk frother grated on his ears. When he finally set a tray down on the counter – complete with a fresh plate and flatbread, and the coffee and tea – he had to force a smile, the sensation making his face feel strained with effort. He was sure that didn't do much for their confidence in Muddy Paws Café, but he no longer cared. It wasn't often he lost his cool; he needed to get it together.

By the time the women had taken their tray and were comfortably seated by the window, Dwayne had cleaned up the mess.

'You okay, mate?' he said.

'Yeah, fine . . .'

But he wasn't fine. Comments like that . . . This woman had *no* idea what she was talking about.

'Why don't you take a break?' Dwayne suggested. 'You've been at it non-stop all morning.'

They owned Muddy Paws Café together. Technically, Dwayne owned the largest chunk – he'd put up most of the money to open it using an inheritance, and Lucas had contributed what he could on top of that, which wasn't much. But they had done all the planning and preparing together – had talked about it for years before taking the leap – and Dwayne wouldn't hear of anything but Lucas becoming his business partner and co-owner, regardless of the mismatched investments.

'Thanks,' said Lucas. The mishap had nothing to do with his busy morning, but he didn't say so; repeating what he'd overheard would make him more irritated. He sighed deeply, as if the act could force the irritation from his body. 'I need to call my parents anyway. I was too busy yesterday.'

'How are they doing?'

'Not great. Mum's stressed out.'

'If there's anything I can do—'

'Thanks, but unless we can somehow work a miracle, there isn't much. We're doing everything we can.' Unhooking his apron, he clapped Dwayne on the shoulder gratefully and pushed his way out from behind the counter.

The group of hikers were leaving, tramping out across the wooden floor, raincoats and jackets rustling, and calling out their thanks. A few of them thanked Lucas as they passed or offered him nods and smiles; one was stuffing the remnants of his cinnamon bun in his mouth and dusting the crumbs from his jacket. The door closed behind them.

Lucas went through to the room at the back of the café, which was much larger and filled with framed, artistic photos of various dog breeds, from Dalmatians to miniature poodles and Alsatians. It opened up onto a patio with sets of tables and chairs spread around, and a timber pergola stretching over the space. He headed outside, round the side of the building and into the shade of the trees.

Round here, they also had a special area for Reina, Lucas's golden retriever. The area was sectioned off from the rest by a tall fence and locked gate. Once, it had been an alleyway running from back to front, but they had one of those on the other side anyway, and so they'd revamped it. He unlocked the gate to get in.

The area was long, running the length of the building, and they'd turned it into something of a garden for Reina to inhabit while they were working – that way, she wouldn't be stuck at home on her own all day, and Dwayne or Lucas could walk her on their lunch break. Sometimes he brought her inside but he couldn't always do that, since he couldn't keep an eye on her 24/7. The ground was coated with a mixture of woodchips and bark, and a doghouse had been built for Reina; Lucas had given it a nameplate bearing a yellow crown. Reina's mini garden was bordered with pink, red and yellow snapdragons, sprouting up from flowerpots, and shaded from the sun so she'd be cool when summer fully hit.

As soon as she saw him, Reina raced forward with gusto, fuzzy tail bouncing from side to side. He crouched down to greet her and ruffled her ears. She shoved her black nose into his hands.

'Hey, girl,' he said. 'Hope you've not been too lonely out here.'

She licked his hands, then his face, furiously. He clamped his lips shut to avoid swallowing a mouthful of doggy saliva.

'Good girl,' he said, reaching into his pocket and throwing her a dog treat. She leaped into the air, catching it between her teeth. 'Nice catch.'

He grabbed a rope toy from Reina's kennel and fooled around with her for a bit before fishing into his pocket for his phone. It was bright and sunny, though the mini garden was covered over with a canvas of green leaves, the cloudy blue sky just about peeking through the gaps.

His mum answered on the third ring. 'Hello?' she barked.

She always sounded annoyed when she picked up the phone – endlessly expecting something else to be added to her plate, he guessed. Reina's head tilted when she heard his mum's voice through the speakers.

'Would *that* be your tone if I was the hunk from your latest Netflix show?' he asked smoothly. Her shows were her escapism; more recently, every time he called, she would tell him about those *dishy Vikings* she'd been watching. He liked to tease her about it.

'Oh, shut up,' she said, but her tone was cheerier now. 'How's work?'

'Not bad—'

'Your dad wanted me to apologise,' she said, before he could continue. He could tell that it had been weighing on her mind. 'Your birthday—'

'It's fine,' he said quickly. 'I understand.'

'It's not fine,' she insisted. 'He hasn't seen you properly in ages, and we should have been there.'

He wished they didn't have to repeat the same lines again and again every time there was an occasion his father had to miss. Besides, Lucas was used to this: his teenage years had been threaded with these conversations, especially as his father's condition worsened over time, like cobwebs clustering over their lives. Lucas's graduation from university had been the biggest event he'd missed, his dad nowhere to be seen as he was in the middle of a particularly bad flare-up of pain that day. He didn't blame his dad for any of it, and these days, he didn't feel the ache inside of him anymore when he thought about those missed moments. The only thing he felt was annoyance when he caught silly comments from people who didn't understand. His father had been a hard worker for *decades* – he'd worked as a landscaper, running his own business – until his body began to behave in a way he did not expect. He could no longer do such manual work; there wasn't much he *could* do in terms of work.

'Honestly, Mum, don't worry about it,' said Lucas. 'How's Dad doing?'

She hesitated, and he heard the heavy sigh on the other end of the line, weighted down with a thousand worries. 'Having trouble walking.' Her voice quaked on the next words, as if shaken by the impact of what she was saying. 'We had a letter and they turned him down again. He won't get any financial help for his . . . condition.' She hesitated on the last word, because they still didn't truly know what was wrong.

'*What?*' Lucas ground out. Reina had brought him her rope toy again, so he pulled it, getting into a tug-of-war with her. The dog growled low in her throat and yanked at the rope; he held on. 'Nothing at all?' he said. '*Why?* He's in constant pain!'

'We didn't score highly enough on their points-based system,' his mum said, sounding downtrodden. 'It didn't seem to matter that we had a letter from the doctor about the pain, and how it affects him. And we're still waiting for the referral to the specialist . . .'

Lucas clenched his fist around Reina's rope toy so hard the dog gave another ferocious tug. This had always been the dance they'd played. His dad's symptoms had grown worse the older Lucas got, and doctors had always put this down to stress, overexertion or injuries at work – even though they all knew in their gut it wasn't any of those things. Something more was going on, and they couldn't get to the bottom of it; it was like digging for a needle on a sandy beach.

'There are no other options?' Lucas asked her. Reina finally succeeded in ripping the toy from his grasp, and retreated into her kennel with it, settling down to chew on it.

'Well, I could force him to get a job and be in constant pain,' his mum said, sarcasm laced into every syllable. She laughed wryly. 'It seems like that's what they want him to do.'

Lucas shook his head wordlessly.

'With the rent going up as well . . .' she said softly, 'I don't know how we'll manage.'

She worked at the cat shelter part-time, doubling as an exam invigilator when it was examination season, so she could be flexible with her hours when his dad needed her. The unfairness of it all made his head hurt, made his palms itch with the desire to fix it, to help.

'The landlord knows about Dad's situation,' said Lucas, frowning. 'Why's he raising the rent?'

'He said he has no choice,' his mum explained. 'His mortgage on the property has gone up, so he has to put our rent up, too.'

Lucas clenched his teeth. He'd heard of this happening to other people he knew; he'd hoped it would never happen to them, but hoping wasn't enough. It was why he wished he could grant them some security, wished he could do *something*. Not that wishes and hopes would get him anywhere. 'But that's not your responsibility!' he said. 'I'll talk to the land-lord myself.'

'No, Lucas. I don't want to cause any trouble.'

'Cause any . . . How would you be causing trouble?'

'I don't want to get kicked out!'

'It might happen anyway if you end up struggling to—'

'What else am I supposed to do?' she snapped. 'I want to keep the peace for now so we don't end up having to leave soon. We can't afford to move into a new rented place right now. Your grandparents are in assisted living and their home is tiny. You're house-sharing with Dwayne. My sister is abroad. There's nowhere else for us to go.'

'I'm sure Dwayne wouldn't mind if—' Lucas began, but his mother cut him off.

'No. There's barely enough room for you two and Reina in that house.'

Lucas rubbed the space between his eyebrows, think-ing hard. He wouldn't have minded sleeping on the sofa, but she was right – making it four people, one of whom had chronic pain, and a dog, in a small house? Probably not the wisest solution, and not fair on Dwayne. Lucas had moved in with him because it made sense financially to split bills and to have somewhere to talk Muddy Paws business.

He watched Reina sniff at the air, tongue lolling happily. It was hard to conjure that same level of joy, though he wished he could. Dogs had such an easy life.

His parents had lived in their rented house since he was a child, and it was their home. Why should they lose it now? He should be able to *help* them. But what could he give? He didn't have enough money to pay two sets of rent each month.

'I'm so sorry, Mum,' he said, because it was all he could say.

'We'll figure something out,' she answered quietly. 'I'm sorry for snapping at you. I'm just so . . .'

'It's fine,' he said. 'What about your copyediting? Could that not help?'

'Oh, well . . .' She gave a breathy laugh, and he could imagine her brushing the hair from her face, like she always did when she was thinking. 'I can't finish the course yet. It's on pause until I can come up with the money to pay for the final module. And I can't get work with most of the academic publishers until I finish it – they'll want to see the qualifications first.'

So much red tape, so many barriers and blockages. And they were quickly running out of solutions. He didn't know what else to tell her.

They said their goodbyes, and Lucas hung up feeling like a weight was pressing on him. There had to be *something* they could do next. Something *he* could do to help them.

# Chapter 4

'I have to get back to work, Reina,' said Lucas, kneeling down to scratch the golden retriever behind the ears. She panted out some heavy breaths, licking his hands with her pink tongue. 'See you later.'

Pocketing his phone, he headed out of Reina's garden, across the patio and inside the building. The front section of Muddy Paws Café was quiet, as it was so sunny and bright out today – ideal for hiking the fells – and Dwayne was behind the counter, scrolling on his phone. The floor was sparkling and free of any pawprints; he must have been cleaning.

When Lucas approached, Dwayne beckoned him over urgently.

'Hey, you *have* to see this,' he insisted, shoving his phone at Lucas.

'What?'

He looked at the screen, at a social media post about something called *Whisked Away*. The post was brightly coloured, glaring, in pastel hues of pink, green, and yellow, and it was decorated with a big, splashy image of a cluster of cakes, biscuits, doughnuts and bread, an explosion of multi-coloured confectionery. The text in the caption read:

*Whisked Away:* the travelling baking show where we pit small businesses against each other for prize money! NEXT UP: the Lake District! Who will bake it best and win £100,000?

Lucas gripped the phone harder. 'A hundred *grand*?'

'Yep. Half for the winning baker, half for the business,' Dwayne clarified, pointing to some more text Lucas hadn't read yet, outlining further details. Dwayne's dark eyes were gleaming with the beginnings of the idea taking shape in them both. 'We could enter. You could—'

'Use the money to help my parents.' Lucas's fingers tightened on the phone. It was a dizzying amount of money, more than he'd ever seen in his life. More than he ever *would* expect to see.

Lucas looked down at Dwayne's phone, at the colourful post and the bright text. This could be his parents' ticket out; with this, he could help them in a way he never had before. They could pay for a private health assessment for his dad, put down a deposit on a house, if he teamed up with his mum to apply. He could give them everything they deserved; he could fix things for them.

'Are you in?' said Dwayne, grinning at Lucas.

Lucas's pulse was pounding fast at the base of his throat. 'You don't even need to ask. Of course I'm in.'

★

On her first shift back at Catpurrcino after Emmie's birthday, Clem spent a solid ten minutes in the car park, sitting behind the steering wheel and clenching a squeezy, squishy cat she kept in the glove box. The car park floor was coated in pink petals, blown over from the cherry tree, and they dusted the bonnet of her vehicle like cupcake sprinkles.

Yesterday had been her day off and she'd done nothing but think about Sylvie's invitation to apply for *Whisked Away* and how she'd left Emmie's birthday meal early. Emmie had sent her a text to say she hoped she felt better soon, and she'd save her a piece of the cake. Clem felt so guilty for leaving.

Taking a deep breath, Clem headed inside. Kaitlyn wasn't here yet; Clem tended to arrive before most of the other staff since she had to make a start on baking and prepping early. In the main room of the café, the feeders were already filled with food and water, the TV displaying a video of mice running in and out of a tiny, door-shaped hole. Duchess, the café's ragdoll, was sitting atop the highest cat tower nearby, her gorgeous blue irises barely visible since her black pupils were so enlarged, her attention fixed on the mouse running around on the screen. On a lower rung of the tower, Lilian the calico was asleep, her nose tucked into her tail.

Eric, their stripy tomcat, approached Clem and gave a long mewl to say hello.

'Morning,' she said, getting down on her haunches to stroke behind his ears. He burst into a series of loud purrs and nuzzled into her fingers. 'Sorry, can't stay and give you attention, little guy. Work's calling.' She gave him a few more scritches underneath his chin and made her way into the staffroom.

Sylvie was already there, at the table, an open laptop in front of her. Another closed laptop sat beside it – this one for the staff to use.

'Clem!' Sylvie smiled up at her, the corners of her eyes crinkling. 'I hope you're feeling better?'

'I am, thanks,' said Clem, wandering to the fridge to grab herself some apple juice. Inside, she also found a piece of cake wrapped in cling film, with a note on reading *for Clem*. She smiled, though a stab of guilt struck her – it must be Emmie's doing. She'd have it later.

'Have you given any more thought to *Whisked Away*?' Sylvie asked, her fingers poised above the laptop keyboard. 'Emmie was agreeing with me, after you left the restaurant. She thinks you'd have a good chance of winning.'

A warm blush crept over Clem's cheeks. She removed the carton of juice and shut the fridge. 'Really?'

'Yes! Don't worry, there's plenty of time to decide. The closing date for entries isn't until next week. Why don't you think on it for a while?'

Nodding, Clem poured some apple juice into a glass and replaced the carton in the fridge. She *knew* she could bake – she had a minuscule but loyal following online who loved her creations, and she'd spent so much time learning. A contest, though? That was something she'd never done before. And this was one that could attract a *lot* more people. Did she want to be perceived by so many? The thought scared her. She rearranged a few cat magnets on the fridge.

'It might be a lot,' she told Sylvie, turning back to her. 'The attention, I mean.'

39

Sylvie's expression softened. She closed her laptop and stood up, crossing to the kitchenette to face Clem. 'I know you find things like that difficult.'

'Is it so obvious?'

'You were a shy little thing when I first interviewed you!' said Sylvie fondly, patting her shoulder. 'So unsure of yourself. But your baking speaks for itself. You have talent, you just need to own it. Don't keep yourself small because you dislike attention, love.'

That was exactly what she was doing, wasn't it? Clem sipped at her cold apple juice. Sylvie was perceptive.

'I have to make a phone call,' said Sylvie. 'I'll take it in the Cat Lounge then open up for the day. You know what you're doing today?'

Clem nodded. 'There are still plenty of frozen dough-nuts, and I've been defrosting them as needed. I'll do more batches of cookies today. Maybe start on those cat madeleines I told you about? They'll be pretty quick so I can do bigger batches.'

'Ooh, yes! Let me see them when you're done.'

'Sure.'

Sylvie smiled at her and left the staffroom. Clem was about to head into the kitchen when she paused, glancing at the staff laptop, which had been decorated with a collection of fun stickers – grey cats drinking bubble tea; kittens being lifted away by pink balloons; and quotes reading: *Caturday* and *my cat is judging you*. She smiled – the last one had been her addition because, according to Emmie, everyone needed to contribute their favourite sticker.

Sitting at the table with her apple juice, Clem flipped open the laptop and brought up the page for the *Whisked*

*Away* competition. There was a photo of the baker who had set it up, Ronan – known as Ronan's Real Bakes online. In the picture, he was cutting into what seemed to be a burning white candle dripping with creamy wax, but it was actually a cake that split perfectly down the middle, revealing layers of chocolate sponge and cream.

The page detailed the prize money and the rules of the contest, including:

> Whisked Away will be streamed online to Ronan's audience and beyond. Past winners have gone on to sign deals for cookbooks, write columns, start their own businesses, work with established brands and star in reality TV shows.

Clem took another gulp of apple juice, hoping to still her nerves. This opportunity . . . It could give her the foundation to finally do what she'd always wanted to do. To make something else of her baking, start her own business, become more independent. But could she do that?

*Don't keep yourself small because you dislike attention*, Sylvie had said.

She should do it. Shouldn't she?

Before she could second-guess it, she filled out the form – her name, address, contact details, the information about the cat café, her social media profiles.

When she was finished listing her social media accounts – the final question in the form – she froze. How popular was Ronan exactly? She'd seen him pop up online lots of times with his incredibly realistic bakes that didn't look like cakes at all – but she had never paid much attention to how large his audience was. Clem pulled her phone from her pocket and checked up on him.

He had over a million followers. Everywhere.

Her head spun. She had, what? A few thousand followers at the most, who were lovely and kind, but . . . The more you grew, the more potential there was for nastiness. She'd never gained enough attention to receive nasty comments but she knew it happened to other people, and the thought of blowing up had always terrified her because of it.

Clem's chest tightened just thinking about it, imagined scenarios playing out in her mind of what could happen if she entered. How her follower account would tick up, with people laughing at her, mocking her, critiquing her the more the number increased – noticing everything she did, her appearance, her skills, who she was as a person. Every round, she would be filmed and ogled, any disasters or mistakes captured permanently on camera.

There wasn't enough air in here, and what little air there was felt stale. She drew in a shuddering breath – it was difficult. Panic sluiced through her and she jumped to her feet, pacing up and down the staffroom with a hand on her belly. She counted the deep breaths, in through her nose and out through her mouth. It took her ten minutes of belly-breathing before she felt calm enough to sit down in front of the laptop again.

Her little corner of the world was, for now, safe and comfortable. Did she want to risk inviting more people like Genie into her life, people who would mock and humiliate her? People who would break apart whatever confidence she managed to build up?

No. She didn't need that at all.

She focused her mind on searching for the delete icon on the *Whisked Away* website – she was going to trash her application. She wasn't going to enter after all.

Seconds later, Clem heard someone calling for her down the hall. It sounded like Miles, their cat caretaker. He kept calling out, so she stood up and went into the hallway to say hello.

'Hey, Clem,' said Miles. He was short, with a head of messy light-brown hair and shiny blue eyes that always put her at ease. 'Sylvie's on a phone call. Can you just help me administer some medication? You don't have to do much. Just hold Kitty in place and keep her calm while I administer. She's usually pretty good but I don't want her wriggling since it's an injection for her allergies.'

'Sure,' said Clem. 'Let's go.'

By the time she'd finished helping Miles with Kitty's medication, Clem was scurrying off to wash her hands and return to the kitchen, since she needed to start baking for the day.

# Chapter 5

Lucas had brought his mum out for a reprieve from the stress she was dealing with – it was the only thing he could think to do. It was early morning and his dad was still sleeping – he often slept in, as he was awake most nights trying to manage his pain – and they'd come for a wander around Lake Windermere, the circular route. The sky was gloriously blue, although it was only half past ten – a great sprawl of azure with the occasional puffy cloud skirting across the sky like blown-around sheep's wool. The April showers finally seemed to be letting up now it was close to the end of the month. They'd followed a footpath into the woodland around the lake, the trees rising up around them from the mossy earth. The lake water sparkled nearby, stones dotting the edges of the banks like puzzle pieces.

'Thanks for this,' his mum said, taking in a huge lungful of fresh air as they tramped across the path. 'I needed it. I don't get out in nature enough.'

'Don't mention it.' Lucas knew, deep down, she wished she could come out here with his dad – to get out of the house together, to feel they were doing something other than coping. But the truth was, his dad was in too much pain and spent almost all of his time in bed or on the sofa now. 'You should join a group or something,' he suggested. 'It'd be good for you. Get you out of the house.'

'I know,' she said, sighing, as they clomped forward in their hiking boots. 'But I get so tired – work and errands and . . . well, you know how it is. Your father feels guilty, wishes he could help.'

Lucas's phone buzzed in his pocket, vibrating against his side, but he ignored it. His mum had stopped to look out over the flowing lake water, the patches of froth pouring over the stones and the smaller scattering of rocks littering the sides like copper coins. She took her phone from her pocket and lifted it into the air.

'A photo for your dad,' she said, snapping a picture. Her hair was pulled into a ponytail and had grown fairly long; she used to style it in elegant waves, but she hadn't done that in a long time now. The highlights had grown out too – she'd long since stopped being able to afford that kind of luxury.

While she took another photo from a different angle, Lucas tugged out his own phone and unlocked it.

He nearly dropped it. He couldn't see the full message without pressing on the notification, but the first lines were clear enough.

RE: Whisked Away Lake District Application

Thank you for your application to Whisked Away! We are delighted to select you for . . .

'No way,' he said loudly.

'What?' His mum turned at once, paling. 'Is it your father – is he up?'

'No, sorry,' he said. He briefly felt bad for making her worry but it was soon swallowed up in the shock of what he was seeing, and he broke out into laughter.

'The contest . . . they got back to me. You'll never believe it!'

'They *picked* you?' she said, becoming shriller with each word spoken. She rushed over, craning to look at his phone, on her tiptoes. She was miniature next to his height; she'd always been short. 'I want to see!'

He pressed on the notification and opened the email so they could read it together. It took forever to open out here – just a white screen for a while – and he wondered if he'd lost signal until, finally, it appeared:

Thank you for your application to Whisked Away! We are delighted to select you for in-person auditions – date, location and details are attached. You will be required to take part in a screen test and create one of your specialty bakes in a live kitchen as part of the audition. We look forward to welcoming you!

'I knew it!' his mother cried, swinging from his arm like an overexcited child and beaming down at the phone.

She pulled away from him, and he took in her features: the greyish bags beneath her green eyes, the fine lines and grooves that seemed to be deeper after the last six months, marking the stress and worry. But threading through it, a gleam of excitement, joy for him.

'You deserve this,' she said, beaming up at him. 'You work so hard, put in so many hours. It's about time you got some recognition.'

'I'm not doing it for recognition,' he said, brushing her comments aside and shoving his phone in his pocket. *I'm doing it for you*, he wanted to say, but he held it in. She might try to convince him to use the prize money on himself, if she knew. Better that she didn't know his plans for the money, should he win.

'I know – you're far too proud. You get it from your father.' Her lips twitched as if she were about to laugh. 'But you *do* deserve some, either way.'

Sunlight burst through a haze of cloud that had momentarily drifted overhead, making Lake Windermere shine like marble. Possibilities were bouncing through his brain so fast it was difficult to keep up with them. What he could *do* if he won . . . Put down a deposit on a house, even if it was only a small one. They'd never have to worry about being kicked out of their home because they couldn't pay the rent. And he could move in, help with his income, contributing to the mortgage. His dad could relax and be left to manage his pain in peace. They could pay for some private health appointments with what was left over. He could help ease their struggles. The hope surged inside him, as if trying to burst free and make his plans a reality.

'I'm going to win this,' he promised her.

'I'd be proud of you even if you didn't,' she insisted. They continued on their hike, boots cracking the fallen branches beneath their feet. 'You don't have to prove anything to me.'

'I know, but I'm going to win it,' he replied. *For you and dad*, he thought.

Dad *was* a proud person, reluctant to accept help or admit when he was struggling or suffering. He'd always been that way, so he wouldn't share his ideas for the money with them. No, instead Lucas would win, and go ahead with his plans.

★

Over the next week, Sylvie was largely absent from the cat café – she'd been visiting the cat shelter, then travelling to a feline care refresher course taking place at a hotel in Leeds – so Clem didn't see her much. On the day Sylvie was due to return, Clem was sitting in the Cat Lounge after the end of a long day, her feet up on the brown leather, checking her socials on her phone and looking up new ideas for bakes. The café was closed, and she'd frozen another batch of strawberry-filled cat doughnuts and cleaned and sanitised the kitchen. Sometimes she liked to relax in here before heading home after her shift, surrounded by the cats. It was pouring with rain outside, the wind pounding the droplets into the panes, and she didn't fancy driving until it eased off. The wood burner was empty; it wasn't cold, but the April showers raged on the other side of the glass.

The Cat Lounge was cosy. Baron was curled on the arm of the sofa beside Clem, and she was running her fingers over his soft, long coat, eliciting soft purrs. Behind her, Jess was standing on the back of the sofa, nuzzling Clem's hair and occasionally trying to eat it.

Clem laughed, reaching round to scratch her on the head. 'Hair isn't edible, Jess,' she told the large black-and-white cat, who was purring more loudly than Baron. 'You have to stop trying to take chunks out of my head, I'm not a cake!' She leaned forward, scrolled through her phone and muttered, 'These look good though, don't they?' A woman was holding a plate of white jiggly cat puddings, shaking the plate to and fro until the heads bobbed about and the ears wiggled. They could be a fun little addition to the café for the summer menu.

She added the idea to her notes app, closed out Instagram, and brought her emails up on her phone. She'd been so caught up in researching new bakes she hadn't bothered to check it – and hadn't looked at her inbox since yesterday.

A bunch of newsletters she subscribed to, random junk mail, and . . .

Clem sat up ramrod straight, choking on her own saliva and coughing to clear her throat. She had to be reading the subject of the email wrong. She read the words over and over. With shaking hands, she stabbed at the message to open the email, scanning over the words so quickly she became dizzy.

> Thank you for your application to Whisked Away! We
> are delighted to select you for in-person auditions – date,
> location and details are attached.

The email continued, providing more details she barely absorbed, because she couldn't get past the fact that they'd chosen her from a pool of applications she hadn't even submitted herself to.

What was going on? She'd trashed the application . . . hadn't she? Miles had interrupted her and had needed help with the cats, so maybe she hadn't. She was a hundred per cent confident she *hadn't* pressed that big, glaring submit button, though.

Jess was eating Clem's hair again.

'Jess,' Clem sighed, too highly strung to really stop her. Should she contact *Whisked Away*, let them know there had been a mistake?

Sylvie appeared in the doorway and leaned against the frame, smiling when she saw Jess licking and chewing at Clem's hair. She was dressed casually in jeans and a white shirt. To a more trained eye, though, the cat-like details were easy to spot: a dainty golden necklace with a pendant shaped like a cat's head, and the bobble holding her braid in place was shaped like a little black paw.

'It's the shampoo scent, I think,' said Sylvie. She nodded at Jess, who was attempting to take another chunk out of Clem's head with her teeth. Sylvie's own hair looked bedraggled and damp. 'She likes when it's freshly washed.'

Clem leaned out of Jess's reach. 'I didn't know you were back.'

'Got back a few minutes ago.' Her smile grew an inch wider. 'I didn't get chance to see you before I left, but I'm *so* glad you decided to enter *Whisked Away*! I'll help you every step of the way, don't worry.'

'W-What?' said Clem, sitting up straighter.

Baron, affronted by the fact that she'd moved, hopped down onto the floor and stretched out on the rug instead of the sofa, his bushy tail waving like a squirrel's. Jess pressed her paws to Clem's shoulders, trying to reach her hair again, and Clem swatted her away gently.

'What do you mean? I didn't enter,' said Clem.

Sylvie paled, and the delight in her expression fell away, leaving behind nothing but horror.

'Oh my God, Clem, I'm so sorry. Before I left, I noticed you left the application form open on the staff laptop. It was filled in except for my section, so I assumed you'd forgotten to ask me to do my section . . .' Sylvie shuffled awkwardly. 'I sent off the application.'

It was as though Clem had stepped out into the spring typhoon. Her ears roared with static and her skin prickled, a cold wave running over her. She mustn't have trashed the application like she'd thought she did, perhaps because she'd become distracted when Miles was calling for her. She was so stupid – she should have double- and triple-checked she'd deleted it after she'd helped him. Instead, she'd gone straight off to the kitchen to get started with work and had forgotten all about it.

Clem stood up, her phone still clutched tightly in her hand, the email like a blazing fire in her palm. She was trapped in a whirlwind, the self-doubt roaring around her. *I can't do it*, the thoughts chimed, repeating like bells.

'Are you okay?' Sylvie said, taking a step closer to her. 'Clem, I know this is daunting, and I'm so sorry for the mix-up, but I think this could be really good for you.'

Clem shook her head wildly, feeling horribly anxious and sick. 'Have you seen how big Ronan is online? How many followers he has?'

'Yes, I did look him up afterwards,' Sylvie admitted, her cheeks pale. 'But, Clem, you won't be doing this on your own. I'll be right there with you, supporting you.'

'Or I could contact *Whisked Away* and withdraw—'

'Is that what you really want? You'd started filling in the application. Some part of you must have wanted to do this, love.'

Clem couldn't argue. A part of her *did* want it. It was just that the doubting and fearful side was louder, clamouring for her attention, drowning everything else out with the what-ifs and the imagined scenarios and the worries. Making decisions was so hard because of it. She found it so difficult to separate her own wants and her own reasoning from the anxious chatter trying to convince her to shy away.

But surely, with her level of anxiety, she couldn't cope with the *Whisked Away* audience scrutinising her – and with what that might bring?

'I can see the cogs turning,' Sylvie said lightly, coming over to Clem and putting an arm around her. 'You never thought you'd be selected, did you? At the restaurant, on Emmie's birthday, you said you didn't think you'd be picked.'

'I did say that . . .' said Clem, surprised and slightly touched that she'd remembered.

'And yet here we are. You *were* picked. They saw something in you – the same thing I saw when you first came to Catpurrcino. Your talent. You can do this, Clem.'

Sylvie's words – *you can do this* – sparked something in her, like a key being turned. She'd been giving too much space to those worried thoughts recently, not fighting hard enough against them, not interrogating them to see if they were true. *I've done hard things before,* she told herself, trying to reframe her anxieties. *I can do them again.*

'Do you want to do this?' Sylvie asked, giving her shoulder a gentle squeeze. 'Forget all the reasons why you shouldn't or why you're afraid. Think about what you'd do if fear wasn't a factor, and answer.'

If fear wasn't a factor? Fear seemed to rule her, sometimes, to the point where she felt like she needed a shove from fate – something to take making a decision away. It had happened when she'd started working here: she'd come in to visit with her mum, and Sylvie had seen her checking her online profiles and complimented one of her cakes. That was how she'd been offered the job interview, and she'd said yes because she didn't want to seem rude when Sylvie was so lovely, even though she was scared.

This might be one of those times. A push in the right direction. She couldn't get Sylvie's words out of her mind. *Don't keep yourself small because you dislike attention.* How had she summed up Clem's personality in one sentence?

Clem didn't like being that way. She didn't *want* to be that way.

'What do you think?' said Sylvie softly, gently nudging her along.

Clem gave a small, barely perceptible nod. 'If fear wasn't a factor . . .' She took a deep, juddering breath. 'I would do it.'

Sylvie spun Clem to face her, the brightness spreading over her face, turning her cheeks pink. 'There's your answer, Clem. What do you say? Do you want to go ahead, or withdraw? I'll support you, whatever you decide.'

'Yes,' said Clem, forcing strength into her voice even as her stomach rolled with the decision. 'Okay. I'll do it.'

She wished she could be this rational all the time, that the logic could *always* crowd out the anxiousness. It happened sometimes but it took so much effort; it was exhausting. She could feel the nerves, like pincers, trying to claw their way up. But there was something else bubbling up too – a dream, an ambition – and it rose faster, winning the fight this time. She pictured what she could do if this all went well, instead of imagining what could go wrong: a little baking business of her own, connections made to help her along. And Sylvie was right; the *Whisked Away* team must have seen potential in her. A swooping mix of nerves and giddiness rushed through her, making her light-headed.

'Yes!' Sylvie clapped her hands together in delight. 'I'll be there for you, love – we'll be in it together, so you don't have to worry about a thing. We'll knock 'em dead if we get onto *Whisked Away*, Clem. You watch.'

In that briefest of moments, Clem believed her.

★

Sylvie had been buzzing with excitement since Clem had agreed to go through with the contest, reassuring Clem everything would be fine, that they'd work together and Clem had nothing to worry about. Clem had spent most of her days following their conversation with a churning gut and very little appetite. Being decisive hadn't lessened her nerves much. The only thing she could do was bake to distract herself – which she got plenty of opportunity to do when she was at work.

Today, she was on her lunch break at Catpurrcino. There was a good number of customers downstairs, most of the seating occupied even in the Cat Lounge, so Clem had decided to come up to the second floor, to a quiet corner tucked away at the back. There was a big arch-shaped window here, allowing sunlight to beam inside, and she sat in the sun with a sandwich and a cup of steaming tea on the table in front of her. One of their biggest cat towers was wedged in the corner, rising almost as high as the tall ceiling. There was only one cat here – Baron, their long-haired Somali cat, right at the top of the tower, fast asleep with his paw pads dangling over the edges. The streams of sunlight picked out the hues of orange and tawny brown in his fuzzy fur. Clem couldn't see his face from down here.

Clem grabbed her phone and visited the *Whisked Away* socials – it was like a compulsion now. They'd announced the contestants to the world a few days ago, introducing them with a series of posts. A photo of Clem and Sylvie had been posted – headshots from the Catpurrcino website – alongside a picture of the cat café and some information on Clem's baking. She couldn't help going back to check it for new comments. She munched at her sandwich; the responses seemed positive so far, which eased the clenching in her gut. Some of their customers were wishing them luck in the comments, too. Maybe it wouldn't be as bad as she'd been expecting?

A notification flashed up on her phone – and Clem nearly choked on her sandwich as a breadcrumb flew down her throat. She coughed, drinking some tea until it settled down.

Genie Maidwell wants to send you a message.

At once, she felt like she'd jinxed herself. Only seconds ago, she was thinking this might not be so bad, but now . . . Clem's eyes were watering and she squinted through the haze, unable to believe what she was seeing. Genie was contacting her, now, after all this time? After what she'd done? Clem's skin turned cold, even though the warm sunlight was splashing across her arms.

If she looked at the message, Genie wouldn't know she'd seen it unless she replied, which she had zero intention of doing. She tapped into it.

*I saw the post about the baking show, you and the other contestants,* Genie had written. *I left it alone back then because I thought you would, too. But apparently you haven't?*

Clem's fingers hovered over *delete* and swivelled over to *block*. But she didn't press either of them. She was tempted to respond to Genie, because she didn't have a clue what this message meant, and a part of her was itching to know. But engaging with her might be a bad idea; it had taken Clem so long to move forward last time. Why drag things up again, years later? So what, if she was on *Whisked Away*? It had nothing to do with Genie. Was Genie trying to ruin this for her? Was she jealous? She'd already ruined one career opportunity for Clem in the past, and Clem still didn't fully understand why. Clem wouldn't let her do that a second time.

She pushed *block*, and looked up at Baron, a fuzzy, sleeping ball of orangey brown on the cat tower. Her fingers were trembling because she was sure Genie's message didn't mean anything good.

# Chapter 6

The day of the auditions arrived – and Clem had barely slept last night. She was running on less than four hours of sleep and a strong coffee her mum had made her this morning, which probably hadn't helped with the jittery nerves. Luckily, Sylvie had offered to drive, and they'd just stepped out of the car and into the early morning sunshine. It hadn't taken too long to get here – *Whisked Away* were hosting interviews and auditions not far outside of Windermere, at the Jade Hotel.

Clem was clutching her squeezy cat again – it was a 'stress toy' she'd picked up years ago because it looked like Misha. It was a stripy cat with a round belly and a pink mouth, lying on its back as if sunbathing. She squished it between her fingers and it made an airy, puffy sound. If anyone asked, she'd say it was a lucky charm.

'This place is . . . amazing,' said Clem, taking in their surroundings. She couldn't believe she would be auditioning at such a grand place – part of her wanted to turn around and flee as all the doubts she'd had about the application pushed their way to the surface.

The hotel was set on sprawling green fields, meticulously and carefully cut, not a blade of grass out of place, gorgeous yellow flowers springing up everywhere. Tidy brick pathways snaked up a slight incline, alongside a weaving water feature and faux stream, dotted with trees and shrubs.

The hotel itself looked like a cross between a mansion and a cottage to Clem – clearly too big and luxurious to be a quaint cottage, despite the charming brickwork exterior. A scattering of side buildings filled the grass, extending out. Huge, modern windows sprawled across the front of the main building, showing off a waiting area filled with plush cream and red seats, and a restaurant with a gleaming bar off to the right. Every surface inside shone and gleamed like glass, from the mahogany bar and beer taps to the cutlery adorning each table. Everything was accented in smooth, rounded gold.

'I bet it costs a *fortune* to spend the night here,' Clem said.

'It's definitely no teensy bed-and-breakfast,' Sylvie agreed. 'I heard it's popular for weddings.'

Clem couldn't believe she was here. She'd never been anywhere so exquisite, and she swiped one of her clammy palms on her dress. They set off up the path, the water feature and smooth faux river rushing pleasantly beside them. Clem was partly paranoid she'd stumble and break something along the way – there were delicate lights wedged amongst the shrubbery, unlit in the daylight, like glass marbles. She clutched her squashy cat again tightly, and it made another sound like a puff of air being exhaled.

A furious barking sound came from behind her. And was that a man shouting something? She could barely make out the words over the water, and turned.

Before she could fully process what she was seeing, a blur of yellow bounced into her field of view, bright and shiny in the daylight.

A huge, furry animal hopped up and down around her legs. Clem cried out, unsteady on her feet, doing her best not to cartwheel sideways. She just about avoided tripping and falling straight into the water next to her.

It was a dog, she realised, and flinched away from the animal on instinct.

She wasn't afraid of dogs, but having a big, excitable creature bounding around her ankles near water was enough to make her tense up. Probably not the best idea to stick close to the dog, unless she wanted to begin the contest as soggy as an overly moist truffle.

She tried to move away a few paces, back up the path, but the dog only followed her, springing up and down. It let out an excitable yip, trying to snuffle around her clothes, its pink tongue rolling around.

Her heart leaped into her throat – what if she fell and broke her wrist and couldn't audition? The dog wouldn't stop bouncing.

'*Reina!* Stop it!'

A man was hurrying towards them, out of breath, and he grabbed Reina – a huge, wheat-yellow golden retriever with a wild, bushy tail swinging from side to side. Bent double and catching his breath, the man clipped a lead onto the dog's red collar.

'*Sit!*' the man ordered.

Clem relaxed and smiled at the dog's happily lolling tongue. Reina obeyed, plonking her bottom onto the brick path, dipping her head slightly as if embarrassed for being told off, and attempting to lick his wrist. Her big brown eyes remained cheeky and joyful, gleaming slightly. They were fixed on Clem's squashy cat toy.

'I'm sorry, I swear she doesn't listen to me.' The man was still doubled over, clutching at a stitch in his side now and giving Reina a quick ruffle on the top of her head, making her ears wiggle and her tail beat hard from side to side.

But Clem was laughing, mainly out of relief. 'Oh, it's okay, she's beautiful. I'm just more of a cat person.' She shot Sylvie an amused look, and she smiled back knowingly.

The man straightened, and Clem's eyes widened. Messy dark hair and equally dark lashes, green eyes framed by heavy brows. She remembered him, and her heart leaped as if it, too, were hoping to take a tumble into the water feature. Warmth crawled up her spine and her neck. Maybe some cold water wouldn't be so bad right now, actually.

'You—' she began, and stopped suddenly. Maybe he didn't remember her? Would it be weird to him, that she remembered their brief interaction outside the restaurant on Emmie's birthday?

Before she could decide whether to ask or not, a second man jogged up behind the first. He had dark skin and a bald head that seemed to glow in the spring sunshine, and he wore a pair of large sunglasses. His black shirt was decorated with red ravens taking flight.

'You got her?' the man in the raven shirt said, also sounding out of breath. 'Hey, good taste,' he added, spotting Clem's dress. She'd chosen her flared white dress printed with little black cats, since they were here representing the café.

'You, too,' she said, smiling and nodding at his shirt. Her neck was still feeling incredibly warm, the feeling spreading to her palms as the first man studied her with those intense green eyes of his.

The man in the sunglasses tipped his chin at his friend. 'Lucky you didn't take a dip. I told you she needs better training, Lucas.'

'She ran off before I could clip the lead on!' the man named Lucas protested.

So this man – this *gorgeous* man – was Lucas? Clem's pulse quickened, but she tried to shut that down, tried to breathe more slowly. She was here for her audition; that was what she needed to be thinking about. Not men with thick dark lashes who looked like they'd stepped out of a TV show about vampires seducing women, or—

'I'm Dwayne,' said the man in the raven-print shirt. He gave them a broad smile, running a hand over his thick beard. 'This is Lucas.'

'I'm Clem.' Her voice came out a little quieter than she'd intended as Lucas's lips tipped into a smile, a slight breeze lifting his dark hair.

'Sylvie,' Sylvie said slowly. 'Don't I know you?' she added, directing that part at Lucas.

Clem was confused – had she met Lucas at the restaurant, too?

'Maybe?' said Lucas.

Sylvie frowned, as if piecing together clues, then realisation must have dawned, because she clapped her hands. 'I do! Lucas Bowen, isn't it? I know your mum – Meredith, works at the cat shelter?'

'Oh yeah, she does.'

'I'm pretty sure you did the catering at my friend's wedding a number of years ago too.'

'That probably was us,' Dwayne chimed in. 'We were doing catering for a while before we set up Muddy Paws Café. Over near Lake Windermere.'

'Oh, I've heard of it – from your mum, and some of our customers,' said Sylvie, beaming.

'You must be from Catpurrcino,' said Lucas, eyes lingering on Clem's stress toy. She tried to hold it behind her, out of sight, feeling silly.

'We are.'

Dwayne whistled. 'Oh hey, that's some serious competition right there. You hear that, Reina?' He gave the dog a pat on the head and scratched her neck. Her tail was pounding the path so hard it was a wonder it didn't split the bricks in two. 'Dog versus cat!' He grinned.

'Don't intimidate them, Dwayne,' said Lucas. 'He's only joking.'

'No harm in a little competition,' said Sylvie, her eyes twinkling. Clem noticed her attention lingered on Dwayne and his rather large muscles, even though she was probably at least twenty years his senior, and she had to stifle a nervous giggle. 'May the best animal win,' Sylvie said. 'What are you going to do with lovely Reina there while you audition?'

'They have pet-friendly rooms,' Lucas explained, 'so she'll stay there for a bit while we audition.'

They entered the hotel together. Clem could almost feel Lucas's eyes on her – like summer heat – as she and Sylvie walked ahead of them, stepping into the reception area. A bright-faced receptionist greeted them, and asked them to sign in before making a fuss of Reina, who tried to leap up so frantically Clem was surprised the woman's skirt wasn't shredded to bits beneath her paws.

'Get down, Reina!' Lucas ordered. To her credit, the dog listened this time.

'Shall we take Reina here across to the farmhouse?' the receptionist crooned, scratching the dog on the top of the head. She didn't seem to mind that the dog had almost torn up her clothes. She gestured at Dwayne and Lucas to follow her outside, before calling over to Clem and Sylvie, 'You can make your way to the conference room. It's down that long hall and up ahead. You can't miss it.'

The two men turned to leave with the receptionist. As he left, Lucas cast an eye over his shoulder at Clem – and her insides skittered as if something was malfunctioning inside her. Those darkened green eyes were enough to raise storms in a person. Or perhaps it was the nerves? She couldn't tell.

Clem followed Sylvie down the long, narrow corridor the receptionist had gestured to, squeezing her squishy cat so hard its belly was flattened. At the far end, a set of huge double doors opened onto a wide room with deep brown carpet patterned with looping cream swirls, like a cinnamon bun.

Clem stared around the room in amazement. The ceilings seemed infinitely high, painted white with huge squares carved out of the middle, each one containing a glittering chandelier. There was a stage at the front of the room, and a huge HD screen showing the *Whisked Away* logo on the display. And instead of the rows of chairs as you'd expect from a typical conference room, the rest of the space was dotted with makeshift pop-up kitchens, each with gleaming dark marble countertops, shiny silver mixers, and built-in ovens.

The hitch in Clem's chest this time was definitely nerves. Up by the stage, a group of people were gathered, talking. She recognised one of them as Ronan, the creator of *Whisked Away* – the light-brown curls fluffed up across his forehead were unmistakable.

'Wow, this is impressive,' Sylvie said. 'They don't do things by halves, do they?'

'I've never baked anything in such luxury before,' said Clem. She was pretty sure the drawers on those cabinets wouldn't squeak like the third one down at home. Or that you'd have to bang the fourth one extra hard to get it to close again.

A young man in a *Whisked Away* T-shirt approached them moments later with a clipboard in his hand.

'Hey, guys!' he said brightly. 'Could I get your names? We'll get you over to your assigned kitchen and Ronan will be up on stage to explain everything.'

Sylvie offered him their names, and they were led to a gleaming mini kitchen in the row furthest away from the stage – closest to the door. Clem exhaled; she was glad to be in this spot, not packed in amongst the others too closely. Lucas had stepped into the room too, giving Clem more palpitations. They kicked up a notch when he and his friend Dwayne were assigned the kitchen right beside her and Sylvie. Nerves about the audition – and the gorgeous man with eyes piercing enough to stop her in her tracks, working right next to her – flooded her. She'd be dead of heart failure by the end of the day at this rate.

More people filtered in, taking up their positions at kitchens spread around the room. Two women in their twenties, hair tied back in ponytails, wearing crisp white shirts and striped aprons. A plump older woman, accompanied by a slightly younger woman in her thirties, both in hot pink. A couple of older men sporting salt-and-pepper hair and beards. And more and more, until every kitchen in the room had a set of occupants. Clem smiled as she caught the eye of the two women in pink; they gave her a thumbs up.

Before long, Ronan was sweeping up onto the stage, a microphone clipped to his *Whisked Away* T-shirt. He raised his arms up to welcome them, smiling, his straight white teeth almost blinding. A hush fell over the gathered group of bakers. Ronan's grin widened, a dimple wedging itself in his cheek. There was some type of clicker in his hand, probably for the screen set up behind him. Clem's insides flipped over when he started to speak.

'Hi, everyone, thanks so much for coming out! We're super excited to have you with us. Now, if you've seen me online, you'll know me as Ronan's Real Bakes . . .'

Clem found it hard to focus as Ronan launched into an explanation about how he got into baking, how he became popular online, and how he started *Whisked Away*. She knew much of this already. She cast a glance over at the little kitchen beside them. Lucas ran a hand through his dark hair. When he spotted her looking at him, his expression made her knees feel as weak as a soft sponge cake. *I really can't let him distract me.* She looked away, determined to focus only on what lay ahead, and on managing her nerves.

Ronan was introducing the other judges, clicking over to a fresh slide on the screen for each of them. There was Viviana Nelson, a bestselling author and baker to celebrities; Clem had seen her on TV. She had light brown skin and long, sleek dark hair, styled in elegant waves. Unlike Ronan, who was an explosion of colour, she was all elegance – a killer black-and-cream suit and matching heels. Next came Laurette Mercier, a woman with smooth, creamy skin who had a baking empire with hundreds of bakeries across the world and her own school in London; Clem wasn't familiar with her. Her ash-brown hair was cut to her shoulders, her clothes polished like Viviana's, but looser-fitting. And finally, there was Jonathan Hale, who was a social media star like Ronan. He looked vaguely familiar with his trendy glasses and cheeky smile, so it was possible she'd seen him online once or twice.

'Now, I'm going to explain the audition process, and what will happen from here if you're selected.' Ronan pushed his clicker, and the screen switched over to a presentation illustrating what he was saying, the text set in the middle. A group of colourful spring flags and pastel cupcakes bordered the screen. 'You'll already know that today, we'd like to see what you can do. Create one of your specialty bakes, one you can finish within the two-hour time frame. You can be as creative as you want. We want to get a feel for your style. All the equipment you'll need is provided at your baking stations, and there are plenty of ingredients, though we know some of you will have brought your own extras.

'We've got the support team here to address any technical issues if they come up,' Ronan continued, and he gestured at a cluster of people standing to the side of the stage, who waved enthusiastically. 'We'll also be recording the auditions to do a screen test, moving around to get some footage as you go.' Ronan pointed to a camera and a couple of staff positioned at the back of the room, in a corner. 'We might get you to engage with the camera, ask questions as you bake, that kind of thing. It'll give us a feel for your on-screen presence, and how it might translate onto the show. Please don't worry about this! We want you to be totally natural. Be yourselves!'

Clem wasn't sure how she could possibly be herself whilst being filmed, especially since the camera was so portable and they'd be moving around the room. She swallowed, trying to bring some moisture to her dry mouth. She was also wishing she had some lip balm stashed in a pocket. And she'd left her chewing gum behind – she didn't want to be chewing excessively in front of people. Part of her wanted to sprint for the exit right now, rather than face the shiny lens of the camera. What if she got anxious when they filmed her and made a fool of herself? What if she did something stupid, and everyone laughed? With a pang, she was reminded of why she most definitely *hadn't* put herself forward for this, why she had decided not to send off the application in the first place. She gripped the squeezy cat, hard, trying to reframe the thoughts. *What if I do everything well?*

'We'll be observing, and one of the judges will wander around to chat to you,' explained Ronan. He clicked the button in his hand, switching over to a screen reading *Let's get baking!* The camera team across the room gave him a thumbs up. Ronan continued, 'Finally, we'll be keeping the doors wedged open for you today, as it'll likely get quite warm in here when the baking starts.'

He motioned towards the door, which had been wedged open with a doorstopper. 'Okay, you can go ahead and start!'

# Chapter 7

The room was filled with the sound of clattering as everyone dug around for the supplies they needed. Sylvie gave Clem an encouraging smile and set to work whipping out ingredients Clem would need.

Clem had chosen something familiar for this stage – something she made every day and was comfortable with: the cat doughnuts from the café. She was putting a slightly new spin on their flavour and look to make them stand out.

She shoved the squeezy cat in the pocket of her dress, and helped Sylvie pile ingredients and tools on the counter as quickly as she could, along with a huge glass bowl she found in a cupboard, adding a stick of butter and some sugar to it. Out of the corner of her eye, she was aware of Lucas and his friend Dwayne bustling around their kitchen too; with a lurch, she wondered what they were making.

The camera was already roving, Viviana Nelson gliding along with it, towards the two young women in pink. One of them began chatting excitedly at the camera and at Viviana, explaining what she was baking with gusto. Clem tried hard not to listen – how was it possible to sound so perky and confident with a camera shoved under your nose?

'Do you want to cream the butter and sugar for me?' she asked Sylvie, trying to keep her voice from shaking.

*Focus. Focus on the practical stuff.* 'You can use the electric whisk there. I'll work on the dry ingredients.'

'Of course,' said Sylvie, springing into action and grabbing the whisk.

Clem tried to filter out the noise – the buzzing of whisks, the hearty conversation going on in front of the camera, the sounds of a busy room filled with people. At the café, she was usually alone. It was exactly why she loved working at Catpurrcino so much: the quiet, the familiarity, the control she had over her environment and the music she listened to, sitting with cats on her lunch break. Here, everything seemed like chaos and wildness. Unpredictable.

She rolled her shoulders to ease the tension, and glanced at the huge clock Ronan had brought up on the screen, as if she expected time to have drained away to nothing already.

In a separate bowl, she added a flutter of flour, some baking powder, and a little salt, whisking them together by hand. 'You can add two eggs – whisk them in one at a time,' she told Sylvie, who nodded, immediately following Clem's instructions.

When that was done, Clem took over. She added her own mixture to Sylvie's and whisked them, forming a swirling, doughy concoction in the glass bowl. The camera was moving again in her periphery. She wished she'd had something else to drink this morning and not coffee; it was churning inside her and she felt horribly sick.

The camera was coming towards their workstation, and Viviana Nelson was striding their way, like a celebrity walking the red carpet. *Oh no, oh no, oh no*, her brain rambled. What should she say? What if she opened her mouth and . . . *No*. She took a deep breath. She was *not* going to puke up her anxiety all over Viviana Nelson's girl-boss outfit. Not if she could help it.

'Milk,' she said dumbly. 'We need milk next, I mean.'

'I'll get it,' said Sylvie.

The camera arrived at their side. Viviana Nelson gave them a smooth smile, her lips perfectly glossed. Sylvie bent to the small fridge built into the kitchenette, and Clem was left to face the glistening, gleaming camera lens – like the eye of some beast.

'And what are you making over here today?' Viviana asked. Her voice was gentle and kind. 'Which business do you represent?'

Sylvie popped her head up in the nick of time and the camera swivelled to her as she broke in, 'We're with Cat-purrcino Cat Café. In Oakside. Clem here is our baker, and I'm the owner.' She passed the milk to Clem, who opened it with a grateful nod and shaking hands, measuring what they needed in a jug.

'Wonderful. That must have *lots* of potential for baked goods – and I love cats!' Viviana replied, winking. 'I have four! What's on the menu today?'

The cameraman had fixated on Clem again, who stiffened. It was as though her shoulders had crawled up to her ears, and she had to force her jaw to relax, unclenching it, and unsticking her tongue from the roof of her mouth. She reminded herself that Viviana wasn't here to intimidate them – she was doing her job, and she was being nice.

'C-Cat doughnuts,' she said.

She didn't remember lifting the milk jug but it was in her hand now. Talking to Viviana was making her feel so out of sorts.

Her entire body was quivering like the leaves of the cherry tree outside the café, only not quite as gracefully. She reached into her pocket with her free hand, bringing out the cat toy and squeezing it. The camera was too busy with her face so perhaps they wouldn't notice it. And she had her lucky-charm excuse ready.

She was about to elaborate, to explain her process and the changes she intended to make to the usual flavour of her doughnuts, when there was a sound. A yell from the corridor outside the conference room, swiftly followed by a loud bark.

Clem jumped about a foot in the air, sloshing milk down her front and losing half of what she'd poured into the jug.

The camera was still on Clem. She turned towards the noise, soaked through with milk, her breaths coming quicker. Their kitchen was positioned so she could see directly into the corridor leading to the reception area.

Reina the golden retriever was bounding down the passage.

She sprang along as if she were riding the summer clouds, a happy dog-grin stretching over her mouth. Behind her came the receptionist – too slow in her high heels and tight skirt to stop the lumbering, excitable dog.

'Reina!' Lucas cried from the workstation next to them. 'Stop—'

But Reina came barrelling through the open doorway. There was a split-second pause where the dog seemed to assess, to decide where it should go, but instead of heading for its owner, Reina came straight for Clem.

She squealed in surprise – Viviana gave a shriek of shock, too. The dog came rushing towards Clem, leaping up at her legs. She was still holding the milk jug and she tried desperately to hold it aloft, keeping it away from the furry chaos. It didn't work – more milk sloshed down her dress. Reina was straining towards Clem's hand, where she clutched the squeezy cat.

'I'm so sorry!' the receptionist was wailing. 'She somehow managed to—'

'Clem! Are you okay?' Sylvie said breathlessly. 'What a daft, silly dog, honestly!'

Clem wanted to sprint from the room – her time was ticking away and she'd lost all her milk, and the dog wasn't calming down. The camera had caught everything. Her cheeks burned with humiliation and she lowered her head, a curtain of dark hair hiding the sides of her face.

She couldn't do this. It was like before. She heard people laughing, the sound sharp and cutting in her ears. *They're laughing at Reina*, she reminded herself. But she couldn't make her body any less stiff, couldn't push down the rising panic that was causing her limbs to tingle. There wasn't enough air in here.

Footsteps, and someone with pale hands was kneeling down and tugging Reina off her. Clem was crushing the squeezy toy in her fist.

'Clem?' said Sylvie, traces of laughter gone from her voice. 'Are you okay?'

She didn't answer. Her lips were locked together like she'd eaten a particularly thick piece of treacle fudge.

More hurried footsteps. 'You silly girl!' Dwayne was scolding, his voice deepening to show his displeasure. '*Sit!*'

A low whine as Reina realised she was in serious trouble.

But whoever was kneeling in front of Clem hadn't gone; she could see dark jeans and black trainers. Her chin was so low it was skimming the top of her dress, her attention fixed firmly on the swirling patterns of the carpet. Her chest was tight and breathing was somehow alien now. If she looked up, tried to interact, she feared she'd fall apart right here and embarrass herself further. Everyone was watching her, probably.

'Hey,' said a soft voice. It was Lucas. He leaned forward, green eyes peering up at her with concern. He gave her a small wave from down there, as if they'd simply met in passing at the bus stop. 'Sorry about Reina. You okay?'

Her head jerked – she'd attempted a nod, but it came out as more of a strange spasming motion. Every breath made her chest tighter.

He lowered his voice. 'Deep breaths. In through the nose, out through the mouth.' He rose to his feet – Clem could only see the tips of his trainers now – and moved away. She thought he was returning to his kitchen, but there was a sound close to her elbow and the jug was removed from her vice-like grip. 'Here. I'll remeasure the milk for you. How much?'

'Half a cup – about a hundred and twenty five mil,' Sylvie said, answering on Clem's behalf – and then came the sound of pouring. 'Thanks so much.'

'Goodness, that startled me!' Viviana was saying, with a titter of laughter. Clem had to work hard not to wince, her neck aflame.

Ronan must have made his way on stage again, because he was calling out across the conference room through his microphone, an upbeat note in his voice. 'Well, that was certainly . . . erm . . . an experience!' There was scattered laughter around the room and this time, Clem *did* flinch. 'Not to worry, we'll get the dog removed and add on an extra ten minutes to the time to account for the interruption. That okay with everyone?'

There were calls of agreement. Clem still couldn't bring herself to raise her head. She could hear the receptionist talking to Lucas and Dwayne about taking Reina back to the farmhouse – apparently, a window had been open and the dog had managed to prise it open even further and escape to the main hotel. On a normal day, Clem would have found this extremely funny, like a scene from some wild animated movie, but her mind was racing and all she could think about was having to continue to audition when the air was being squeezed from her lungs – and they'd caught her on camera with a dog trying to grab a squishy toy from her hand, milk being sloshed all over herself.

'Hey.' It was Lucas again, standing beside her, lowering his voice so the cameras couldn't pick it up. She felt a stab of appreciation for his consideration. His voice was so silky, so calming. 'Are you okay?'

Clem nodded again; it was more noticeably a nod this time.

'I had a friend who used to try to postpone it,' he advised. 'You can panic all you want after this audition, for as long as you like. Tell it to wait until later. Can you do that?'

*Postpone . . . ?* Something like irritation cut through some of the stiffness in her limbs – did he think she could *control* this? – and Clem finally raised her head. But wait . . . the small, logical voice was rising up within her and saying he was right. She *could* control this, she reminded

74

herself. She hadn't let it take over her, not yet. Not completely. That meant she could salvage things. If she could keep it together long enough to audition, and not have a full-blown panic attack . . . Running away never helped, and she'd only feel worse afterwards, and too scared to continue the competition. She'd been there before, and didn't want to go back. *I'm in control.* If she broke down later, it didn't matter. So long as she didn't do it here, in front of these cameras.

She did some more deep belly-breathing, trying to tune everyone else out, to think rationally. *I'm okay. No one is laughing at me. They were laughing at Reina.*

Reina the golden retriever had disappeared down the corridor, heading to the farmhouse. Lucas had measured out the milk for her again. She may be damp, her dress smeared with spilt liquid, but it hadn't ruined anything. They had been given extra time. She repeated all of this in her head several times, like the chorus of a song.

'Carry on, everyone!' Ronan was calling over their heads. 'Filming is never predictable anyway – it's good to give you a taster, get you used to the chaos!' He laughed, and some of the others joined in. Clem attempted a weak laugh that came out sounding all wrong – strangled.

*They aren't laughing at you*, she reminded herself.

Sylvie gave Clem's shoulder a reassuring squeeze. 'Let's get cracking. We can do this. Everything'll be fine, Clem.'

The camera moved away from them, and the crew seemed to have decided Clem had been given enough attention – and humiliation – for one day, because they focused on the other workstations. Clem and Sylvie worked on mixing their wet and dry ingredients together, before transferring it all to a pastry bag. Clem was doing everything on autopilot, trying to shove down the simmering anxiety beneath her skin. *Later. You can panic later.* She forced herself to remain detached.

When their doughnut pans were filled, they shoved them in the oven to bake – then set to work making more. Soon they'd filled some more doughnut pans.

Focusing on the baking, on the motions, had helped soothe her somewhat, even though her shoulders were tight and rigid. Clem glanced across at the workstation beside them, where Lucas and Dwayne were baking. A strong cinnamon scent was in the air, and it looked like they were making iced cinnamon buns – one of her favourite treats in the world. They looked *divine*, fat and doughy and beautifully swirly, with a layer of pale yellow on top. Maybe a lemon coating? Lucas caught her looking and smiled at her – she smiled tentatively, her stomach performing a wide loop.

'Are you feeling okay?' Sylvie asked Clem, touching her lightly on the arm.

'I'm okay, thanks,' said Clem. 'Just . . . need to keep occupied.'

'We'll be grand. Your cat doughnuts are always excellent. All the customers think so.'

'Technically they aren't *proper* doughnuts, though,' Clem said, looking down at the doughnut pans set out in front of them. 'They aren't fried or anything . . . It's quicker to make them like this in big batches, like we do at Catpurrcino. Do you . . . do you think that'll matter?'

'Not if they taste like they usually do,' said Sylvie, dusting her hands on her apron. 'It's all in the taste, and everything you bake tastes incredible. *And* they'll look incredibly cute. It'll be fine!'

Clem nodded, hoping she was right. Her shoulders were hurting from the stiffness and her chest still felt constricted.

The decorating was Clem's favourite part – giving the doughnuts little almond cat-ears and adding the colourful candy melts to their surface to give them character. Her hands were shaky after what happened earlier, but she managed. When she was done decorating everything and the timer had run down, they had an assortment of cute cat-shaped doughnuts with little almond ears, and iced bodies in all colours: black and white, pale brown, grey, pearl white, light pink, baby blue. Each cat had a teensy nose and a smiling mouth – and whiskers, of course.

When Ronan clambered up on stage again to end the audition, he was beaming, his cheeks aglow with enthusiasm. 'Well done, everyone! The taste-testing will be done in private so we can discuss – but we have refreshments set out for you in the dining hall, so feel free to head there before you make your way home. You'll hear from us shortly if you've been selected for the show. Thank you all so much for coming!'

# Chapter 8

As they headed out into the reception area, Sylvie turned to Clem and said, 'I might go and grab some refreshments, but you could wait in the car if you don't fancy it? I can bring something out for you. I'm so hungry – I blame those baking smells! It's about lunchtime too.' She checked her shiny gold watch.

Many of the other contestants were heading for the dining area, too. Clem was grateful Sylvie hadn't suggested they eat in there – the tension was returning to her body and she was ready to nap at home with Misha sitting in her lap for about twelve hours. The tension and anxiety had collected inside of her like a ball of string and she needed to release it. Before either of them could continue their conversation, someone interrupted them.

'Excuse me . . .' said a voice.

They both turned. Lucas was standing there. His friend Dwayne had disappeared – maybe in the dining hall with everyone else. In the gleaming, bright lights of reception, Lucas's dark hair had a slightly brown tint and his eyes seemed extra green, reminding her of wild moss. A shudder ran up Clem's spine as if someone had let in a draught.

'I'm sorry about what happened in there,' said Lucas. He pushed a hand through his hair, making it more chaotic and messy than it already was, strands sticking up at all angles. He appeared dishevelled, and even more attractive, Clem thought, her insides swooping like a leaf caught in the wind. 'I left the window open a fraction for Reina in the farmhouse because it was stuffy. I didn't know she'd prise the whole thing open and get into the conference hall . . . She's a bit of a wild dog. She's good though, just a bumbling idiot. She wouldn't hurt anyone. I think she was after Clem's squeezy cat – she has a toy just like it.'

Sylvie waved a hand. 'No harm done. I'm sure you didn't intend for anything like that to happen.'

But Lucas was watching Clem, as if he was waiting for her approval.

'It's okay,' she said sincerely. 'Really.'

'You know . . .' said Sylvie, glancing over her shoulder at the hotel, where some of the other contestants were scattered around, talking. The entrance to the dining hall was set far back from the reception; already there was the clinking of cutlery, the sounds of voices and people helping themselves to food. 'If you aren't having anything to eat inside, why don't you come to the cat café with us for a coffee?'

'The cat café?' Lucas clarified.

'Sure, why not? Your mum's told me a lot about you but I don't think you've ever visited us! I'm sure your dad would love it, too. She really wants to bring him along sometime. She's mentioned it a few times. Why don't you come along, and see it for yourself?'

Clem had a mad urge to stamp on Sylvie's foot when Lucas wasn't looking, but held herself back. Why was she inviting him to the café? She also didn't understand why Lucas would need to look at the café first, if his dad was interested in visiting. Couldn't he come himself?

'Dwayne's heading over to Muddy Paws, and I . . .' said Lucas, trailing off.

'Oh, did you already have plans?' said Sylvie.

Lucas glanced at Clem, shifting on the balls of his feet as if weighing up his options. Her neck was warm under his gaze, and she was suddenly flustered. What should she do? Should she say something? He'd been kind to her, during the audition. But he was the competition, going up against them for the prize.

'I was going to go see my dad,' he admitted. 'But you're right . . . we have always thought he'd like the cat café. Wouldn't be so bad to report back to give him some encouragement . . .' He trailed off. 'And I suppose I can't miss an opportunity to scope out my enemy.'

Clem's stomach performed a twist. It wasn't entirely unpleasant. Why was he looking at *her* when he said that? Was he flirting, or fooling around? She couldn't tell.

Sylvie laughed, and her tone was light-hearted. 'Great. You'll love it and you can tell your dad about us, try to convince him to come. I think it'd be good for him. Lots of people find visits to us therapeutic.'

Lucas paused again. Clem could see the conflict in his face, weighing up what Sylvie had said. She felt like she was missing half of this conversation. Was there a reason his dad would need something therapeutic? She wondered what was wrong with him and felt a surge of empathy for Lucas – it sounded like his father was going through something difficult.

'I can't stay long,' Lucas clarified. 'Let me message Dwayne and ask if he can take Reina home for me.'

★

Not that he'd tell Dwayne this – he'd think it was some kind of betrayal to dogs and the Muddy Paws Café – but Lucas had always wanted to visit Catpurrcino, and not only because he thought it might be enjoyable for his dad, who had always been a cat lover. But just to see what it was like. He told himself this was the only reason he'd come, and *not* because of Clem and the way she'd looked at him with those big hazel eyes. They made their way through the latched gate beyond the gift shop, into the main café room. After reviewing the café's rules, Lucas had insisted on paying the cost of admittance since he wanted to grab a coffee while he was here.

Muddy Paws Café was quite basic, with wooden floors scratched by the feet of a thousand dogs, and matching tables spread higgledy-piggledy throughout each room. It was always noisy, with low music and occasional barking, talkative hikers in every corner. Catpurrcino was like some sort of Zen retreat by comparison. The front window was wide and sprawling and a glossy black cat with a white diamond on its forehead was sitting at the window seat, washing its paws and face. There were towers for the cats all over the place, and shelves for them to climb dotting the walls, like a bizarre obstacle course. He spotted at least four different cats scattered about: one fluffy smoky-grey cat basking in a bucket-shaped bed, another stripy one with a bobbed tail strutting over to a feeder with confidence, a calico rolling in a patch of sun and trying to catch its own tail. Across the room, there was a counter spanning the length of the wall, with another smaller gate leading behind it, blocking the cats off. Glass cake displays were set out and he recognised some of Clem's cat-shaped doughnuts from the audition smiling up at him. There were biscuits and cookies iced with cat faces, too.

As they moved further in, Sylvie's phone began to buzz in her pocket, and she fished it out, glancing at the flashing screen. 'I need to take this,' she said. 'Sorry. Why don't you sit down and get yourself a drink? I won't be long – five minutes?'

'Okay,' said Lucas, looking uncertainly at Clem.

'I'll be super quick.' Sylvie disappeared behind the counter, through another door and out of sight.

Lucas was left standing with Clem. He wondered what Dwayne would have to say about this development. He could imagine his friend's grin when he found out Lucas had spent some time alone with Clem. Especially after what happened during the audition. The cameras had honed right in on that. His jaw worked; he was conflicted. It had been *his* dog, and his fault she'd been splashed with milk and become so anxious she'd shut down. So he felt to blame, and he had to help put it right. Even while he knew it wasn't something he should be doing, not during a competition like this when they were all going up against one another. He couldn't have just ignored her, though, left her to struggle after Reina had behaved like that.

He wondered why she'd entered the competition at all; it didn't seem to be easy for her, being in the spotlight.

'Um . . . shall we sit down?' Clem said, leading him to a table close to the window seat, surrounded by two comfortable-looking cream armchairs. There was a bucket of cat toys pushed up against the wall nearby – dangly, feathery things and fake mice. When he took a seat, she hurried on, sounding flustered, 'Oh, I'll get our drinks. What do you like?'

'A mocha would be great. Thanks.'

She nodded and scurried away.

He watched her placing the order with a dark-haired woman behind the counter, who glanced at Lucas and gave him a little wave. He raised his hand in return. His wallet was digging into him in his back pocket, so he pulled it out. A large ginger cat bounded up by the window, and Lucas turned, setting the wallet down on the plush window seat behind his chair so he could stroke the cat. The cat began to purr, loud and rumbly.

When Clem came back to the table, she had a pot of tea for herself, his mocha, and a cat-shaped doughnut with grey icing balanced on a tray. He stood up to help her set it down.

'Thanks,' she said breathlessly, dropping into the arm-chair opposite him. 'I got you one of these, too . . . in case you wanted to try . . . Um, to thank you for before, at the audition.'

She gestured at the iced doughnut; it had a little face, complete with black whiskers. Clem's ivory skin was prone to flushing a luminous pink and he couldn't help but notice it made her look even more beautiful, like she'd stepped out of a hot shower.

But he didn't want his thoughts to go down *that* particular track. Too dangerous.

'You didn't have to do that,' he said, surprised by her thoughtfulness. 'Thanks. You make everything here?' he added, partly to fill the silence and partly to distract him-self from her face. He dumped a sachet of sugar from the tray into his mocha.

'Yes,' she said, pouring some tea into her cup and swirling in milk. 'All the baked goods.'

The black cat that had been at the window earlier wandered over and weaved its way to Clem's legs, brushing against them and her shiny black shoes. Clem reached down to scritch the cat's neck. 'Hello, Salem,' she said softly. Even her voice was delicate, like wind chimes tinkling.

'I'm sorry again about what happened with Reina,' he told Clem. He was still feeling guilty. 'I know the camera caught what happened. But at least it's only for the judges' eyes at this stage. No one else will see it.'

'I hope not.' Clem chewed her lip. She looked more worried, and guilt churned inside him – he wanted to put things right. 'On second thought, maybe it put the judges off? It might be for the best if I don't get through anyway. I'm not great on camera, honestly . . .' She trailed off.

Lucas raised a single brow. 'But your doughnuts look really good.' He lifted up the one she'd brought across to him and took a bite. The icing was perfectly sweet and soft enough, the vanilla flavouring delicious – and the almond ears added a nice crunch, and an extra nutty taste, which complemented the fluffy inside. He couldn't help the moan that escaped him at the sweet, soft taste. 'They taste great, too,' he added.

That pinkness was back in her cheeks again. He wanted to trace the circular curve of her cheek with his thumb. These urges he felt around her kept stopping his brain in its tracks. It had been so long since he'd had those kinds of desires – but there was something about her that drew him in, made him want to be near to her.

He needed to stop thinking like this, get his head out of the clouds. What was her deal, anyway? Why was she so reluctant to be part of a competition she'd already applied for?

'If you don't mind me asking, why did you enter?' he said. To him, the most logical thing to do if you didn't like doing something was to avoid the situation – not dive headlong into it. It was why he'd given up on dating; it had never been the best experience.

She gave a half-shrug, which didn't quite explain things. 'Why did you?' she said.

'The prize money,' he said simply.

'I imagine that's why most people entered. The practical reason . . .'

'But not you?'

She opened her mouth and closed it again, thinking. 'Well, it's complicated. That's part of it . . .'

He wanted to ask why she wanted the prize money, what she intended to use it for. If she was so anxious about being on camera, but entered anyway, there must be something she wanted badly enough, and he was curious to know what it was. But Clem changed the subject: 'Do you think you'll make the next round of the contest?'

'Who knows?' He sat back in his seat, assessing her. She seemed so certain she wouldn't be selected because of what had happened with Reina, but she was so talented. 'You might get through, you know,' he added.

She huffed out a sigh. 'I know . . . I bet they're thinking what happened with Reina will make for great viewing.' She took a sip of her tea, looking at him over the rim of the mug. 'They got you on camera, too. Afterwards, when you helped. They could pick both of us.'

'They could do. We'd be rivals then.'

She stiffened.

'I didn't mean that in a confrontational way,' he said quickly. 'It's just—'

He didn't get to finish, because Sylvie had emerged from beyond the counter, the gateway banging shut behind her. She dodged around a big ginger cat lounging on the floor as she made her way over to them, smiling.

'All done,' she said. 'I'll grab a coffee and join you.' She headed towards the counter to get herself a drink.

Lucas took a gulp of his mocha. The black cat took this moment to weave around his ankles, and he gave it a quick stroke before straightening up. 'Would being my rival be so bad?' he asked Clem.

'You make it sound like we'll be sparring with whisks.'

'We might,' he said, finding himself smiling at the image, and she snorted into her tea.

# Chapter 9

After Lucas had left the café, Clem made herself another cup of tea – she'd head home after this. It was only when she finished the dregs from her teacup and cast her eyes over the main room that she noticed something small, black and square-shaped over by the window. Thomas was curled up beside it, his big ginger body reminding her of a fuzzy children's toy.

She crossed the room. It was Lucas's wallet – he'd forgotten it. Thomas was half-sleeping on it; she tugged it from beneath him. The cat looked up, giving her a chirpy *mew*, and she tickled him behind the ears.

Would he come back for it? But if he was driving to Muddy Paws Café, he probably wouldn't notice until he arrived; he'd be too occupied on the roads.

'Guess I'll have to find some way to contact him, Tom-Tom,' she told the cat, giving him a pat on the head and retrieving her own phone from her pocket. She googled the café and found a number, dialling it.

Someone picked up on the third ring. 'Muddy Paws Café?' It sounded like Dwayne. She hadn't expected anyone to answer.

'Hi, is that Dwayne? It's Clem—'

'Clem! Hey. What can I do for you?'

'Lucas left his wallet here at Catpurrcino,' she explained.

'Ah, shoot, he's not here,' said Dwayne. 'Went over to see his folks. They live over in Keswick. He could probably swing your way again on his way home. Let me give you his number; you can text him.'

'Oh, okay . . .' Clem had anticipated Dwayne contacting Lucas himself, but then again, he was probably busy, and if Lucas would be driving this way again anyway, it was easier.

Dwayne rattled off Lucas's number – she put him on speaker so she could add it to her contacts – and Clem said goodbye and hung up. Something was stirring in her again, like bubbles rising in a fizzy drink. She had Lucas's number. Thomas had gone to sleep on the window seat, his head tipped to the side, exposing a smiley mouth. Taking a deep breath, Clem tapped out a message to Lucas so he'd come to collect the wallet.

★

Lucas did swing by to pick up his wallet, meeting her in the car park at the back of Catpurrcino. He was out of breath by the time he jogged over to her from his car, his dark hair poking up at all angles, making him appear windswept and beyond handsome. The surge of giddiness she felt at the sight of him with his dark hair askew in the breeze was hard to tamp down.

'Here's your wallet,' she said, holding it out for him.

'I can't believe I left that here,' he said. When he took it, their fingers made contact, sending vibrations up her arms and into her core. Lucas tucked the wallet into his pocket and shoved his hair away from his forehead. 'Thanks for finding it.'

'Dwayne gave me your number,' she explained, feeling winded. She could smell his cologne, fresh and masculine with notes of cedarwood, wisping towards her on the wind. 'I don't know if you mind. I can delete it—'

'Keep it,' he interrupted, with a shrug. 'You never know.'

*Never know what?* she wanted to ask, but he was already talking again.

'I better get off,' he said. 'Dwayne is probably sick of babysitting Reina. I'll be seeing you.'

'Okay . . . bye.'

He raised a hand, turned, and hurried back to his car, leaving her with a faint sense of disappointment that he didn't stay – and curiosity about what he meant by *You never know*.

★

By the following week, Clem was feeling like a nervous wreck, waiting to find out if she'd made it through the auditions. She alternated between desperately wanting to be selected – because she could put the money towards building her own baking business, and to moving out – and wanting nothing more than to *not* be chosen, and to spend the rest of the summer months hiding in the garden with her cat. She wasn't sure she could handle another incident like the one with Reina, and at least *that* one hadn't been shared with *Whisked Away*'s audience. How would she cope if she made it through auditions and had to be filmed regularly, uploaded in high-definition for the world to see?

It was a bright sunny day in May, the sky a stretch of eggshell blue, and she was sitting in the Cat Lounge on her lunch break at Catpurrcino, absently munching at an egg and cress sandwich. Her phone dinged, and an email notification flashed up. She usually kept her email app disabled on her phone, but she'd turned it on so she'd know right away if something happened with *Whisked Away*.

Clem snatched up the phone from a patch of sunlight, putting her sandwich down and placing a plastic cover down over her plate so hard Baron looked up, startled, from the seat opposite hers. He'd been sitting there watching her eating her sandwich intently, hoping for a morsel, and he now offered her a disgruntled look, his fuzzy ears leaning back.

'Sorry, boy,' she said softly, giving him a blink – the friendly gesture all cats knew. The long-haired cat blinked his green eyes once, slowly, and started licking his paws and rubbing at his head, cleaning behind his ears.

With quaking fingers, Clem unlocked her phone screen – the email was from *Whisked Away* and the subject line read *congratulations!* It was as though a dozen marbles were cascading through her body, clacking into one another. She'd got through – and the Catpurrcino Cat Café would be in the contest, officially.

She raked over the email, skipping from one line to the next, skimming it. *Congratulations, the Catpurrcino Cat Café has been selected . . . Ronan and the other judges were impressed by your baking and the attention to detail . . . Attached are further details of the next stages of the competition . . . Dates are final . . .*

Clem jolted to her feet, caught between excitement and immense anxiety, and had to force herself to walk slowly as she took her food and half-empty mug behind the counter. Jess danced around her ankles, hoping for her leftovers, her black tail high in the air.

Had Lucas received one of these emails, too? A sudden, horrible thought occurred to Clem. Was this really down to her baking skills, or what had happened, and how he'd comforted her in front of everyone – on camera? Did *Whisked Away* simply think that together, they made good TV? Ronan had mentioned the importance of screen presence. If he'd got through as well, maybe that would be why . . .

Even though she'd just consumed half a mug of tea, she was parched.

Faye, who was steaming milk – the noise of the machine whooshing and hissing – glanced up at her and frowned. 'Something wrong, Clem?' she asked.

Clem shoved her way behind the counter, throwing away the rest of her sandwich. Her appetite had gone. 'Where's Sylvie?' she squeaked, bouncing on the balls of her feet.

'In the staffroom.' Faye finished up with frothing the milk and hovered there, uncertain. 'What is it?'

'The contest . . . we got through.'

'You did?!' Faye shrilled. A few of the customers at the nearest table to the counter looked over curiously, distracted from playing with Eric, whose bobbed tail was wiggling with excitement as he studied the feather toy hanging above him. 'Oh my God – that's amazing!' Faye continued, breaking into a huge smile. 'You have to tell Sylvie – she's doing finance, I think—'

Clem nodded and disappeared before Faye could finish, depositing her mug and plate into the sink on her way by the kitchen, and hurrying into the staffroom, almost tripping over her own feet in her haste down the corridor. Even though she was apprehensive, worried about the true reason she'd got into the contest, she couldn't help the smile that formed on her face. She found Sylvie where Faye said she would be, sitting at a plastic chair in the staffroom, her laptop in front of her and a bulging planner open on the table.

'Oh, hi, Clem,' said Sylvie, glancing up. She looked surprised to see the smile on Clem's face, and sat up straighter. 'What is it?'

Stepping further into the room, Clem brought up the email on her phone again and held it out to Sylvie. 'Look!'

'That's . . .' Sylvie stood up, taking the phone from her and scanning over the contents of the email, as Clem had. 'This is wonderful!' she cried, grabbing Clem's hand. 'I knew you could do it, Clem!'

Clem could feel the smile slipping from her face. *Had* she done it, though, on skill alone – or had she merely given them some good entertainment during her audition? How was Lucas feeling about all of this, she wondered?

Sylvie must have noticed the hesitancy, because she said, 'Don't worry, Clem, we'll be fine. I'll be there with you the whole time. They've given us plenty of details here so you can plan ahead. I have total faith in you. This is so exciting! It'll be fun.'

Excitement swirled within her again, and Clem bounced on her toes – it was strange, to be so giddy and apprehensive all at once. She hadn't felt like that since she'd first landed the job at Catpurrcino.

'Do you think Lucas and Muddy Paws got through . . . ?' Clem ventured.

'I'm not sure.'

'Maybe I should ask him . . . I have his number. Dwayne gave it to me when he left his wallet here at the café.'

There was a glint in Sylvie's eye now, and Clem wondered if her attraction to Lucas was that obvious. 'He won't mind you asking,' Sylvie said. 'Get in touch with him! They're nice lads.'

'We're going up against them – is it weird to be friendly?'

'A little friendly competition – there's no harm in that. It doesn't mean we can't make friends along the way, does it?'

Laughter and jeers echoed in Clem's ears as she thought back to university, how she was humiliated. Sylvie was such a joyous person, sunny and trusting, like Emmie. Clem, on the other hand, couldn't help but wonder about people's motives since then. And her anxiety was like a chatterbox in her ear at the best of times – questioning and offering up what-ifs and doubts.

But Lucas, he'd helped her, at the audition, hadn't he? That could have risked his own place in the contest, taking his focus away from his own baking, and he'd done it anyway. None of the others had. Surely it meant he was a kind person.

She fumbled with her phone, the eagerness to contact him warring with her mounting anxiety. The anxiety won this time.

'I'm sure I'll find out eventually,' she decided, slipping her phone away.

★

## Whisked Away Competition Rounds

*Before we introduce our Whisked Away contestants in the Lake District, we'd like to share the details of the upcoming rounds so you, our audience, can join in at home! We'd love to see photos of any creations you make as you watch the rounds!*

*Here's what we'll be asking our contestants to do ...*

*Round 1: Biscuits! We'd like our contestants to design biscuits to introduce us to them, and what they do! This could be a staple biscuit already made by the business, or, if they don't do biscuits at all, a batch of biscuits to show us what they're all about ... Think biscuits shaped like birthday or wedding cakes, for added creativity! We want a glimpse into what makes the business special.*

*Round 2: Bread! We want the best seasonal bread creations possible – think focaccia, flatbread, fruit bread, and sourdough! Our contestants should link this to their business in some way. As we shift over into summer, we want something ideal for a picnic!*

*Round 3: The final round! Here, we want our contestants to make their standout bake of the contest ... a spectacular diorama, in cake form, of the business they're here to represent and what it means to them. Our winner will be chosen during this finale – based on both the diorama and the bakes that came before!*

*The dates and times are as follows ...*

Clem was sitting at her desk at home, tossing her phone between her palms. Misha was curled in her lap, her nose tucked into her tail and her little head tipped to the side. She was snoozing contentedly, her mouth slightly parted, as if she were smiling. Clem stopped palming her phone and unlocked the screen, staring at it again, stroking Misha's soft fur with her free hand, which helped to quell some of her nerves.

Outside, the sun was setting, spilling pink and orange light into her bedroom, the thick pink clouds outside her window promising another bright day tomorrow. Her mum was at work, off photographing a wedding; spring and summer were her busiest seasons.

For the last thirty minutes, she'd been staring at Lucas's number, trying to work up the courage to send him a message. The email she'd received from *Whisked Away* about getting onto the contest didn't say anything about the other contestants, or who they'd be. They would be doing full public announcements soon – something that made her skin tingle with fear – but the desire to know whether Lucas had got through, to talk to him now, was nibbling away at her, even though she'd held off before.

At first, she'd thought there was no need to message him again. If he'd got through, she'd find out soon. And if he didn't, she probably wouldn't be seeing him again. She had been surprised by how much the thought made her heart sink. And that was what was prompting her to stare absently at the digits of his phone number.

There was a picture of him in the little bubble beside his name that had been making her feel quivery – and it was part of why she was hesitating. In the photo, he was standing behind a café counter, wearing a loose-fitting dark grey shirt and a white apron. Someone had clearly made him laugh before taking the picture, because his smile was dazzling, showing his top row of teeth. There was a menu on the wall behind him, and a row of shelves, faded so only Lucas stood out. The image of him was sharp, making his dark hair and green eyes pop.

She typed out, *Hi Lucas, it's Clem*, then promptly deleted it, hissing through her teeth in frustration.

Misha's head lifted, her pupils growing in size as she caught the sound.

'Sorry, sweetie,' said Clem, rubbing her fingers onto the top of Misha's head. 'Go back to sleep.'

When Misha realised the sound wasn't anything threatening, she stretched out a paw, her whole body shaking with her stretch, and lowered her head again sleepily.

She needed to bite the bullet and do it. She furiously typed: *Hi Lucas, hope you don't mind me getting in touch. It's Clem by the way,* she added quickly, because she had no idea if he'd saved her number to his contacts when she returned the wallet. *Just wondering if you got through in the contest? We heard back and we got through.*

Before she could talk herself out of it, she jabbed the send button. At once, her palms slickened with sweat. Maybe she shouldn't have asked. He might try delving into her reasons for entering again, and she'd have to admit she hadn't, that it was all just a twist of fate, a decision taken out of her hands because she wasn't brave enough to do it herself. She rubbed her palm over Misha's fur, giving the cat a belly rub as she exposed her fluffy stomach to Clem, beginning to vibrate with purrs.

The sound soothed Clem. She tried to focus on something else while she waited, looking up some ideas for new recipes and thumbing through her scrapbook of ideas, but she couldn't help checking every five minutes to see if Lucas had seen her message or replied.

Finally, an agonising hour later – Misha had moved to curl on Clem's bed, tired of her being so fidgety – he replied.

He'd written:

Hey Clem, I recognised your number. We got through too.☺

Clem reread the message four times. Maybe it was his overly attractive picture hovering in the top-left making her hormones spiral out of control, but the smiley face was sending her head spinning.

Before she could tap out her answer, he'd sent another message:

I'll be seeing you at the first round.

# Chapter 10

The official announcement of the *Whisked Away* contestants came a week before the first round was due to be filmed in May. Lucas was on his break at the Muddy Paws Café, sitting out in the back, where wooden picnic tables and taller seats and barrel-tables with giant yellow umbrellas were framed by trees and bracken. It had been a busy day – it was sunny, bright, and the weather was warming up nicely, spools of sunlight flecking the tables like pirate's gold, and lots of families, tourists, and local workers had been out taking full advantage of the balmy weather. Now, with it being school pick-up time, it was much quieter: an elderly couple were sitting in the shade with their snoozing Dalmatian resting at their feet while they sipped iced teas, and a young couple drinking coffee had their heads pressed together over a hiking trail map.

Lucas had been checking his phone all day when he could, and the announcement was finally live. His and Dwayne's headshots were splashed under the words *Muddy Paws Café*. His stomach leaped in excitement and he grinned at the prospect of the prize money, and what he could do with it – how much easier life could be for his parents.

He *had* to win.

He glugged some of his mocha, scanning the rest of the contestants. There would be five groups of two, with one group being voted off each round until the final, where three groups would go up against one another to win. The other contestants outside of Muddy Paws included a family-run cake business, a breakfast bakery known for their pies, and a quaint little farm shop he'd heard hikers rave about.

And then there was Catpurrcino. His thumb traced Clem's headshot. Beside her, in Sylvie's headshot, she looked confident and smiley, standing at the counter, a paw-shaped clip scraping her hair into place. But Clem's smile looked a little nervous, hesitant, and she was tipping her head, as if to try and hide behind her silky black hair.

He took another sip of his mocha and opened up the comments on the announcement. The more he scrolled through them, the more the smile edged from his face. Because most of Ronan's loyal fanbase were interested in one thing: Lucas and Clem.

> Did you see the clip they shared from the audition?
> Oh my God, it was SO cute, I can't stand it.

He swallowed. They'd shared clips? He'd been so busy working, and looking for the announcement specifically, he hadn't noticed.

> He's such a green flag. They better get together by the end of this!
>     The way he looked after her! I'm here for it!
>     They better not get voted off. I want to see what happens.

He couldn't stop scrolling, even though every other similar comment made him feel uneasy. He chucked the rest of his mocha in the nearby bin without standing up, almost missing. The elderly couple grinned at him when the cup met its mark. He smiled absently.

There were a few comments about the other contestants, wishing them good luck, or people mentioning if they'd had cakes or pastries from them before. They were overwhelmed by the comments about him and Clem, though.

He scrolled the *Whisked Away* social media accounts and looked for the clip from the audition. Sure enough, they'd shared clips of everyone who'd got through, including the moment where Reina had come barrelling into the conference room at Clem, and the aftermath.

The clip played out. He understood why they were doing this – it was good publicity for the contest. Spinning a storyline could ensure people stayed invested and kept coming back to watch more. If it were just him, he'd be fine with that. It was business.

His thumb tracked across the screen until he'd frozen the video on Clem, her head bowed down, face not visible beneath a curtain of dark hair. She looked fragile, like a flower coiling in on itself and withering beneath the rain.

Lucas's chest twisted. It *wasn't* just him. She'd been thrust into this spotlight too. Had he made it worse, by helping?

His mind argued with itself. She'd signed up; this was to be expected. And yet she hadn't wanted this extra attention. Lucas and Reina had made it worse for her.

Suddenly, he got to his feet, pulling up the cat café on his phone. He only had another hour left at Muddy Paws. The cat café was open for a while longer. He fired off a text to Clem.

> Are you at work? Can I talk to you after your shift? Heading to see my parents then driving back your way.

As he shoved his phone into his pocket and hurried inside Muddy Paws, he told himself this was business – an excuse for him to discuss the contest and what they would do about this attention – even if the reasoning was as flimsy as paper. Because really, he wanted to make sure she was okay.

★

Clem had agreed that Lucas could come to the café, which he was relieved about. She said she'd be there until closing because she was batch-prepping some more cat doughnuts. When he arrived, the sun was sinking lower and casting the roads into shade. Thick grey clouds were moving across the sky now, blowing in on the breeze. He messaged Clem to say he was here. The café sign was already switched to closed, but when he tapped on the door, she opened it at once, ushering him inside and shutting it behind him.

Her hair was scooped up under a hairnet, pulling her fringe out of her face and exposing its heart shape, and she was wearing a pink apron decorated with little cartoon cats, all rolling around, sleeping, or playing with balls of string. He wasn't prepared for the whooshing sensation in his stomach: he'd still had the image of her from the audition in his head, hair concealing her face. She looked more dainty and beautiful with it pulled back, highlighting her dewy skin and hazel eyes.

'You saw, didn't you?' she said. Her forehead was creased with dismay, her bottom lip pouty, and he wanted, madly, to kiss away the worry in her features.

*Stop it*, he scolded himself internally. *Focus.*

'The announcement? Yes—'

'And the clip!' she said shrilly. 'They posted that just after. I can't believe it . . . I think they said they *might* use audition footage but I thought it was unlikely . . .'

She was talking extremely quickly, making it difficult to keep up.

'I haven't been able to focus. I completely wrecked a batch of doughnuts. Sylvie and the others have gone; Emmie's at Jared's and I said I'd close up. I just can't stop thinking about—'

'Slow down,' said Lucas softly, bringing her to a halt.

His words seemed to have encouraged her to assess him. Clem took a step back, drinking him in. The way she was looking at him made his skin surge with electricity, and she hadn't even touched him.

'Sorry,' she said, quietly.

'You don't have to apologise.'

'Why . . . why are you here?' she asked tentatively. They were still hovering in the entrance, where a huge poster of the cat café's rules looked down on them, beneath a big green pair of cat's eyes. An alcove looked in on the reception area and the gift shop. A woman was sitting at the reception desk, headphones dangling from her ears as she stared down at her phone.

'I . . .' He trailed off. It had seemed urgent that he come here to see if she was alright but he couldn't say so, could he? Not without burrowing deeper into his feelings about her. And if he went down that route . . . No, not a good idea. He had wanted to make sure she was alright, nothing more. 'I thought we could discuss strategies. For dealing with this,' he said.

She opened her mouth, then closed it again, looking confused.

'But we're going *against* each other in the contest.' Clem looked upset all over again, her brows knitting together, and she cast an anxious look at the receptionist behind her.

'Yes.' He sighed. 'But they seem to have singled us out.'

'I know.' She was pouting and all he wanted to do was run his finger over her mouth, brush the frown into something happier. 'I don't understand why.'

'It's probably the cats and dogs thing,' he replied. 'It's a good angle, for the show . . .'

'You better come inside . . .' she said, waving at him to follow her. 'Sylvie won't mind if we chat somewhere.'

She led him through the gift shop and reception. The woman in headphones glanced up but when she saw Clem, she simply said hello and waved Lucas onward. They headed through the door and the latched gate, until they were in the main café.

A cat was immediately visible on one of the chairs at the nearest table. It was huge, with black-and-white markings, and only just about fitted into the seat, its tail dangling off as it snoozed softly. Its head was buried beneath its black paws. Clem took Lucas behind the counter, where she said hello to another woman, fair-haired and smiling at them, before they walked down a narrow hallway and into a staffroom.

'It's quieter here,' she said.

The room was painted in a mixture of bright ivory and off-white, with brightly coloured chairs set around a break table. There were framed photos of the café's cats on the walls – as if these cats were the staff, rather than the humans. A kitchenette with tea- and coffee-making facilities and a small sink was set against the wall near the door.

'Listen,' she said, 'I appreciate you coming here but I don't think there's much we can do . . .'

'I know,' he agreed. 'If this is the angle they're going to spin, we'll have to deal with it. But are you prepared?'

'What do you mean?'

'It might get harder from here.'

Clem grasped her elbow tightly. 'I know it might. I can't back out now . . . Sylvie is counting on me . . . What are your strategies?'

In truth, he didn't know. But he'd studied film; maybe he could at least give her some advice?

'Think of it like acting in a movie,' he said, and when she looked terrified, he hurried on, 'Hear me out. When you're on camera, on-screen baker is your persona. Act the role – or that cliché, fake it till you make it.'

'I'm not an actress,' she said weakly.

'But you obviously wanted to enter this contest for a reason. Whether it's the money, the opportunities that might come – whatever it is. Maybe it's better to think of it like this: you come to work here, at Catpurrcino, right?'

'Yes . . .'

'When you're working in the kitchen, you're in that persona, right? Professional baker. Employee. If you talk to a customer, you're professional baker Clem. It's the same thing. When you're on camera, you have to slip into a different persona. Contestant Clem.'

She was gnawing at her lip so hard it might bleed. 'Have you done acting?'

'Ha, no. Studied film at university. I worked some live-action roleplay events as a caterer and picked up a few things, though. Think of it like that. Like roleplay.'

'I'll try,' she agreed, though she didn't sound sure.

He wanted to offer more advice, but didn't know what else to give. She still seemed so worried, her hand hooked over her elbow and her foot tapping nervously against the floor. There was an odd mixture of emotions building inside him, like waves crashing forward to reach a shore – to reach her. Because he wanted to reassure her, make her feel better, and there was this pull towards her that he didn't really understand.

'It'll be fine,' he said, because it was all he had. 'Don't worry.'

And he couldn't help it – he stepped forward and gave her shoulder a reassuring pat, almost turning it into a squeeze before he moved away quickly, shoving his hands into his pockets. *Idiot*, he thought. He hadn't been thinking.

She stared at him, wordless, then, surprisingly, she smiled, her hazel eyes sparkling, and those waves inside him crashed even more loudly.

★

Several days later, Lucas was spending a morning at home, preparing for the first round of the contest. He was in the room that served as their designated Muddy Paws office, which held two desks – one for him, one for Dwayne – and a couple of swivelling office chairs. A big canvas picture of Reina leaping through a green field holding a frisbee took pride of place on one of the walls. They'd been sitting here developing ideas for a solid few hours, so Dwayne had gone out to grab some cold drinks to stave off the muggy weather, which was making the air close and sticky. Lucas leaned back in his chair, swinging to one side in it, absently.

A familiar name flashed up on Lucas's phone when his chair rotated to face the desk again, giving him pause. *Georgina.* What did she want? He hadn't heard from her in a while. Since she'd moved away, they didn't talk like they used to – hadn't for years. Childhood friends for over ten years, drifted apart not only in distance but in their bond, too. They met up occasionally, if he happened to be in her neck of the woods, or if she was visiting home. And he'd talked her through a few bad break-ups when she was still settling into her new home. Maybe she was visiting again and that was why she was contacting him?

*Georgina:* Are you around, Lukey?

    *Lucas:* What, like right this second?

    *Lucas:* And stop calling me Lukey. It makes me sound five years old

    *Georgina:* No, I mean in general. Soon. I'm coming home for a bit

    *Lucas:* Yeah, I'm around

    *Georgina:* Okay

    *Georgina:* It'd be nice to see you and catch up. I've missed you

He frowned down at his phone, reading the words over twice. She hadn't said something like that in a long time. Where had this come from?

> *Lucas:* Is something wrong?
>
>    *Georgina:* Nah. I just feel bad we aren't close anymore

Lucas didn't know what to say to this – so he didn't answer. When they'd been closer as friends, she had never been particularly affectionate, never saying she missed him or she loved him in the way some friends did. She wasn't a hugger, didn't display her feelings through touch or words. She'd been like that throughout their childhoods.

Until she suddenly told him she had romantic feelings for him – and he couldn't reciprocate. How could he, when she was like a sister to him? He remembered playing tag with her in the school playground, forming a fake band with some of their schoolfriends, swimming lessons, going to the same high school. For her, it had always been more. A crush, grown into something deeper over years.

Was she thinking down that track again? His phone vibrated against his hand; he checked the screen.

> *Georgina:* Are you seeing anyone?
>
>    *Lucas:* Why are you asking me this?
>
>    *Georgina:* I'm curious. We hardly talk now
>
>    *Lucas:* No

> *Lucas:* But why does it matter? I hope you're
> not thinking of asking me out
>
> *Lucas:* Sorry, Georgina. I don't mean to be
> harsh but we've talked about this before

It took her a long time to respond, and she'd been pretty quick up to now; she must be puzzling out a response, digging around for the right words like she was searching for seedlings. He sighed, scraping a hand over his neck and stretching it out. He didn't want to go down this road again – they weren't heading in the same direction and he'd only disappoint her, like he had before.

Back then, he'd thought maybe he should distance himself from her for good, a clean break. Only, he hadn't been able to, not completely, after so many years of friendship. The gradual distance between them had helped; he'd expected things to peter out after she moved away. Yet here she was again.

Finally, his phone vibrated again.

> *Georgina:* No, I'm not going to ask you out
>
> *Georgina:* I wondered, is all. It'd be good to
> see you, when I come. I could visit you at Muddy
> Paws. I haven't been there in ages

Now it was his turn to take his time replying, fingers hovering over the touchscreen as he figured out what to say. He hoped she didn't think there was a chance something more would bud between them. He should make that clear, as gently as he could. Eventually, he typed out:

> Okay, let me know when. Always good to catch up with old friends.

There. It was a subtle enough reminder that she was a friend, almost a sister, to him, and not a prospective romantic partner.

Even so, it irked him that after all these years, Georgina couldn't seem to let go of her feelings for him. He didn't know if a friendship could survive that.

# Chapter 11

The first round of the contest came around *fast*. Lucas hadn't been able to keep his attention off social media in the lead-up to it; he usually didn't bother, save for updating the Muddy Paws Café accounts every so often with events or offers. People were still acting like he and Clem were fictional characters in some TV drama they could theorise about, not real people. *I hope they get together!!* some of them squealed in comments sections. If this was how people were behaving before they'd truly got started, how were they going to act in the second round, or the third, if he and Clem were still in the competition? He'd had no idea Ronan's fans were so rabid or that people cared so much about the contestants of *Whisked Away*.

He was standing outside Muddy Paws Café with Dwayne, rucksacks on their backs, waiting for the coach that would be picking up the contestants. They'd decided to close up the café on the contest round days, even though it meant losing money – hopeful that any progress in the competition meant more business on the other days when they remained open.

'Are you still checking your phone?' Dwayne said, clucking his tongue in disapproval. 'Get off it, mate. It's not worth looking.'

'Clem's probably looking.'

'You're worried about her,' said Dwayne slyly.

'Shut up. I'm not. It was an inane comment.' But Lucas felt a sharp twang, like an elastic band being snapped in his ribcage. He sucked in a breath, unable to help it – he *was* worried about her. What would she be thinking as she read these comments?

'Inane my backside,' said Dwayne.

Lucas ignored him. Maybe Clem wouldn't show up for the first round, with all this going on? It seemed like it was going to be a *lot* to deal with for both of them.

About five minutes later, the coach came driving smoothly down the road. It was a sleek white thing with dark, tinted windows, shining in the early morning light as if they'd been washed until squeaky clean that very morning. When the door swung open with a whoosh, they hopped on, and a driver in a *Whisked Away* shirt wished them a good morning and pointed them to their seats. Little pieces of paper were sticking up from the top of each seat, with their names written on.

They said hello to their fellow contestants as they passed, nodding and smiling and exchanging good mornings. Dwayne was in the seat by the window, Lucas in the aisle. They sat down and the coach rolled away from Muddy Paws, past the moored ships at the port and the glittering surface of the lake. Out of curiosity, Lucas checked the empty seats across from theirs, and the names written on the paper.

*Typical.* They had to have done it on purpose.

*Catpurrcino,* the papers read.

Clem would be sitting directly across from them. He dug around in his rucksack to take a swig of water.

'Oakside next, I imagine,' said Dwayne, giving him a suggestive grin. He leaned forward. 'What were you looking at? Who's sat there?'

Lucas tried in vain to shove Dwayne further back in his seat, but it was too late.

'Ahh!' Dwayne laughed. 'I see they're aligning the lovebirds perfectly—'

Looking at his friend's shirt choice for the day – white, with Dalmatian print, this time, in honour of their café's name – Lucas warned, 'If you end up coming in a lovebird shirt next time, I swear—'

'*Ooh*, great idea, I hadn't thought about that . . .'

Lucas bopped him in the arm with his water bottle.

All too soon, they were arriving in Oakside, red-brown brick buildings springing up either side of the road, and climbing the hill to the cat café. It was still early, the sunshine hazy and partly concealed by clouds, birds cheeping happily in the trees. Clem and Sylvie were standing beneath the café's awning, Clem's hair night-black and standing out more prominently through the dark film of the window's tint.

His stomach flopped like a pancake being turned. She had her arms folded, as if to contain something. It was cool so early in the morning in spite of the recent warm weather, so she was wearing a dark jacket and a long pleated skirt with a shirt tucked in loosely. A quote was printed on the front of the shirt, reading *life is better with cats*, surrounded by the outline of a cat's body and tail. When she boarded the bus behind Sylvie, the earthy colours she wore were revealed. He'd never seen anyone look so good in greens and beiges before, or maybe he'd simply never paid attention.

Lucas cleared his throat. Being Dwayne's friend was clearly making him pay too much attention to other people's clothing choices.

'Ah, here we are,' said Sylvie when they reached their seats, and she slid in, sitting next to the window. 'Right across from Team Dog!' She beamed over at Lucas and Dwayne.

Dwayne waved at them and elbowed Lucas, who gave a weak, 'Hi.'

Clem smiled softly and sat down, shoving her backpack beneath the seat. She kept her hands planted in her lap the rest of the journey, her head angled toward Sylvie and the scenery flashing by the window. Lucas was acutely aware of the small distance between them, as if her body was giving off crackling waves of electricity that he could feel.

He kept his own gaze fixed on the landscapes – the hills and the sheep and the towering craggy mounds rolling by. He tried not to look at her, if he could help it.

Wray Castle in Claife was their final destination. Lucas had visited the castle itself once, in school, but he'd forgotten how imposing it was. They circled into the car park, passing a series of flowers in spaced-apart clusters along the grass, and he peered out of the window. The Gothic-style castle rose up from behind a high stone wall, some of its jagged towers and stone walls etched with arrow slits, the windows pushed deep into the structure. The entrance was huge and arched, sitting between two of the towers. He couldn't see much else; the stone walls concealed the rest from view.

The contestants filed off the bus, into the coolness of the early morning. Birds were singing their melodies in the trees and a thin layer of mist hung over the surrounding landscape.

'Nice location,' Dwayne said at his side. 'Wonder how Ronan swung this one? Didn't they film a movie here?'

'Dunno,' Lucas replied. The back of his head was warm, as if Clem was a physical heat behind him.

A huge white tent had been erected on the sprawl of bottle-green grass near the castle. The tent was glowing in the sunshine that had just managed to break through the shrouded clouds. It wasn't a run-of-the-mill tent, either: it was luxurious and long, with an entrance at one end, less wide than the rest and topped off with spring bunting. There were several pointed sections along the top, like miniature roofs or wizard's hats, and each side of the tent had a transparent film running along it. Towards the back, there was a canopy to provide shade, and some empty tables.

A short distance from the tent, there was another, much wider canopy offering a patch of shade to a cluster of empty tables and chairs. Each table was draped with a white cloth; this must be for the small audience invited for each round to taste-test their bakes and to get footage of real people enjoying their creations.

The camera crew were already here preparing, and staff in black *Whisked Away* shirts hurried about like bumblebees in search of pollen. Lucas caught sight of a row of kitchen counters in pale green, and twinkling fairy lights, inside the main tent.

'This way!' a woman called, gesturing at a gate in the fencing, leading onto the grass. 'Come along, we'll get you into the tent now.'

The group tramped forward, over the grass. Clem was walking behind him. He cast a glance over his shoulder. Her hazel eyes were wide and there was a pink tint to her cheeks that made his neck prickle.

'I'm disappointed we aren't going *inside* the castle,' Lucas commented. He was still looking at Clem and she turned towards him, offering up a faint smile.

'It's too small,' Dwayne said. 'For a big tent and all those workstations, at least. And it's a visitor attraction so we'd be in the way of everyone else, even if we *could* fit inside.'

They were ushered into the tent entrance, and Dwayne whistled.

The entrance segment to the tent was decorated with a zig-zag of glittering fairy lights that touched everything with their golden light, like fireflies. It reminded him of a garden centre, with plenty of shadowy corners provided by the leafy plants, making the lights glow more brightly. The plants were interspersed with pot animals: white swans, painted badgers, cream-coloured rabbits, hedgehogs, and jewelled turtles with flowers bursting from their backs.

'No dogs or cats. Scandalous,' Dwayne muttered in disapproval, as the group of contestants were guided through.

Lucas replied with a wry smile. Behind them, Sylvie laughed.

The mini garden led straight to the workstations. Two rows of wooden green workstations were set out neatly, with plenty of space between them and a walkway up the middle. It was spacious and bright in here, the transparent parts of the tent allowing in plenty of light. There were a few eggshell-blue fridges gleaming along the outskirts, along with more decorations: copper pans hanging from the walls, teacups and fake cakes stacked on more shelving. One big, wider counter spanned the back of the tent, and to the left was a kettle and coffee-making facilities.

The woman from *Whisked Away* got them set up at their individual workstations. 'You'll have everything you'll need here,' she told them. 'Oven and hob, ingredients, mixer. Take some time to familiarise yourself with the stations before the judges get here.'

Clattering and chatter followed her words as everyone got acquainted with their set-ups. Lucas rummaged around in the workstation with Dwayne. She was right: they were well equipped.

'They're near to us again,' Dwayne muttered, nodding at Sylvie and Clem. They were at the workstation directly beside Lucas and Dwayne, and Lucas was finding it difficult not to focus on Clem's skirt swishing as she moved, because it made it too tempting to look at her.

Within ten minutes, Ronan and the other judges had breezed into the tent, followed by the camera crew. As usual, their styles could not be more different: Ronan's curls were bouncy and he wore a pale green chequered suit with a baby-pink tie. Viviana was in a long black dress, with a cropped white jacket draped across her shoulders, gold buttons shining. Beside her, Laurette was in a pair of fashionable dark shorts and a flowery blouse, and Jonathan had on his trademark designer glasses and a perfectly pressed navy shirt.

'Good morning, all!' Ronan called out, clapping his hands together and grinning around at them as they fell silent. 'We hope you're prepared for round one! Let's begin.'

# Chapter 12

*Biscuits.* Lucas grinned as he set to work. It was the perfect way to start: he and Dwayne planned to make the strawberry and white chocolate shortbread that was so popular with the humans at Muddy Paws Café, and on the side, they'd make a set of dog biscuits humans could eat and enjoy, to reflect the dog treats they gave away for free. Dwayne was already whipping out the ingredients they needed, and Lucas set the oven to preheat at the right temperature.

When he glanced up at Clem not a few minutes later, the camera was sweeping by, homing in on her. Jonathan was accompanying it and asking her questions.

'How are we feeling about round one, girls?' he asked, pushing his glasses up his nose. 'We know everyone is feeling *really* excited about you two!'

Did he mean Sylvie and Clem? Or was he talking about the comments made online, about Muddy Paws and Catpurrcino? Lucas wasn't sure.

Clem must have asked herself the same question, because she dropped the carton of eggs she was holding at once. The eggs splattered and cracked around her Converse, coating the front of them in gooey egg, the rest of the stringy liquid layered on the fake wooden floor. Lucas hitched in a breath. Without thinking, he whizzed around the side of his workstation with their own carton of eggs, which had been sitting on the countertop.

'Here,' he said softly, holding the carton out to Clem. 'Take what you need.'

As he spoke, he was now wondering if he should have remained at his own workstation. The camera had swept from the spilled eggs to eagle in on him, filming their interaction. He wanted to swat it away when her eyes widened, but he restrained himself, and tried to keep his back to the lens, shielding her.

He hadn't meant to do this. Lucas had acted on impulse, automatically, as if he were working at Muddy Paws.

'Th-Thank you,' Clem spluttered. She glanced from him to the camera, looking like a nervous squirrel at risk of being spooked. Reaching for the eggs, her fingertips brushed his as she took the paper carton, sending icy shivers down Lucas's spine, even though warmth was building in the tent from the ovens.

It was on the tip of his tongue to offer to help her clean up the eggs splattered on the ground. But he held it in. He was wasting his own time. This wasn't a charity bake sale, and he wasn't working in catering and helping a colleague, either.

'Get back here, mate,' Dwayne was calling to him, right on cue. 'Focus on your own bloody biscuits!'

Jonathan laughed, and the cameraman moved to Dwayne to catch him in the shot, too. Clem's cheeks had flushed pinker, rose-red in intensity. ''Scuse me,' she said, hurrying past Lucas to grab a nearby sweeping brush for the mess of eggshells.

The rush of air in her wake made him catch his breath, her long skirt brushing his legs as she hurried by.

Shaking himself, he rushed to his own workstation. What was he *doing*? His brain seemed to have forgotten he wasn't at work. Lucas told himself that was all it was: a knee-jerk mechanism learned from years of co-owning a café. It hadn't meant anything. Or had he spent too long helping his parents, his default setting becoming helper? This was a competition; he needed to get his act together and win the prize money. Behaving in this way would make those comments online worse, too.

'Focus,' Dwayne hissed at him. He'd already greased a baking tin and lined it with paper.

'My bad.'

'And you say you aren't interested in women,' said Dwayne, with an eyeroll.

Snapping to attention, Lucas began blending the butter and sugar to a pale fluffiness, adding a splash of vanilla while Dwayne measured out the flour. As they worked, it was like Clem was a burning presence nearby, hot sunlight peeking from behind a building – he was aware of her even when he wasn't looking at her. The camera was still fixed on the Catpurrcino workstation, and he caught the tail end of an abrupt comment from Sylvie, directed at Jonathan Hale: '. . . silly to speculate, really – and they're the competition anyway!'

Not long after, the camera moved away to focus on other workstations near the front of the tent. Lucas blew out a breath, glancing over at Clem. Now the camera was away from her, she seemed to have visibly relaxed, the tension dropping out of her shoulders.

Dwayne had added the flour to their mixing bowl and was swiftly combining it with Lucas's other ingredients to form dough. Together, they floured their fingers until they were coated in white, and patted the dough into the pan Dwayne had already lined. 'I'll dock it and get it in the oven,' said Dwayne, rummaging around for a fork.

Lucas nodded. They'd already decided the strawberry compote was his job – he always did it best – while Dwayne sorted out the white chocolate. He forced himself to tune out the room, and to stop his focus from straying to Clem as she bustled up and down her own workstation, skirt swishing.

When their crust was baked and Dwayne's white chocolate was setting in the fridge, the camera roved over to them, the lens glinting as it caught the sunlight starting to spill in through the transparent side of the tent. Lucas tried to occupy himself but his strawberry compote was still heating and there wasn't much to do but stir it occasionally and aggressively clean the workstation so he looked busy.

The cameraman – and Jonathan – soon swept over to their workstation. Jonathan quizzed Lucas on what he was making today, and he was happy to answer, but all too soon the line of discussion went down a track Lucas didn't like.

'Your café, Muddy Paws, and Catpurrcino, the cat café, have proven quite popular already!' Jonathan said. 'What's more, you seem naturally drawn to one another. Have you become . . . friendly outside the competition as well?'

A snarky retort of *no comment* whizzed across Lucas's mind, but it made him sound so petulant – he wasn't speaking with a journalist – so he decided against it. Maybe they'd chosen to have Jonathan quiz them on purpose; he was a social media personality. He must have seen the speculations, realised they could use this as an angle for *Whisked Away* to make it more exciting. Draw it out during the rounds. Most of the team had probably realised that.

'I imagine everyone here sees this as a friendly competition,' he said instead, reminding himself of a politician trying to dodge a fraught topic he didn't want to give a straight answer to. 'We're not mortal enemies.' He smiled at the camera and stirred his compote some more, the strawberry-jam scent wafting up his nostrils.

But this only gave Jonathan another angle. He was practically frothing at the mouth when he replied, in an overly jovial voice: 'But cats and dogs *are* known to be mortal enemies, aren't they?' He laughed. 'Still, they say opposites attract!'

Thankfully, his strawberry compote was thick enough now, so he removed it from the heat and pretended to asked Dwayne if the white chocolate was setting okay, even though he knew it wouldn't be ready yet. Jonathan lost interest in him and drifted away to the workstation to their left, followed by the camera. Over at the Cat-purrcino workstation, Sylvie was melting chocolate, and Clem was meticulously decorating some biscuits she'd shaped into neat cat-head and pawprint shapes. There were a few discarded ones nearby, broken up into bits, as if she'd decided they weren't good enough – or she'd made a mess of them out of nerves; he couldn't tell.

When the baking was done, they lined up behind the counter at the back of the tent with their bakes in front of them. By this point, the day was getting on, and the tent was hot and sticky from the ovens and the people. Dwayne had undone the top few buttons of his shirt, and Lucas's scalp was prickling with sweat.

The staff placed them in a strict order behind the counter, rather than allowing them to stand where they wanted. And Lucas found himself shoved shoulder to shoulder with Clem by a member of the crew with long, pink acrylic nails. He was so surprised when they scratched his arm accidentally, he bashed into Clem with some force.

She stumbled, and he reached for her without thinking as she tripped, his arm going around her and pulling her upright.

Clem looked up at him, wide-eyed, cheeks cast in a hue of delicate pink. He could smell sugar and butter on her clothes, and instead of stiffening at his touch, he could have sworn he heard her let out a soft sigh of relief. He was reminded, stupidly, of those scenes in old movies he'd seen where a man grasps a woman around the waist.

He released her at once. 'Sorry,' he said, motioning at the cat biscuits she'd been lovingly working on. She'd almost crashed into them, and that could have sent them tumbling to the floor and breaking into pieces. 'I thought you might break them . . .'

Clem raised her eyebrows. The flush remained on her cheeks. He wished he could read minds. What was that look she was giving him? What was she thinking?

Lucas had to suppress a groan when a shaft of sunlight caught the camera lens that had turned to them. The camera was watching them yet again, pointed straight towards them. Had it seen that interaction too?

Clem looked like she wanted to say something else, but instead she snapped her mouth shut and focused on the front of the room, on the judges. They were side by side, like the lead singers in a band arriving to a sea of delirious fans – all were beaming and looking round appreciatively, and Ronan called out, 'Now, are we ready?'

There were some nods and a scattering of applause for the judges as they stood before the table.

'A pair of you will sadly be going home today,' said Ronan solemnly, like he was delivering a eulogy. 'Now, we'll be judging you, as we will in each round, on your method, your flavours and how things taste, your presentation and creativity, and how well you've showcased your unique business.'

The judges began at one end of the line and moved along it, followed by the eagle eye of the camera lens. They taste-tested the bakes, made comments, thanked the participants for their work, asked follow-up questions. Lucas could feel Clem's leg bouncing beside him the closer the judges got to them both.

Ronan came to a halt in front of Lucas and Dwayne, flanked by his fellow judges. They looked down, assessing the shortbread: layers of crumbly crust, strawberry compote, and chocolate, with a swirling chocolate design on top. They'd presented it like they would in the café – on a long wooden block, with a black price label wedged into a silver stand. To go along with the regular rectangular shortbreads, Lucas had made smaller biscuits shaped like dog treats.

'Those are human-friendly, don't worry,' he assured the judges, and they laughed.

Each judge tried a piece of their shortbread, biting into them with gusto – and they tried the dog-treat-shaped ones, too. Lucas watched their faces for any indication of what they were thinking, barely breathing. The only sounds were furious crunching and chewing.

Viviana let out a sigh of contentment and smiled. She held up the final piece of her shortbread as if it were a jewel she'd plucked from a treasure chest. 'These are excellent,' she said, popping the last piece into her mouth. 'I've never had such delicious shortbread. And the ones shaped like dog treats are a lovely touch, even if they do make me feel like I'm eating something I shouldn't!'

'We don't actually sell those,' Dwayne clarified. 'We have jars of dog biscuits on the counter, so we wanted to replicate the experience of being at Muddy Paws.'

'Clever,' said Ronan, who had swallowed the final piece of his own shortbread. He dusted crumbs from his collar. 'That was incredible – the blend of strawberry compote, white chocolate, and the shortbread makes for some interesting textures and flavours. Divine! Can I have another one before we move on?'

He snatched a piece before either of them could reply.

When Ronan had devoured the shortbread in a few bites, the judges shuffled away to look at Clem and Sylvie's cat-shaped biscuits.

'Ah, Catpurrcino!' said Ronan. He jabbed a thumb at Lucas and Dwayne. 'The cat café, up against their natural rivals!' The other judges laughed – even Sylvie joined in.

Clem's smile looked slightly strained. Next to him, her leg was still bouncing; if anything, it had picked up speed.

'Now, Clem,' said Ronan, his pearly white teeth on show as he beamed down at her. 'I've seen your profiles online and I already think what you do is *remarkable*. And these look exquisite, so much attention to detail. Now, don't worry, I'm not playing favourites – it has to taste good, as well!'

Ronan leaned over the biscuits, taking his time select-ing one. The paw-print biscuits Clem had made came in a variety of pastel colours, and the cat-face sugar cookies looked professional grade. Every line was done with precision, from the two-tone colours of the brown-and-white cats to the little whiskers and the tiny, smiling faces – not a segment out of place or messy. They looked like something you'd see sold in a gift shop.

The judges chose their biscuits and bit into them. Lucas glanced across to Clem – there was a dimple in her cheek, but she wasn't smiling anymore, as though she was biting down on the inside of her cheek.

'Lovely,' said Laurette, hand held over her face as she chewed.

'Not quite as punchy in flavour as Muddy Paws over here! But it's nice and subtle,' said Ronan.

'And the artistry – they look perfect. You're a masterful decorator, Clem,' Viviana added.

'Clem's very talented,' agreed Sylvie, putting her arm around Clem and squeezing.

Jonathan nodded, finishing his own biscuit. 'So well done, it was almost a shame to eat one and ruin your lovely work!'

'Thank you, Clem, Sylvie,' said Ronan.

The judges moved onward, and Lucas heard Clem's audible exhalation of relief.

★

The judges were conferring – Clem's heart was pound-ing so hard in her ears she could barely hear the other contestants and their murmured conversations. When

125

the judges returned, they took their positions again in the centre of the tent to announce who would be leaving them this round. Viviana and Laurette had their arms crossed, making the judges look like a row of police officers. She swallowed, her throat dry, wondering if she would be the one to go – because in spite of her nerves, she was proud of those biscuits and wanted the recognition. And the judges had used the words *artistry* and *masterful*, sending tingles down her spine, making her cheeks hurt as she smiled. She still couldn't believe they were talking about *her*. Her, Clem, a university dropout turned baker, being called a masterful decorator? It didn't make sense. And if she *wasn't* voted off . . . Well, she'd feel bad for the person leaving, because they'd probably wanted to be here a thousand times more than her – she'd hesitated about even entering.

'We're so sorry . . .' Ronan drew out the pause for effect, a solemn expression painted across his face, the camera capturing it all. 'Just Desserts,' Ronan announced. 'You'll be leaving us today.'

Clem couldn't help the rush of joy, mingling with the guilt about her reluctance when all of this started.

Their instructions when someone was eliminated had been to form a group in the middle of the room, consoling whoever was going as the camera caught the moment. The bakers from Just Desserts approached the judges to shake their hands, looking crestfallen at leaving so soon, and Clem moved forward with Sylvie and the others to surround them.

After goodbyes and condolences had been given, they left the sticky heat of the tent. Outside, the sky was a cloudless, eggshell-blue. Noon had passed now and the sun was at the beginning of its descent. Clem still couldn't relax, not until this next stage was done. She'd made it through, but she couldn't believe she'd dropped her eggs in the tent, and was on high alert to avoid another mishap. She was standing next to Sylvie, and they were each holding a plate of their biscuits. The next job for the contestants was to serve up their bakes to one of the tables across from the tent. They'd been empty before, but now they were filled with people sitting in the shade and chatting. The camera team were set up nearby, ready to film everything. Clem's ribcage was tight.

The staff took charge, pointing them onwards in pairs. Clem watched as Lucas and Dwayne were sent over to the tables, where they delivered their biscuits to a sweet-looking elderly couple. The woman's face was radiant as she looked down at the shortbread, and Clem caught her mouthing *Thank you* to Lucas. He grinned at her, a dimple puckering in his cheek, and something within her somersaulted. She couldn't stop looking at him. Every movement he made was as gorgeous as his face.

All too soon, it was her and Sylvie's turn. They crossed to the tables, heading for the one the staff had pointed to, the cameras following their every movement like a persistent shadow. Clem kept her focus on her plate – and her feet – to avoid dropping anything else today.

'Here you are,' said Clem, placing her plate down on the tablecloth. Good, she'd done it without making a mess.

'Thank you . . .'

The voice was tentative. But Clem knew it from some-where. When Clem looked up, she froze, her hand in mid-air above the cat-shaped biscuits.

Ash-blonde hair tumbling in a silky, straight sheen down her chest. Piercing blue eyes. A small nose, with a stud gleaming on the right nostril. She was unmistakable, although it had been over five years since Clem had seen her. The once-friend who had humiliated her, broken her confidence.

'Hi, Clem,' said Genie.

# Chapter 13

Clem couldn't decide if Genie's smile was genuine, or cunning. Like a fox, Genie could be pretty and glossy, but sly, if she was after scraps. What was going on? Why was she here? There was no time to ask and Clem certainly didn't want *that* particular conversation to be caught on camera, either. She had to get away as quickly as she could before the film crew noticed anything odd here.

'Hi,' said Clem stiffly. 'Excuse me . . . I have to . . .'

She hurried away after Sylvie, the excuses dying in her throat. Clem raced across the grass, towards the others. She didn't once glance back to see Genie's reaction, or if she was following.

'Who was that?' Sylvie whispered to her.

Thankfully, the camera wasn't focused on them anymore, as the next pair of contestants were taking their biscuits across to the crowd.

'Someone I used to know . . .' said Clem slowly. Her insides were blazing, like she'd been run through with a hot poker, and there was a roaring sound in her ears threatening to drown everything else out. 'I don't know why she was there . . .'

'Maybe she heard about you being in the contest?' Sylvie suggested.

Numb, Clem nodded. 'Maybe . . .'

But why had she joined the audience – or more accurately, *how*? Clem had heard they would be a mixture of the camera team's family, and friends of the contestants. Genie hadn't been her friend in a long time. Why was she here? Did she know someone on the film crew?

When the guests had been served and were enjoying their baked goods, the *Whisked Away* team led Clem, Sylvie, and the other contestants across to the canopy running along the side of the tent. Clem was mildly dizzy, and wished she'd brought her squishy cat so she could clench it, but she'd been afraid of another Reina-style incident.

Refreshments had been laid out for them to enjoy: fluffy triangular sandwiches, bread sticks with assorted dip, tubs of creamy pasta, bowls of crisps, slices of bright watermelon, sausage rolls and miniature pies, and various colourful fruit juices and fizzy drinks. There were huge cool boxes filled with ice for keeping drinks chilled. Clem was grateful this part wasn't being filmed – Genie's face was imprinted on her memory, as if she'd stared too hard at the sun and it had left a garish mark.

The audience was on the other side of the tent, out of sight, having their reactions and responses to the bakes filmed, but she couldn't let her guard down even if she wanted to. What was she up to, coming here? Clem assessed the refreshments but was too uneasy and swirly inside to touch anything, including the strawberries, which looked plump and delicious. The sun dipped behind a cloud, making everything duller.

'You did such a great job, Clem,' Sylvie said, helping herself to a paper plate and napkin, and selecting a few sandwiches.

Clem smiled, hoping the alarm about Genie wasn't showing on her face. She tried to school it into neutrality. 'Thanks, so did you.'

'Hey, congratulations,' said a voice.

Sylvie and Clem turned. Dwayne was standing behind them, Lucas a few steps away, looking unsure if he should approach. Around them, the other contestants were milling around, grabbing plates and pouring out cups of orange juice and fizzing Coke.

'You too!' said Sylvie. 'The dog versus cat game continues!'

'It's more fun this way,' said Dwayne, reaching around Sylvie to grab a bottle of water. He threw one to Lucas, who caught it. Clem lifted her eyebrows at his reflexes. Why had that done all sorts of things to her chest, making it feel tangled and jumpy?

Clem drifted to the side table to get some orange juice while Sylvie and Dwayne chatted absently about their cafés. By the time Clem had finished pouring herself some orange juice and grabbed some ice to dump into the plastic cup, Lucas was at her elbow, fumbling with his water bottle, as if something was on his mind.

Her heartbeat was loud and furious in her ears; it wouldn't settle down, still stuck in panic mode because of Genie. What was she doing on the other side of the tent right now? Was she being filmed by the crew, and telling tales about Clem to the camera? What if she'd somehow found out Clem hadn't really chosen to enter the competition herself initially, and had come here to reveal that to everyone? *No*, Clem told herself. There was no way she could know; only Clem and Sylvie knew. She took a swig of orange juice, the ice cold against her teeth, trying to dispel her speculations. It was cool and refreshing and eased some of the panicky heat inside her.

'Why did you do that, back there?' she asked Lucas, desperate to stop thinking about Genie.

'Do what?' he asked her.

'You know . . . you helped me, twice. With the eggs, and when I tripped . . .'

'Oh.' He scraped a hand along the top of his neck, ruffling some spiky strands of dark hair.

She'd never wanted to mimic someone's actions more – to run her own fingers along the bottom of his hair – and she had to look away. Everyone was speculating about them online already, and she was developing a crush. How could she not? He was gorgeous, helpful, kind. But she should quash this before it got out of hand. There were too many things to worry about already.

'Sorry about that,' he said. 'I didn't really think, if I'm honest.'

She didn't understand. He must have seen those comments online, like she had. Sylvie and Dwayne had drifted away from them to help themselves to some mini desserts – jelly and cupcakes – spread out on another table nearby, which some of the other contestants were clustered around.

'I guess I did it automatically,' he elaborated, with a shrug. 'Habit, from work at the café and . . .' His sentence petered out.

'It's probably not a good idea to help me,' she said, 'even though I do appreciate it.'

'You mean because of what everyone's saying about us, online?'

'Well, yes.'

He sighed. 'I know what you mean. I don't want them to get the wrong idea either . . .' He cleared his throat. 'But we're part of this competition together, whether we like it or not, aren't we? We have to interact at some point.'

'I know.'

He smiled at her. 'Though maybe I'll try to restrain myself . . . with the helping.'

She couldn't help it – she laughed. Because that conjured up *many* different kinds of thoughts in her brain about *not* wanting him to restrain himself with her. For a split second, she allowed herself to slip into a daydream where he came over to help her in the tent, and instead scooped her up, lifting her onto the workstation so her legs dangled over the sides, before leaning in for a delicious kiss . . .

*Nope. Absolutely not.* This was not a daydream she should indulge, even if he did look as delicious as the best kinds of dessert.

'Sorry,' Lucas added. 'I hope I didn't get in your way.'

'Of course you didn't. It's really that automatic?' she said, pushing aside her wild imaginings. 'Helping others?'

Now he looked uncomfortable, shifting on his feet in the grass, and she wasn't sure why. 'Maybe? I dunno.'

'It's fine,' she said quickly. 'Like I said, I do appreciate it. I just wish people weren't talking about it all over the internet . . .'

Genie's laughing face swam in her mind – the way she'd thrown her head back and mocked Clem, years ago – and she took another swig of ice-cold juice. It should hurt less by now, but it didn't. She must have heard about Clem making it onto the contest. But she didn't even live in Cumbria anymore. So why was she here now? Had she moved back permanently, or had she only come to bother Clem during *Whisked Away*? Clem swallowed; she wasn't sure how she'd feel if there was a risk she'd bump into Genie more frequently.

'Maybe try to avoid helping me on camera,' she suggested to Lucas, shoving aside her Genie-related worries yet again. They were like an overly persistent bluebottle fly, and less pleasant than her daydreams about Lucas, which seemed more appealing suddenly. 'Don't give them any more fuel,' she added.

'Don't feed the trolls?' he said, with a light smile, which she returned. 'Sure, but . . .' It was his turn to hesitate now, and she looked at him curiously. He gave what sounded like a nervous laugh, and the sheepishness transformed his face, making him look several years younger. And downright adorable. 'Well, are you okay being the centre of attention on-camera, by yourself, if something happens, like it did with the eggs?' Before she could process what he was saying, he was carrying on, in a rush of words: 'If the attention's that bad for you, maybe it's better to share it?'

When Clem finally realised what he was getting at, a lump rose so quickly to her throat, she had to take another drink of juice to fight it down. He was offering to shield her from the attention.

'Why would you do that?' she said. 'Do you like being on camera?' Maybe he was a natural at it? He did seem more confident than she was. She thought of what he'd said at Catpurrcino. 'Or is this one of your strategies, for handling it?'

'It could be?' he said. 'I see how it freaks you out, whereas I really don't care what people say, or think, about me.'

'Really?' Clem studied the smoothness of the orange juice in her cup, swirling it absently, the ice cubes reflecting the light like orbs of glass. The offer was kind. 'I wish I could be more like that.'

The words were out before she could stop them. She feared if she looked up at him, he'd see right through the windows of her eyes and into her soul. She barely knew him, yet he was so perceptive, and it made her open up to him. His attention was strange: not mocking or negative, but . . . piercing and sharp, like being exposed to a sudden rush of snowfall.

'I've mastered the fine art of not giving a fuck. You should try it, too.'

He said it so casually, so smoothly, she burst out laughing, so hard and for so long that her belly ached. She deeply wished she could learn not to care about other people's opinions of her, but she didn't think her brain was capable of it. Wow, it felt good to laugh, alleviating some of her stress about Genie sitting on the other side of the tent. Lucas laughed along with her.

'So, you're offering to . . . what, be more of an idiot than me next time?' she said, lips twitching. She looked up at him, and the smile he sent in her direction made her stomach swoop, swift as a bird in the sky.

'I could do that,' he said. 'Why not? It's a good strategy, right?'

'It is.'

'I'll be sure to make enough of a fool of myself that they completely lose interest in you.' He glanced over his shoulder. 'Maybe we can get them to focus on Sylvie and Dwayne instead? They seem to be getting along.'

Clem snorted. 'Isn't she too old for him?'

'Hey, different strokes, different folks. You never know.'

As if they'd been called over by the conversation, Dwayne and Sylvie approached. 'Are you going to say hello to your old friend when they're done filming, Clem?' Sylvie asked.

Clem couldn't help it – she flinched at the suggestion, and the joy Lucas had stirred up in her fizzled out. 'Oh . . . um . . . Maybe?' Clem fumbled for an excuse. 'Actually, I'll be right back.'

She darted away before they could stop her, into the shaded area beyond the tent. She probably should have mentioned where she was going, but hopefully they'd guess she was simply going to the bathroom – her usual way of getting out of awkward or uncomfortable situations. It never failed her.

They were allowed access to the toilets inside Wray Castle. Clem dashed across the lawn and up the winding path that snaked through the outer walls, up to the entrance. The paved area up here was wider than it appeared, and a set of wooden picnic tables had been positioned either side of the castle. To the right, another path weaved past a row of green hedges and flowers, heading deeper into the woodland surrounding the castle.

Clem hurried between the two chunky towers, through the massive arched doorway. The toilets were either side of the main doors. When she entered them, though, it was far more cramped than she'd been anticipating – there was barely enough room for two people to stand in front of the sinks.

She stood in front of them, gathering herself, and checked her phone. The battery was lower than she'd realised, since she'd forgotten to charge it up last night.

She couldn't stay in here forever; if someone came in there wouldn't be enough room for her to remain here, composing herself. She would stay in here for a little bit, in case they made the contestants mingle with the miniature audience. If someone came in, maybe she could wander around the grounds? And when the coach came, she'd hurry on board before Genie could see her. She wasn't sure what she'd do if Genie came to any of the other rounds of the contest, but for now, she wanted to keep as far away from her as possible.

★

Lucas frowned as the contestants boarded the bus that would take them home. The audience members had gone too. The rest of the *Whisked Away* staff were working on packing up their things and loading them onto a separate bus. Sylvie was hovering by the bus's open doors, her phone pressed to her ear. Dwayne had already boarded and was peering down at them through the window, occasionally glancing across the lawn from his vantage point to see if Clem appeared.

The sun was no longer shining – a layer of grey tumbleweed clouds had moved in, and the bright emerald hues of the grass and shrubs had dimmed. A pinprick of quickly fading light hung over the castle's towers like a halo.

'She's not answering,' said Sylvie, jabbing her thumb on her phone screen to end the call. 'Where is she? I have to get back to close up the café for the evening . . . And it's forecast thunderstorms later.'

Her brows were drawn together in concern. And she looked completely worn down and exhausted; it had been a long day for them all.

'It's okay, I'll go look for her,' Lucas offered. 'You get on the bus. We can always make our own way back on the ferry. I know the way to the pickup point. It's not far to walk from here.'

'Are you sure . . . ?'

'It's fine – I have your number.'

'Thank you . . .'

Lucas turned, hurrying across the grass. He checked the tent, even though she was unlikely to be there, and zig-zagged his way to the entrance of the castle. It had been an increasingly muggy afternoon, close and cloying, so perhaps she'd gone inside to keep cool, although that didn't account for why she wasn't answering her phone. His mind flashed with possibilities. Was she injured? Collapsed? Surely one of the staff would have found her. But there were a lot of woodland paths branching off in different directions around the castle. What if she'd gone down to the lake, tripped and fallen in? Got lost?

It was dark and gloomy in the entrance hall of the castle. He went into each of the rooms on the ground floor – the dark-wood room on the right, the other brighter rooms with fancy windows and children's activity areas set up. One room was acting as a miniature donation-based bookshop for the National Trust, with a children's corner bursting with stuffed cats and fuzzy rabbits. But he didn't find Clem there either.

He went to the main entrance again, called her name at the door to the women's toilets. No one answered.

A woman made to enter the toilets, and he asked if she could check if Clem was in there. She came out shaking her head.

He checked elsewhere. Outside, there was an eco-friendly café to the right of the castle, set back from the picnic benches, so he checked in there, too. It was full of hikers and visitors to the castle. There was already a queue and he had to stand in line to ask the staff if they'd seen Clem. But she hadn't been here.

He left, the smell of roast coffee replaced by the fresh air and the twang of pollen tickling his nose. By now he'd been looking for nearly twenty minutes without any luck.

Lucas made his way to the front of Wray Castle, standing on the raised, paved area, and called her name again. When he headed to the far wall, craning his neck over it to see if he could spot her from this height, he did notice one thing.

The bus was gone.

A text message from Sylvie came shortly after:

> Driver gave me five minutes and I got off to find you but couldn't see you, so we had to go. Did you find her yet? Should I call Mountain Rescue, do you think??

Lucas honestly didn't know the answer. Had she been gone long enough to call them? The air was getting chillier now and those clouds overhead were darker, fatter, like ink stains on paper.

He turned on the spot, in a circle. The dirt tracks and paths around the castle were set up with a children's activity where you 'hunted down' different types of wildlife, with signposts displaying information about the animals. Maybe Clem had gone on a walk around the grounds, following the trail? But why hadn't she come back? He followed one of the trails, the one marked with a hedgehog.

# Chapter 14

It had been foolish of Clem to come this way. Someone had come into the toilets and it hadn't been practical to stay in such a small space, so she'd decided to take a walk around the grounds, at least until the little audience went away, Genie included. Originally, she'd followed the hedgehog trail. One of the signposts had been on its side, as if blown over. She'd turned left, thinking that was the way to go to follow the route. But it must have been wrong because she'd become completely and utterly lost. And when she'd unlocked her phone, it had flashed up a warning about her low battery and died before she could call or text Sylvie, the screen blackening.

Lake Windermere was like the ocean, sprawling and blue-grey, lapping up against the small shores. She thought if she followed it round, she'd eventually come to some signs pointing the way to Wray Castle – and she could follow those to the entrance. It was as good a plan as any, she told herself, as her chest throbbed. She didn't like being out here alone with nothing but the rush of the lake water for company; it was unnerving with the clouds closing in. There weren't any hikers around to ask directions, and her phone being dead was making her extra panicky, a sick feeling in her gut. She tried to tell herself it was unlikely she'd become a missing person statistic, that her mind was getting carried away and she'd be fine.

She thought of Misha to calm herself down, with her shiny green eyes and long white whiskers.

'Be home soon, Mish,' she said quietly.

She headed up an incline, her shoes sliding in some mud. She moved aside to correct herself, but her foot caught in the root of a branch and she tripped. She landed on her backside in the dirt, covered in grime. Clem hissed out a curse at her own stupidity.

'Clem!' came a voice.

She turned, still on the ground, and saw Lucas running towards her. She groaned. This wasn't the most elegant position to be in. And it was gorgeous Lucas who had come across her. But she was glad he was here, the relief like a lovely, soothing wave over her fears.

'Clem, are you okay?' he said breathlessly, coming to a stop beside her. 'Are you hurt?'

'I'm fine. I fell over.'

He offered her his hand. She was embarrassed, spread-eagled on the ground beneath him. He'd already helped her several times today and she was a grown woman, even if she had messed up and made a mistake. She repeated, 'I'm fine, thanks,' and pulled herself to her feet without his help.

There was no point in attempting to dust herself off; there was mud caked into her shoes and across the hem of her skirt. Clem put some weight on her ankle and thankfully, it didn't hurt. She hadn't injured anything, even though she'd fallen awkwardly.

'I would have found my way back eventually,' she told him. 'There would have been signs.'

He frowned, looking bemused. 'Right . . . but Sylvie had to close up the café, so I came looking for you.

She didn't want to leave you, said there are thunder-storms forecast. She felt bad about it.'

Clem hesitated. Seeing Genie had unnerved her. She exhaled, trying to dispel her unease. 'Has everyone gone?' she asked him.

'What? You mean the bus?'

'No, the audience, the ones who were taste-testing?'

He still looked confused, but then comprehension dawned on his features like clouds parting. 'Wait, is that why you ran off? To avoid the audience?'

'I didn't run off. I went to the bathroom, but it was cramped, so I came for a walk and lost my way.' She knew he was right, and something twisted in her chest. She'd been in the bathroom because she'd run away to avoid Genie.

'Well . . . yeah, the audience is gone. Everyone else, too.'

Clem ogled at him, panic sluicing through her anew. 'Everyone else? Sylvie too? Wait, so the bus—'

'It's already taken everyone home.' He was tugging his phone out of his pocket, and tapping away at the screen. 'I'll let Sylvie know you're okay.'

'But . . . how are we going to get back, without a vehicle? I didn't bring my car and I'm guessing you didn't either?'

'We'll take the Green Cruise – the ferry,' he said. 'We could walk to a main road for a bus, but it's quicker to get to the ferry point and take that across to Waterhead Pier.' He looked down at his phone screen. 'We're just in time to make the last one of the day.'

'You know how to get there?'

'I think it's that way.' He turned back the way he'd come from, gestured with his hand. 'If we go back the way I came, there are some signs. Come on.' He hesitated, assessing her with that expression of his that made her feel like she was being X-rayed. Or undressed with his eyes. She shivered. 'You good?' he asked. 'You seem cold.'

'I'm fine, honest.'

'Okay.'

They began to walk, traipsing up the path. He guided her onto a main path and, mercifully, a wooden sign sprang up pointing the way to the ferry point for the Green Cruise. A breeze ruffled their hair and clothes as it whispered through the surrounding trees. They passed through a latched wooden gate, Lucas holding it open for her, and Clem being careful not to slip on any more muddy areas.

'I hope Sylvie wasn't too worried,' said Clem. 'I did intend to be right back.'

'I'm sure she knows, don't worry.'

Clem glanced at the sky. A faint yellowy glow managed to peek its way out from behind the scudding clouds, which were increasing in number and growing blacker.

'Let's hurry,' she said. 'It might rain.'

They walked briskly through the trees, along the sloping, paved paths, dodging tree roots and particularly hazardous thick mud.

'They won't cancel the ferry if it rains, will they?' she asked Lucas. 'If there's thunder?'

'I don't think so. It's the last one and the rain'll probably hold off for a little while. They only cancel for extreme weather and it's not that bad yet.'

Clem let out a breath of relief. At least they wouldn't be stuck here permanently.

'It would have been fun to camp out at the castle, though,' Lucas joked. 'Live like some historical rich land-owner for a night.'

'As if,' said Clem, snorting. 'They wouldn't let us! We'd be chucked out like the peasants we are.'

Soon, the trees parted, the gleaming lake still a fixture on their right, rippling in the wind. An ancient stone structure – somewhat like a small house – jutted out of the mud, its large stones covered in moss. Clem didn't know its purpose; there were no doors or windows that she could see. Some kind of ruin, perhaps?

'Ah, we're here,' said Lucas, smiling at her. He rounded the side of the stone ruin, and Clem followed.

Up ahead, a wooden boardwalk stretched out from between some jagged stones, and out across the lake. Faint raindrops were visible on the lake's surface now, and soft kisses of rain dappled her cheeks. There was a sign wedged onto one of the wooden beams of the board-walk, reading *For Green Cruise, wait here*, in rough and blocky handwriting.

'I'm glad we made it,' said Clem, sinking down onto the boardwalk and sitting on the edge, her feet dangling over the rain-speckled lake.

'We've got some time to wait, though,' Lucas said.

'That's fine. I've never been on a ferry before.'

'Really, even with living here? Then you want the best seats. That'd be on the top, if you can brave the weather. The wind can be rough up top.'

She smiled. 'It's not that bad.'

He took a seat beside her on the boardwalk, legs and feet dangling beside hers. In the distance, across the lake, the land rose up like the peaks of mountains, patchworks of green grass interspersed with spindly trees and darker lines marking paths and walls. A collection of white buildings with grey roofs was visible on the opposite shoreline, and a gathering of boats were bobbing in the water like little chess pieces that had been toppled over.

'Are you OK now?' Lucas asked Clem.

'What do you mean?'

'Well, you went off to get some space. I assumed something was wrong.'

'Oh. I'm fine now. I feel bad for worrying Sylvie.'

'Shit happens,' said Lucas, with a shrug. 'Last time I came here, I ended up with my leg in a cast.'

'What?' Clem said, laughing. 'How?'

'We were on a school trip – high school. English, learning about Beatrix Potter and the poets, and all of that. Me and my friends broke away from the group to sneak into the woods, and one of my closest friends at the time, Georgina, she dared me to climb this *huge* tree. I did, but I lost my footing and fell. Ended up breaking my leg. She felt bad about it afterwards. If I'd gone any higher, it could have been a lot worse.'

'It really could have been. And there were no teachers around?'

'No, though we didn't go far. And they soon found us – Georgina was screaming, said my leg looked weird. I think I scared her.' Lucas smiled, looking out across the lake as another boat crawled past them, leaving a trail of white behind it as it headed for some other town somewhere. 'I never did it again, though.'

'Because of your friend?'

'No, my parents, actually.'

'Were they angry with you?'

Lucas hesitated. He was quiet for so long, she wasn't sure he was going to answer; maybe it had been an uncomfortable question? She opened her mouth to say he didn't have to respond, when he answered.

'Not angry. Distraught. My mum was, anyway. My dad's always had health stuff going on, so she has to deal with that . . . and me, falling out of a tree? She must have been terrified. And when I got home, she had to look after two people, instead of one. Normally, it's us two, looking after Dad.'

Ah. Clem was starting to understand him better. 'It must be tough,' she said. 'Is he okay now?'

There was another long pause. Eventually, he said, 'No, not really. We're trying to figure it out. Get him the help he needs.'

Lucas was no longer looking amused by the tale; it had transformed into something else and he looked troubled. Clem didn't continue the line of conversation in case he didn't want to discuss it. She wondered if this was where his caring side came from, why he felt the need to help others when he saw them struggling.

The rain pattered off the lake around them, bounced off the boardwalk. It was picking up in pace, the air cooling. Clem shuddered.

'Are you cold?' he asked, already shrugging off his jacket.

'Oh, no, you don't have to . . .'

'It's okay. It'll be blustery on the ferry. Especially if you want the best seats in the house. Here, hold up your arms.'

She did as he asked, smiling as he draped the jacket over her. It was baggy on her, but she could smell the mix of his fresh, earthy scent and baking – sugar and butter and all things sweet – on the material. She tugged it closer around her chest. He had a way of making her feel looked after, safe. The way she felt when she was cocooned at home in a blanket with Misha snoozing in her lap. She liked that feeling.

He tugged up the hood for her, to keep her hair dry. The gesture made her soften and melt like chocolate.

When the ferry finally arrived, cruising across the water, they rose to their feet and waited as it pulled in. The attendant – a jolly-looking old man with a thick salt-and-pepper beard, and rain-speckled glasses – looped some rope around a wooden pole to secure the boat. They clambered on board, and paid for their ride across in the bottom compartment.

'Come on,' said Lucas, turning for the steps. He led Clem up to the top deck, where their feet clanged against the metal flooring.

Lucas had been right – it *was* blustery up here, the sky a blanket of steel overhead. Her clothes whipped around her as she walked between rows of blue plastic seats. He was only wearing a T-shirt now and she felt bad, hogging his jacket.

'These seats are relatively dry,' he announced, sitting down. 'They must have brushed them off before we got on board.'

'Do you want your jacket back?' she asked. She took a seat beside him, near the front of the boat.

He waved her away. 'You zip up. I'm fine.'

She zipped up Lucas's jacket, right up to her chin, and pulled the hood further forward, securing it with the toggle. It *was* blustery up here with the boat in motion.

A few minutes later, the attendant appeared behind them and draped them both in a thin blanket.

'Here you go, lovebirds!' he said, in a booming, jovial voice. He reminded Clem of Father Christmas with his twinkling eyes. She was going to correct him – they weren't together – but he carried on, 'We don't want anyone getting poorly now! It's raining. Keep dry. We'll be taking bets downstairs on how long you last up here!' He chuckled and moved away.

'I'm made of steel!' Lucas called, although he contradicted himself by drawing the thin blanket more closely around him and shuffling closer to Clem.

Clem kept tight hold of the blanket, too, so it didn't blow away. The ferry was already moving away from the boardwalk, and out onto the broad stretch of Lake Windermere, the wind kicking up and slapping at Clem's cheeks. She was acutely aware of how close Lucas's thigh was to her own, almost touching. Their shoulders were brushing. And her skin had electrified, pulsing with feeling.

A gust of wind rippled around them – Lucas's dark hair was dancing around his head like it had a life of its own, and Clem burst into laughter at the movement of the spidery strands.

'What?' he said, smirking.

'You look funny. Your hair.'

'Hey, I give you my jacket and now you're mocking me? Rude.'

She continued to laugh at the faux pained expression on his face. She was surprised by how much better she felt, even though she'd seen Genie earlier and got herself lost around the castle's grounds. With Lucas, everything seemed lighter somehow.

'Thanks for coming to find me,' she said.

He turned to her. There was something in his expression she couldn't read. 'Of course. Sylvie was worried about you . . .'

'What about when we get across the lake?' she said, looking out at the expanse of greyish water stretching far and wide. 'Windermere isn't far – don't you live around there? It's where Muddy Paws Café is, right?'

'Yeah, but don't worry. I'll order a taxi for us to share, and I'll come with you to Oakside first.'

'Oh, you don't have to do that. Then you have to come all the way back here—'

'It's alright.' He grinned. 'I've got you this far. Might as well take you all the way.'

She reeled, interpreting his words in an entirely different way and feeling queasy and giddy as she imagined those possibilities. Lucas didn't appear to notice; he was looking out across the lake, watching a bird zoom across the sky towards a cluster of spindly trees. There were flecks of raindrops caught in his hair and gathered on the side of his face, and even in this blustery weather, with his hair whipping around in a frenzy, he looked like the most handsome person she'd ever seen. She wouldn't mind spending more time with him. She wanted to kiss the rainwater from his lips, to see what that would feel like. What he'd taste like.

Instead, she turned her attention to the water, the rippling waves spreading from the boat, far out into the distance, to dry land.

# Chapter 15

Clem was sitting in the back of the taxi. She couldn't help but wonder if they'd sent the smallest, stuffiest taxi in the universe on purpose – she would have taken another top-level ferry trip over this. It was warm and claustrophobic, and she had the window fully wound down to let in the fresh air. The taxi driver was extremely interested in what they'd been doing today and had asked them a dozen questions as soon as they'd clambered inside. Clem would have paid him double to be quiet; her ears were already hurting from the wind on the top of the boat. They'd already bypassed Windermere, Lucas insisting on making sure she got to her house in Oakside safely. Lucas's jacket was folded on the seat between them.

Lucas turned to her. His hair was fluttering in the wind whipping in through the window, and her stomach performed a jump. 'Do you need to text anyone to tell them you're on your way?' he asked her.

'Oh . . .' She trailed off, fumbling for an answer.

Was he asking if she had a boyfriend? No, no, that was silly. It was because he thought someone might be worried about her at home, if she was late. That didn't necessarily mean he was asking about a boyfriend; he could have meant a housemate or family. She tucked her hair behind her ear. Should she tell him she lived at home with her mum? Would he judge her, think she was immature?

'No, it's fine,' she said carefully.

'That's fair. My folks are usually too wrapped up in themselves to notice me too,' he said lightly, grinning at her.

Wait . . . He lived at home too? She blew out a breath and laughed. 'Oh my God, really? Mum notices everything I do – our cottage is *tiny*. Baking at home is a bit of a nightmare so sometimes I visit the cat café to use the kitchen. Sylvie's fine with it. And it means me and Mum don't get under each other's feet.'

Lucas nodded knowingly. 'Ah, it was like that before I moved out too. Cramped.'

*Before* he moved out? Heat rushed up Clem's neck – like the hot sun had emerged, though it was much cooler outside. She'd misunderstood. She wanted the sticky taxi seats to swallow her up.

'You . . . so you don't live with your parents now?' she said.

He shook his head, apparently not noticing her embarrassment. 'No, but . . .' His gaze travelled to the window, to the stretched-out moors and the silhouettes of the mountains towering up and shielding the sky. 'I'm working on it.'

'Working on it? You mean you *want* to move home?'

Something passed across his face. He looked . . . sorrowful? Clem wanted to reach out and take his hand, to unpack what was really going on in his head, to understand. She'd been feeling like a failure for being at home, and here was someone who was working on going back? He looked a couple of years older than her, at most, so wouldn't he value his independence, his space, particularly if he'd become used to that? She waited for him to continue.

'It's why I entered the contest,' he said eventually. 'They need my help, and if I could get together a deposit, buy a place with my mum, we could all live there together. Me, her, and Dad. They wouldn't have to worry so much anymore.'

He still wasn't looking at her, as if he was determined not to, after revealing something so personal. And she was glad, because she was sure her face had cycled through ten different emotions one after the other. Why did he always take her completely by surprise, to the point she was breathless with it?

Clem's own reasons for entering the contest now seemed muddy, a mess. She'd thought she would move out, get her own place, start a business. In truth, she had the means to move out into a rented house right now. She gave her mum money towards bills, but the cottage's mortgage had long since been paid off, and she'd been able to save up enough for a deposit on a rented property, plus a little extra and some emergency funds. She'd been hesitating, telling herself it wasn't enough, she needed to be sure she'd be secure. That she needed *more* first, before she could be truly ready. The truth was, she was afraid. She still remembered how hard she'd found everything after what Genie had done, and the anxiety attacks that punctuated her life like scars. She couldn't bear the thought of moving out, gaining her independence, having another massive setback and having it all crumble beneath her.

'I hope you can help your parents,' she said softly.

The vulnerability on his face was gone when he looked at her again, and a sly smirk spread over his features instead. 'So that means you hope I win the contest?'

'No!' she said, laughing.

'Well, I have to win for my wish to come true . . . So, if you could just lose, I'd appreciate that.'

She smiled, but it was slightly strained under the weight of her thoughts. She wasn't sure what Lucas would think if he knew the truth – that Sylvie had submitted the application, and it was all a big mix-up that Clem was part of *Whisked Away* at all. And what did Clem really want from the contest, now she was in it? It wasn't the money.

Lucas's motivations had shone a light on her own reasoning for being in the contest, and now she was confused. After all, she'd doubted whether or not she should enter, and Sylvie had ended up taking the choice out of her hands. She shuffled uncomfortably in the leather seat.

'I might lose anyway,' he said. 'Cakes aren't my forte. And that's the big finale.'

'Well, I'm bad at bread, and that's the next round,' she told him, shrugging. 'We have to do our best.'

He was silent for a while. 'Why did you rush off back there?' he asked her eventually. 'Why avoid the audience?'

Clem glanced at the taxi driver to check he wasn't listening, but music was playing from the speakers in front of him, and he was singing along, tapping his fingertips on the steering wheel and checking his satnav as it chattered directions.

'I . . .' He'd told her why he'd entered the contest, and his reason – so *moral* and full of principle – had softened her like sponge cake. 'I saw someone I knew.'

154

'I'm guessing it wasn't a good someone, given how you reacted?'

Clem shook her head. 'She did something to hurt me, years ago.' A wry laugh escaped her. 'Maybe that's an understatement. It derailed me completely.'

Lucas frowned. To Clem's utter gratitude, he didn't ask her to elaborate. 'Why did she show up at Wray Castle?'

'I have no idea. We have a . . . difficult past.'

'I know what that's like,' he said.

'I panicked when I saw her. I thought she was there to mess things up for me again . . .' Clem twisted her hands in her lap. 'I couldn't face talking to her. I still don't really understand what happened between us. One day we were close, best friends. And the next, she did something so cruel I never spoke to her again.'

'You never talked to her about it?'

'Not exactly. Things felt clear enough in her actions.'

Lucas was silent, looking out of the window with a thoughtful expression on his face, the daylight casting shadows on his dark stubble. Clem could almost read what he was thinking. He was likely wondering why she didn't talk to Genie, since she'd showed up in the audience. She squirmed in the leather taxi seats, her clothes sticking to them and making her more uncomfortable. Clem was wondering that herself. After all this time, why couldn't she confront Genie? Back then, she'd felt too broken with anxiety to face up to it all and challenge Genie. Shouldn't she be able to now?

'Did she say anything to you?' asked Lucas.

'Just hello. I couldn't really figure her out. I rushed off before we could talk properly.'

'I wouldn't worry. Maybe she was there to make amends? If she shows up next time, I can always talk to her with you. Or . . . be nearby. In case you need support.'

Her mood lifted at his encouragement. 'I . . . Thank you.'

The taxi was finally rolling into Oakside, and Clem directed the driver to the secluded road where their cottage was positioned, far across an open field. The rain was growing heavy now, where before it had been fine, with thick droplets splattering into the taxi. She wound the window up.

'It's not a proper road . . .' she told the driver as he crawled forward. 'We're on a dirt track round there, so I'll get out here.'

The driver pulled up to the closest brick wall, where the road made way for a dirt track on one side, and a fence and the field on the other. Ahead of the dirt track, in the distance, Clem could make out their cottage and the rows of plant pots outside.

'Thanks, Lucas,' she said, unclipping her seatbelt. 'See you.'

'Wait, you didn't take my jacket – do you have an umbrella?'

'It's okay!' She shoved open the taxi door and climbed out.

The rain was only getting fiercer, pounding down on the dirt and bouncing off the wooden fence at her side, and off the taxi's windows and doors. Raindrops pelted her skin and her clothes. She shrieked, shoving her phone down into her bra to keep it dry and functional, and rushed forward to make a run for it, dashing alongside the hedge that lined the track.

Up ahead, the track weaved left, and she turned, the taxi shielded from view by trees now. But she could hear footsteps pounding behind her, and she paused. Already, her hair was stuck to the sides of her face, and her clothes were quickly getting wet, too.

Lucas rounded the corner, holding an umbrella. His green eyes were blazing with something fierce – determination? Concern? Her breath caught again as he hurried forward. She laughed as he held the umbrella over her, but the sound faded when he gripped her hand, pushing the umbrella into her grasp. He wasn't smiling, and still held a serious aura, as if he were charging into a burning building to help her, rather than handing her an umbrella.

'It's a little late for that,' she said, glancing up at the umbrella over their heads. 'I'm already wet.'

His hand tightened around hers. 'Could have been worse,' he said softly.

Lucas wasn't letting go of her hand, and she found she didn't want him to. The rain pattered furiously on the umbrella overhead, and the petrichor scent in the air filled Clem's nose. Why was it so soothing, standing here with his hand on hers, with his moss-green eyes locked on her own? Had she ever met someone – outside of her cat, of course – who could calm her down like this, make her feel so at peace, so unbothered? The taxi was waiting and the rain was pounding, but she didn't feel worried at all.

'The taxi . . .' she said lamely.

'He said he'd wait for me.'

He'd inched closer. She could trace the fine pinpricks of dark stubble where he'd shaved, skirting along his chin and jawline. Tentatively, she reached up with damp fingers, not knowing where she found the courage; her anxieties had receded, like the raindrops snaking into the grasses. His other hand met hers, guiding her, his fingers threading through hers. The pads of her fingers touched his cheek, tracing the softness down to the scratchy stubble. And he leaned over, pausing, as if to check this was okay. The green in his eyes was bright, like summer foliage.

She couldn't speak, let alone think, and let her body make the choice. He closed the distance and kissed her.

She melted into him, against the softness of him, his lips warm and inviting. Her hand tracked down to his neck, pulling him closer, as if she wanted him as close as the droplets on her skin. Her brain was buzzing with static – no worries, no fear or anxiety, just this delicious, pleasant blankness, like she'd sunk into a hot bath. She could barely remember the last time her mind had been this quiet, this free. His mouth moved against hers tentatively, gently, a question she kept answering with *yes* as she pressed her lips against his.

Inside, she was dizzy, wild, like she was spinning out of control.

When they finally parted, her mouth was tingling, as if missing him already.

There was still no room to question anything, nothing but *yes* echoing around her mind and her heart.

# Chapter 16

Clem was curled on the sofa with Misha, wrapped in a blanket and holding a strong cup of tea. It was almost ten and her mum had gone to bed already, to wake up for an early photo shoot in the morning. Clem had spent most of her time after she'd dried off chatting to her about today's round of the contest – and strenuously avoiding mentioning Lucas and the taxi ride home. And that kiss.

Now her mum had gone to sleep, an itchiness was settling over Clem like a scratchy blanket.

She absently stroked Misha, who was curled into a ball in Clem's lap, her nose between her paws. Reality was pinching at Clem like cat's claws. Clem had *kissed* Lucas. It had been wonderful and calming and everything she'd needed at the time, relaxing her mind and her soul. But people were talking about them already. What if someone found out they'd kissed and it ended up online? She was fighting the impulse to check social media to see what people were saying, even though the first round and their biscuit-baking wouldn't be posted for people to watch for another few days.

Her phone vibrated with a message. She grabbed it from the arm of the sofa. It was Lucas.

*I have an idea,* he'd written.

How soon was too soon to reply? She didn't want to look like she'd been sitting here waiting for a message from him. She drank half of her tea, trying to concentrate on the TV, droning absently across the room above the fireplace, some show about people with far too much money complaining about ceiling beams in grand houses. But her mind chittered on: what was his idea? Something to do with the contest, or that kiss?

Four minutes passed. It was enough time not to seem desperate, she figured.

*What is it?* she typed.

He clearly didn't care about timing himself, because he replied at once.

> Next round is bread and you said you're not good at it. I'm no good at cakes and that's coming up later.

Clem was encouraged by his speed, so she stopped hesitating and responded right away with:

> Okay, so what's the idea?

He wasn't going to mention the kiss. Should she bring it up, ask if it was going to make things awkward? In hindsight, maybe it hadn't been such a good idea . . . She chewed on her cheek as she considered, but soon a reply came through reading:

We could help each other out. You teach me
what you know about cakes and I'll help you with
the bread.

She stared at her phone, her hand resting on Misha's
soft back and tracing the stripes. Misha gave a wide yawn
and stretched out her front paws, claws extending and
piercing Clem's pyjamas.

*Clem:* Is that allowed?
   *Lucas:* Nothing in the rules or terms about it.
And trust me, I read them all. Three times. Some
people are doing family recipes, so they can't
exactly ban us having help or getting advice,
right?
   *Clem:* You're very thorough, ha
   *Lucas:* I'm glad we're not up against the
Grasmere gingerbread. That would be
seriously un-fun. Do you know how
popular it is?
   *Lucas:* Anyway, what do you think?

Clem paused. Thoughts were crashing and cascading
through her mind like ocean waves. The kiss, now the
offer of them teaming up to help each other with their
weak skills. Ronan's audience already wanted them to
get together, and wouldn't this add fuel? And yet . . . the

last time she'd tried to make the bread she had in mind for the contest, it had failed spectacularly, coming out more like something from a bricklayer's arsenal than a baker's kitchen.

> *Lucas:* Unless you can manage the bread? I mean, you've got skills so I know you could do it

Was he worried he'd offended her now? In spite of herself, in spite of the fact they were competing, she wanted to spend more time with him. She wanted to kiss him again.

> *Clem:* My skills don't really stretch to bread, haha. I'm bad at it. I tried lembas bread once, and it nearly broke my mum's teeth. Think she actually had to go to the dentist after.
> *Lucas:* A Lord of the Rings fan!
> *Lucas:* RIP your mum's teeth though
> *Clem:* Safe to say I felt like a colossal failure for letting the elves down
> *Lucas:* Is that a yes?

Clem looked down at Misha, stroking the soft spot between her ears. Misha lifted her head and yawned massively, exposing a set of pincer-sharp teeth and looking up innocently with big, green eyes. Clem groaned and rubbed the bridge of her nose.

Misha extended a paw, stretching it out onto Clem's abdomen. Clem's phone buzzed again and she checked his message.

> We don't have to tell anyone. It can be our secret. I promise the online trolls won't find out. If they do, I'll handle them Bilbo style.

Clem laughed.

> *Clem:* What, by hiding until the wizard gets there?
> *Lucas:* Something like that
> *Clem:* Okay, but no one can find out we're helping each other. Don't feed the trolls like we said?
> *Lucas:* Deal

She considered asking him about the kiss, too – what it meant, how it might change things – but she couldn't bring herself to do it. Maybe, like their helping each other out, it would remain their little secret.

★

Clem huffed out a breath of frustration, tucking her hair behind her ears. She was in the little kitchen in their cottage, trying to get in some bread-making practice for round two of the contest, which would be happening next month. And it was *not* going well. The radio was tuned to a classical station – she couldn't concentrate on anything with lyrics right now. Misha was sitting in the corner on the wash basket, tail curled around her and watching her with wide, green eyes, as if judging her every move.

'I'm glad you find this so amusing, Mish,' said Clem, huffing out a breath and going over to give the cat a cuddle and a kiss on the head. When the embrace went on ten seconds too long for her liking, Misha protested with a little mewl, and Clem let go. 'Shame you're not good at anything other than making biscuits out of blankets, otherwise you could have helped.'

Ingredients were packed up next to the sink, and shoved into the wall. Various test batches of bread were spread out along a tray on the counter – all of them had come out wrong. Some of the bready shapes resembled battered and beaten cat heads, but they were a far cry from the kitten rolls she'd been hoping for. They looked more like something an animal charity should be concerned about.

It was too small in this cramped cottage kitchen. It hadn't mattered so much when she *hadn't* been part of a competition, and was baking the occasional thing for fun at home. But when she needed to keep practising, it wasn't ideal. She stood at the sink – already full of dirtied equipment – sunlight filtering in through the small window. Clem popped a failed roll in her mouth absently and chewed. This one was too doughy and claggy, but at least it tasted good.

She was considering asking Sylvie if she could use the cat café's kitchen today when her phone buzz-buzzed on the counter, illuminating the screen. A call?

She checked the screen and a muscle jumped in her throat. Lucas.

She answered quickly. 'Hello?'

'Hey, Clem.'

'What's wrong? Did something happen? Is the video up?'

'No . . . Ah, sorry. It's not been posted yet.'

She let out a long breath. The video for the previous round was meant to go up today, which meant they could expect a flood of comments and commentary. Clem wasn't looking forward to it – she was bracing herself for it, like you'd brace for bad news – and the bread-making practice had been her way of distracting herself, even though she'd agreed to Lucas's help too.

'Did I catch you at a bad time?' he asked her.

'No, I was . . . ah, failing at bread again.'

A smile crept into his voice. 'That'll be because you didn't consult the breadmaster over here.'

'Is breadmaster an official title?'

'I'm thinking of asking Dwayne to make it part of my job title,' he quipped. 'You want to practise together today, if that's what you're doing?'

The suddenness of the suggestion caught her off guard. 'Today?'

'Sure, I'm not busy. It's my day off.'

'Okay, but . . .' She trailed off. 'My kitchen here is tiny. I was thinking of going and using the one at Catpurrcino . . . It's bigger. Do you want to come?' Realising what she'd said, she hurried on, 'Wait, what if someone sees you? The guy from the dog place, visiting the cat café.'

There was a pause on the other end of the line as if he were considering. 'I'll wear a disguise.'

'A disguise?' she repeated, snorting out a laugh.

'I don't have a cat costume though – can't pretend to be your new mascot or anything. A cap and sunglasses will have to do.'

Clem's smile was hurting her cheeks at the image of him dressed in a giant cat costume. 'Okay.'

'I'll meet you at the cat café?' he said.

'Alright, I'll wait for you in the car park.'

# Chapter 17

Lucas was like a movie star trying to hide from the paparazzi as he pulled his baseball cap down and adjusted his sunglasses. It was a bright sunny day, the sky free of cloud cover, so at least the get-up was fitting for the season. When he pulled into the car park and climbed out, Clem waved at him from over by a black hatchback. And he couldn't help it: the kiss in the rain flashed across his mind. He couldn't stop thinking about it – about her. He didn't know what was the matter with him; he'd never been any good at making the first move and he hadn't been planning on getting involved with anyone. But when he was around her, it was like everything turned upside down, including logic and sense.

She crossed the car park to meet him.

'Hi,' she said. 'Sylvie said it's fine for us to use the kitchen together whenever we like, to practise.'

'That's good of her.'

'Emmie is usually here too – she lives in one of the flats upstairs – but she's out for the day with Jared, so Sylvie asked me to top up the feeders and water.'

It was a Sunday, so the café was closed, but Clem let them in through the front door. They passed through the cube-shaped entrance, through the gift shop and reception area, and into the main café, where Clem raised the latched gate so they could step inside.

The room was bright and airy, sunlight flooding through the main window. Lucas glanced around – it was like playing a spot-the-cat game whenever you stepped inside this place. They weren't immediately visible, but if he looked close enough, he could pick out the cats. A long-haired tawny, fluffy cat was curled in a basket-shaped shelf, no eyes or face visible – just a giant ball of fur. A black cat's green eyes gleamed at him from beneath a chair. A calico snaked out from beneath a table and hopped onto the window ledge to bask in the sun, watching a bird wheel across the sky, her pupils dilating.

'I won't be a minute,' said Clem.

'Okay.'

Lucas took a seat by the window, reaching out to stroke the calico, who nuzzled into his hand and rolled over, exposing a fluffy white stomach. He tickled it absently while Clem made her way around the room, topping up feeders and giving the cats fresh water.

His thoughts drifted to his dad as he scooped his fingers through the cat's soft fur. They'd had a cat when Lucas was a small child – he barely remembered it – and his dad had apparently adored her, though she passed away relatively young. Which was why his mum thought he'd love it here. A pet wasn't an option right now; his mum had too many commitments already and his dad was always in pain. Plus, they couldn't afford it if they wanted to. But coming here might be comforting to him. He added a conversation with his dad to his mental notepad – he should suggest it, the next time he spoke to him.

'Done,' said Clem, reappearing. 'Shall we go into the kitchen?'

He nodded, giving the calico one final belly rub and getting up to follow her through another gate and behind the counter. A narrow hallway led them to a series of doors and into the kitchen.

It was large enough for several people, even though he knew it was only Clem who worked in the kitchen. A large commercial oven took centre stage, alongside a set of appliances: a shiny metal stand mixer and a set of scales. A series of racks and shelving units contained plenty of utensils, tools, and equipment, where Clem could easily access them, and there were stainless steel workstations set close to the mixing equipment. There were cooling racks and a refrigerator too.

'You're pretty well equipped here,' he said. 'Roomy, too.'

'Sylvie was thinking of hiring a cook but she's happy with just baked goods for now.'

'What shall we practise first?' he asked her. 'What were you thinking of doing?'

'I call them kitten rolls. It's a Hokkaido milk bread recipe – originated in Japan and it's become popular elsewhere. I wanted to arrange them in a bread basket, and do a bigger loaf shaped like an adult cat. That one will be tiger bread. It's meant to represent our partnership with the cat shelter, and . . . Well, last year, there was a stray cat hidden in the wall outside during a snowstorm. She was pregnant.'

'I think I remember my mum telling me about that,' said Lucas.

'Yeah, some of the kittens were adopted out – Jared took one in. Sylvie took in the mum and one of the kittens. I thought I could represent that event,' Clem explained.

She sighed. 'I might be being too ambitious, though . . . I can't seem to get it right.'

'Let's give it a try. I can help.'

Clem donned an apron from a hook by the door; it was decorated with lots of chubby-cheeked cats and hearts. She threw him a spare one – green and decorated with brown cats this time – and began gathering up the ingredients they'd need.

'I still don't understand why you offered to help me,' she told him, as they washed their hands.

He was wondering that himself. Had it been their kiss, making him want to spend more time with her? Or that automatic urge within him, to lend a helping hand when people needed it? Had he become so used to helping his parents during his life, he now did it with everyone? He hadn't thought about it until he met Clem.

'I dunno, I thought it would be mutually beneficial,' he suggested lamely.

'We're in competition, though,' she pointed out, 'so you could have easily left me to struggle.'

'Right. It's a contest, yes – but let's make it a fair one,' he said. 'I want you to compete at your best, and I'll compete at mine. No one else will stand a chance.'

That drew a laugh from her. God, he loved the sound.

'What about after that? We fight amongst ourselves?' she asked.

'To the bitter end, with whisks drawn for battle,' he said sombrely, hand against his chest.

She giggled again. 'Okay.' She pulled up the notes app on her phone. 'I'm doing one main loaf I'm confident with, but for the mini ones – the kittens – here's the recipe. I'm struggling with it. Again, maybe overambitious of me, but . . .'

'Let's give it a whirl.'

They set to work. Clem made the tangzhong paste first, mixing the flour and water in a pan and placing it over a medium heat, following the method until it was thickened and at the right temperature. She covered it with plastic wrap and set it to chill in the freezer. Lucas was hovering at her side like a shadow the whole time, observing, while she explained what she was doing.

'It's the dough that never works out right,' she said, when the paste was chilling. 'Shall we grab a coffee first, then try it? Sorry, I should have offered you one earlier.'

'Sure. Coffee sounds good.'

'Have you always baked?' she asked him, as they removed their aprons and left the kitchen, heading through to the main café room again.

He shook his head. 'No, I didn't start until just before me and Dwayne opened Muddy Paws. I offered to learn so we could save some cash at first. It became habit. My dad liked a lot of the stuff I was making, so I'd make extra to bring to him.' He made his way through the counter's gate, and chose a seat nearby, sliding into it, his foot catching on a toy mouse one of the cats had left there. It jingled happily.

'It sounds like you're close,' she said.

'We are.'

'What would you like to drink? A mocha again?'

'Please.'

She nodded, turning to make the drinks. Lucas didn't notice there was a cat on the opposite chair, concealed by the top of the table, until a stripy cat popped its head up and stretched out, ears tilted. He laughed as it blinked up at him.

'Hey, you. Nearly gave me a heart attack.'

'Sylvie always jokes that death by cat isn't a bad way to go,' Clem called over the noise of the milk frother, and Lucas laughed.

When the drinks were made, Clem deposited them on the table – a frothy mocha for him, dusted with cocoa powder, and a milky tea for herself. 'Here you go. I can't do coffee art like Emmie, so you'll have to settle for a boring, non-decorative mocha.'

The striped cat had already hopped down onto the floor, helping itself to some water from a dispenser, so she slid into the seat across from him. She whipped her phone out of her jeans pocket, checking the screen.

'You worried about them posting the video of the first round?' he asked.

'A little.' She set it on the table, as if determined not to look at it again, but her hand twitched towards it. 'I've already had some comments on my own profiles. New people finding me, talking about *Whisked Away*. It's weird . . .'

'Ah. I don't use social media much. And all my accounts are private.'

'I kind of wish I wasn't on it at the moment,' she clarified. 'But I like posting baking videos and I sometimes help with Sylvie's cat café accounts. Pictures and videos of my baked goods usually do pretty well. But with the contest . . .' She took a deep breath. 'I don't like the extra attention.'

'Putting yourself out there is good,' he said. 'In a way, that's especially true if you don't like attention. It makes you more confident. You never know what opportunities will come from this. People get book deals and morning TV shows out of things like this.'

'I'm not sure I'd want that!' She looked frightened at the very idea.

'Why not? We could spin out the dog-versus-cat angle.' He grinned. 'Everyone would love it. We could even write a dog-versus-cat comic book together.'

Her cheeks flushed, turning a familiar shade of pink. 'That's more Emmie's area than mine.'

He'd never seen anyone look so beautiful while they were embarrassed before. Lucas took a gulp of his mocha to avoid looking at her.

It was refreshing, how calm Catpurrcino was compared to Muddy Paws: no scuffling of paws or yipping or barking, no animated hikers arguing over maps and walking routes – even when the place was open for business, it was tranquil. The striped cat had now finished drinking, and it rolled onto its back on the wooden flooring, stretching out its front paws.

Clem was checking her phone again, and her face paled in shock. She nearly dropped it. 'It's up!' she squeaked, already scrolling.

'The video of the round?'

She nodded, hair whipping around her ears.

'Going straight to the comments probably isn't a good idea . . .' he cautioned, reaching into his pocket for his own phone. Normally, he'd take his own advice, but she looked like she was going to burst into tears, which made him want to know what people were saying.

It was clear right away what was giving her that expression.

Did you see the way he swooped in to help her? SO dreamy. Don't get what he sees in her though, she dresses like a kid and her nose looks squashed?

It'll never work out anyway, dogs hate cats, haha!

He's way too good-looking for her!

Shut up, they're both good-looking – those babies would be stunning.

I doubt she's his type.

He was usually pretty thick-skinned, but Lucas's palms tingled with unease at seeing strangers from across the country talk about them so openly. The more complimentary comments had a bizarre undercurrent to them, like they were speculating about their favourite characters on a TV show and didn't realise Lucas and Clem were real.

When he looked up, Clem's eyes were gleaming with tears. She sniffed and blinked them away.

Lucas shuffled in his chair, unsure what to do. 'Hey,' he said, trying to sound reassuring. 'Don't cry . . .'

Clem gave a shaky laugh, scooping her hair behind her ear. 'I'm going to be such a mess by the end of this . . .' she muttered, as if to herself. She blinked away more tears. 'Or maybe I am already. Such a mess . . .' She caught herself, glancing up at him. 'Sorry. This is so ridiculous.'

'An Eton mess?' he countered.

'W-What?'

'Mess isn't necessarily a bad thing. You know, like an Eton mess. Those are pretty good, right?'

The laugh that broke free was more genuine this time, lighting up her face. But it soon faded, like a light bulb dimming. She frowned down at her phone and poked at her own nose. 'People used to make fun of my nose all the time. I haven't heard that in a while.' She took a long breath, but her shoulders stayed hunched over.

'Your nose is adorable. Ignore them.' He wanted to add *your entire face is perfect* but he bit the comment back.

She stared at him, a delightful flush on her cheeks. 'Maybe we shouldn't have . . . You know . . . when you took me home . . .'

She gestured vaguely, and he knew she meant the kiss. He'd been wondering whether they should have done it, too. He'd been caught up in everything – in her. In how he felt. Should he have acted on those emotions?

Clem took a sip of her iced tea and watched one of the black cats chase the ginger one up the length of the cat café.

'Look,' he continued, 'I'm sorry I kissed you, if that's what's bothering you. Maybe I—'

'It's not!' she cried. 'I wanted to kiss you, too. It's just . . .' She trailed off, as if fumbling for the right words. She looked on the verge of more tears and his chest constricted.

Clem looked down at her phone and scrolled. Her face dropped and she gasped. 'Oh my God . . .'

'What is it?'

'How? How did they . . .' Her hands were shaking so much the phone was jerking around in her grasp.

'Let me see.'

He reached for the phone, and she snatched it away from him, looking thunderstruck, as if he'd tried to hit one of the cats.

'I'll be able to see it anyway,' he said gently, 'if it's in the comments. Come on, Clem, they're talking about both of us. We're in this together, so let me see.'

His choice of words seemed to bring her back from whatever panic she was feeling. Slowly, she leaned over and pushed her phone across the table towards him.

'It's not about both of us. You see that link?' she said, so quietly it was almost a whisper. 'The one people keep posting? Go to it, and you'll see.'

Lucas looked down, tapping on the link. It brought up a video, but it didn't look like it came from the competition, as it was too dark. He glanced up at her, seeking permission to play it. Clem hid behind her hands. The cats continued to chase each other around the room, paws padding furiously on wood. One of them leaped up onto a table.

'You'll see it anyway, like you said,' Clem told him, voice muffled by her fingers. What little he could see of her face was rapidly turning beetroot red.

He turned his attention to the phone and pressed play. The picture was murky at first, and he caught snippets of a pavement, and a pair of baggy black-and-white trousers shoved into some fur-lined ankle boots.

'I feel ridiculous,' said a young woman's voice. She sounded light and excited, but with an undercurrent of uncertainty. 'I should have put the costume in a bag, and changed into it when I got here.'

'Don't be silly!' came another voice, laughing. Lucas still couldn't see anything except the murky pavement and patchy black-and-white trouser bottoms. 'You look perfect. It's a themed hen party – overdressed is the whole point.'

'But you look plain!'

'I'll be changing soon enough. I told you, my sister is bringing a spare costume. It's not like I *meant* to spill red wine everywhere.'

'I still don't get why your sister is having a themed hen party in a student area in *Cumbria*,' the first girl complained. 'It's quiet here. There are way more exciting—'

'We're here! Go on, you go in first.'

'*Me*?'

'Sure, the other girls will spot you straight away. The sooner we find them, the sooner I can change so we match!'

'Okay, okay, don't shove me!'

The camera was obscured by an arm before it panned upwards, revealing a nervous-looking Clem. The only reason he didn't laugh was because he already knew something was off about this whole situation.

Clem was dressed in a one-piece cow costume, her body covered in a patchwork of white fabric and black splodges. The front of the costume, across her belly, had a huge pink circle stamped across it, complete with a dangling set of udders. She'd also pulled the hood up so a set of floppy ears hung either side of her head, and two yellow horns stuck up from her temples. She was visibly younger here in this video, the lines of her face softer and her hair longer beneath the hood, poking out and trailing down her torso. She was looking worried and Lucas's insides clenched, because whatever happened next, he was guessing it wasn't good.

'Are you filming this?' on-video Clem asked.

Lucas glanced up at present-day Clem, who had abandoned her tea. She was half turned away from him, her elbows propped on the table, eyes shining with tears as she watched the ginger cat and the black cat playing with each other nearby.

'Why are you recording?' asked on-screen Clem.

'I haven't seen her in forever. I want to get her reaction to your costume!' Was it his imagination, or did this other girl stifle a giggle at Clem's expense? 'Go on.'

In the video, Clem took the other girl's word for it and pushed open a set of double doors leading into a building. It was still fairly dark, but it looked like a function room or events hall. The camera followed Clem's progress down the hall, the video getting brighter as they moved beneath the indoor lighting.

It clearly wasn't a hen party like her friend had said.

Rows of chairs had been set out in the room, in front of a lectern and a large projector showing an image of a landscape and the words CONSERVATION CAREERS. Many of the chairs were already filled and other people were helping themselves to flutes of champagne and some snacks that had been set out around the edges of the room.

When they started to notice Clem standing there in her loose-fitting cow costume, fluffy boots at her feet, laughter broke out. Someone called out, sounding half amused, and half baffled: 'Who hired a mascot?'

He wasn't sure if Clem was going to move; she was rooted to the wooden floor, rigid, her arms locked at her sides. She turned on her heel and ran, but the hood must have fallen down, concealing her vision. She barrelled into a long table by the door, crashing into a cluster of champagne glasses and sending them careering sideways, smashing onto the floor. Her legs were quickly soaked through with champagne.

Behind the camera, the other girl was laughing; Lucas had never heard such a cruel sound. On-screen Clem yanked her hood down and, clearly in tears, fled the room.

The video cut out.

Slowly, Lucas set the phone down between them.

Clem turned away, leaning down to stroke the big ginger cat that had come strolling over to her. He couldn't see her face; her hair was covering it.

'Why would your friend do something like this?' said Lucas, his anger at the way she'd been treated making his voice rise.

'Good question,' Clem mumbled. She straightened up, her face still incredibly red, and snatched up her tea, taking a long drag. She still wasn't looking at him, instead watching the ginger cat as it rolled onto its side, tail twitching. She sounded as if she were speaking around a lump in her throat. 'We were at university when that was filmed. She knew I wanted to work in conservation. Maybe she thought it was funny? She'd made friends with some other people . . .' Clem's voice quietened again. 'Could have been their influence? Some of them thought I was weird. I don't know. I thought about it after, and she must have spilled that red wine on herself on purpose, because she knew it was never a themed party we were going to. I've never understood why she did it. We were close. I trusted her.'

Lucas scowled. 'Doesn't seem like a good friend to me.'

'I thought so too. That's why we stopped being friends after this.'

'How long ago was this video?'

'I was twenty, so . . . about five years ago? Ironically, I was so scared back then of this video getting out and spreading further – going viral – but it didn't go far outside the university. But that was enough for them to mock me, wherever I went on campus. The stress was enough to make me drop out. I was pretty ill for a while. Kept imagining applying for jobs in the area, people remembering the video and . . .'

So that's what she'd meant, when she'd said her life had been derailed. But Lucas's mind was rushing over everything she'd said, and the video. 'I went to uni here, too,' he admitted, though he must have been a year above her. 'I used to do catering for some of the events.'

'Why would she post this now?' said Clem, and her voice cracked. 'I don't get it. Because of the contest?'

'Maybe jealousy?' he suggested. He was so furious with this other girl, his words spilled out of their own accord. 'You got through the round, you've got talent as a baker, you work at a pretty unique place, and you're beautiful – there's a lot to envy. Maybe she was trying to mess up your success. She could have felt threatened by it.'

Clem stared at him, her tea halfway to her mouth. 'I'm . . . You think I'm beautiful?'

He hadn't meant to lay out all his thoughts like that. The most logical conclusion came next: 'Well I kissed you, didn't I?'

She opened her mouth to speak again, but before she could, Lucas's phone buzzed. He checked the screen and saw the word MUM flashing at him. Dread gripped him. When he unlocked it there were six missed calls and some messages. He must have missed them, while he was in the kitchen with Clem.

*Dad been taken to hospital,* the first one read. *Call me.*

# Chapter 18

Lucas stared at his phone. His body had turned featherlight and his ears were ringing, drowning out all other sound, including Clem's voice – she was saying something to him. The messages on his phone were variations of the first one: *call me when you can, Lucas,* and *We're at the hospital now.* The third one elaborated: *He had a fall. Can you come?*

He was frozen to his seat. The ringing was growing louder in his ears, vibrating along his skin. He'd been here messing around, helping Clem with her baking, and his dad had been taken to hospital. What was he *doing*?

This was exactly why he'd told Dwayne he wasn't interested in dating. His family needed him and no girlfriend had ever been okay with that. On top of that, Clem was competing against him, and he *needed* that prize money for his family. For his dad, who was now in the hospital; he didn't know what state he was in or how badly he'd been hurt. They needed a diagnosis, and a secure home. What had he been thinking, helping Clem like this?

Her words finally cut through the shrill ringing in his ears. 'Hey, is everything okay?' she was saying.

'I have to go,' he said mechanically. He was talking as if from a great distance, like he was hovering somewhere near the ceiling.

'Go . . . ?' she echoed. 'But . . . what about the dough? We haven't tried it yet. You said you could help me get it right?'

*Dough* . . . That's right. He rose to his feet.

'Try using cold milk from the fridge, rather than warm,' he offered. 'It speeds up the yeast. And prove it once.'

'Are you sure? The recipe said—'

'Yeah, I heard it once from this renowned baker on TV.' His words rushed out. His head was elsewhere, somewhere across the fells in a hospital room where his dad could be lying, hurt. He was speaking quickly, eager to get the words out and leave.

Clem nodded, and she got to her feet, too, her brow knitted in concern. 'Okay . . . I'll try it. But where are you going?'

His voice cracked when he replied. 'My dad's in the hospital. I have to go.'

★

Somehow, the call from his mum had brought whatever was swirling between Lucas and Clem like pollen into sharp focus, as if he were looking at things through an enhanced camera lens, and it was too personal, too intimate, suddenly. She'd offered to come with him to the hospital but he'd said no. He drove there hunched forward over the wheel, swearing at anyone who was meandering way below the speed limit. It wasn't uncommon for tourists or visitors to drive slowly, take in the views of the sprawling vistas, scatterings of sheep, immense lakes, and rough peaks extending to the sky. Today he had no patience for them.

It seemed to take hours to get there. When he finally pulled into the car park and raced inside the building, he was still pent up, shoulders aching with the tension. He only unclenched his teeth slightly when he found his mother waiting for him at his father's bedside. Lucas drew the curtain around the bed after him and his mother hurried over to embrace him.

'Is he okay?' Lucas whispered. 'What happened?'

'He's right here, and he's fine,' said his dad gruffly.

Lucas hadn't noticed he was awake. He broke away from his mum's embrace and turned to his father, who was sitting up in the hospital bed, propped up by a small mountain of pillows. His father was in pain all the time day to day, but from the outside, he looked in perfect health. Even now, in the hospital, he didn't look unhealthy – just tired, the wrinkles etched more deeply around his blue eyes, though they still managed to twinkle with a mischief that didn't reflect his age.

'He fell earlier today,' said his mum quietly. She looked shaken and she'd spilled something down the front of her shirt, as if she'd been rushing around to get here quickly. Lucas grasped her hand tightly. 'I had to go out to run some errands . . .' She took a deep breath. 'I feel awful. Maybe I was gone too long . . .'

'Rubbish,' said his dad, waving an idle hand in the air. 'You can't stay cooped up all the time, Meredith, and I don't expect you to.'

'But . . .' His mum chewed on her bottom lip. 'Richie . . . You've always had the dizziness problem, but you've never fallen like that. What if you'd been on the stairs?'

His mum had a good point; it could have been much worse had that been the case. Lucas's insides constricted at the thought. But his dad brushed off their worries.

'I'm absolutely fine – no damage done. Just cuts and bruises. Stop looking at me like I'm about to drop dead, or I'll have to come back and haunt you when I do.'

Lucas smiled, glad he was well enough to crack jokes. His mum didn't, her lips pursing into a line.

'Never mind me,' his dad said. 'I'm bored of talking about me – I've been doing it with the doctors for too long today. And Lucas needs to focus on the contest, not on my problems. What are you baking for the bread round? Have you made a move on that girl yet?'

'Richie!' his mum said, moving closer to the bed and poking him in the leg through the blankets. 'Don't ask him that—'

'Hey, stop poking me, woman. No foreplay when I'm bruised—'

'Can you save those particular jokes for when I'm *not* here?' Lucas interjected.

His words drew a laugh from his mother, as if a dam had broken and all her tension had spilled out. Her posture visibly relaxed as she clutched his father's hand and gave him a kiss on the side of the head.

'I'm making a bunch of different bread for this round – flatbreads, muffins, all sorts,' Lucas told his dad. 'You'll have to taste-test for me when you get out of here so I can get the flavours right. When can you go home?'

'They want to monitor him in case of concussion,' his mum explained to Lucas. 'He banged his head. I'm sorry if I frightened you, Lucas. I—' She cut off. 'I was scared he might have hit it too hard, had a bleed—'

'Mum, it's okay,' Lucas said. 'I'm glad you got in touch. I'm sorry I didn't see your messages straight away. I was . . . practising for the contest.'

'If I'd known this fall would lead to an official taste-testing role, I would have done it sooner,' said his dad.

'Richie!'

'I'm joking, Mer—'

A hard vibrating sound filled the air – his dad's phone was buzzing from the corner of the bed. He pulled it towards him from near the pillows.

'That's probably your sister, Rich . . .' his mum began. 'I told her what happened.'

'Why don't you two go and grab a coffee?' Lucas's dad suggested. 'This might take a while.'

'Do you want anything?' asked Lucas.

He shook his head, mouthing *no, thanks* and swiping to answer the call.

Lucas steered his mother away from the bedside, and together they weaved through the shiny hospital corridors, past a huge rainbow painted on the wall in honour of the healthcare staff, the sound of their footsteps echoing off the walls. They soon arrived at a spiralling set of stairs that took them down to the ground level, and through past the reception desk. The canteen was through another set of double doors nearby, the sounds of clattering drifting out, and the smell of food cooking mingling with the clinical scent in the air.

Inside, his mother sat at a table while he ordered them coffees and bought her a sandwich. When he set the tray down and sat opposite her, she'd hooked her handbag on the back of the plastic seat.

'Thanks,' she said, accepting the coffee gratefully and wrapping her hands around the cup. There were only a handful of other people here: a few elderly couples chatting over cups of tea; an old man leafing through a creased newspaper; a man in scrubs immersed in a book, probably on his break.

'You should try to eat.' He pushed the sandwich – chicken and stuffing, her favourite – towards her.

She nodded, reaching for the packet and unwrapping it, but she didn't make any move to eat it, simply fiddled with the edges, crinkling them over. The laughter and the joy brought on from his father's jokes had vanished in the space of a few corridors. 'I don't know what to do anymore.' Drawing in a great breath, she let it out again heavily. 'I'm always in my overdraft. Your auntie suggested moving somewhere cheaper but we don't have the funds to move, and even if we did, our entire lives are here. My job. *You're* here. I don't want to uproot everything. This is our home.'

'No,' said Lucas quickly. 'Wait a bit. You might not need to resort to that.'

His mum took a bite of her sandwich and raised her eyebrows. She swallowed and said, 'Lucas, I hope you're not planning on—'

'Mum,' he interrupted. 'I'm going to help you if I can, so hold out for now.'

'The competition money, if you win, is *yours*,' she told him. She gave him a stern look, as if she was telling him off.

'Exactly,' he answered. 'Mine to do what I want with.'

She didn't reply, instead drinking some of her coffee and shaking her head as she tucked into the sandwich.

His attention turned to one of the elderly couples in the corner, both eating a different slice of cake. They each cut off a small chunk, swapping them with each other, so they could each try a different flavour. With a sharp pang, he thought of Clem, and had to shove the thought to one side guiltily. His family needed him. What had he been doing, anyway, in helping her? If he got closer to her, he could let his guard down and spoil his own chances of winning. That would only hurt his family.

'He's struggling, you know, your dad,' his mum told him. 'I know he goes through cycles, but I think he's really low right now. Fed up.'

'He needs proper help,' Lucas said. His phone buzzed but he ignored it.

'I can't eat that. You have it,' said his mum. She'd finished one half of the sandwich and pushed the other half towards him. He accepted begrudgingly, but at least she'd eaten *something*. 'I know he needs help,' she continued. 'But you know how it's been, Lucas. We didn't realise there was a serious problem for a long time, until it was debilitating, and now we keep hitting up against obstacles every time we try to sort things out.'

'He needs a specialist.'

'And he's on a waiting list. Who knows when it'll be?' She sighed, draining her coffee mug. 'Until then, we're stuck.'

Lucas leaned back in his chair, shaking his head. That prize money could change everything: allow him to get together a deposit, get his dad a private appointment so he didn't have to wait for an aeon for the specialist help he needed. Lucas had to get serious and stop messing around. He'd been taking this too lightly, as if it were a simple village bake-off, when it was much more. He realised as he studied the older couple eating the cake that he liked Clem. Liked her a lot. The kiss kept floating across his mind like summer clouds, bright and glaring. But it was a gut-punch, because liking her had made him foolish, illogical.

Liking her would be his downfall.

★

Clem was still at the cat café. To try to distract herself from her worry about Lucas and his family, she'd got on with the baking. But her head wasn't truly in it. She'd formed the dough balls and shaped everything until they had cute little ears and paws, and she'd followed the other steps – utilising Lucas's advice – and waited until her miniature dough-cats had doubled in size. She brushed them with some beaten egg and baked them, but because she was so worried, she overdid them, and some of them came out burnt at the edges. She'd forgotten to cover them with foil so they didn't brown too much. What's more, they were extremely dense and chewy, not as airy as they needed to be. Milk bread was meant to be like eating a cloud, not . . . whatever *this* mess was. Why weren't they coming out right?

His tips . . . had they been genuine? No, that thought process was stupid. Why would he lie?

Unless he wanted to sabotage her. Her thoughts flitted to Genie, the big sign reading *CONSERVATION CAREERS*, and her stomach bottomed out. Would Lucas do that? Offer to help to make sure she didn't get through in the contest? To ensure he would win?

Surely not. And especially not with his dad being in hospital. She was just being silly because she'd been hurt once before by someone she cared about.

She couldn't think about this right now. Thinking she could at least practise the decorating, she attempted to paint faces on the kitten buns, but she messed them up, and some of them ended up looking as worried as she felt. One of them looked borderline hysterical.

In the end, she brought the kitten buns that were relatively okay into the Cat Lounge in a dish. The wood burner in the grey-brick fireplace was empty – in spring and summer they had no need for it, but in winter it could be incredibly cosy in here, with logs burning and a fire crackling and the cats spread out across the room, drawn to the warmth. Only a few of the cats were in here – Binx was coiled atop one of the cat towers, green eyes briefly assessing her before he tucked his face into his grey fur and went back to sleep. Kitty was curled on the rug with her paws tucked in, her beautiful Bengal colouring vibrant in the sun spilling in through the windows, eyes opening and closing lazily. Jess was in one of her favourite positions on the back of the sofa, snoozing with her black tail coiled around her.

Clem leaned into the leather – making Jess chirp in greeting. She stroked the cat's head and checked her phone. Lucas hadn't replied. She'd texted him earlier asking if everything was okay and she thought he would have answered by now. She felt a horrible lurch – was something seriously wrong?

Now her phone was in her hand, it was too easy to compulsively check on what was happening with *Whisked Away*. She couldn't bring herself to watch

the video of the round of the competition – she had
no desire to see herself bumble through things again –
but judging by the comments, the show was spinning a
particular angle.

> This is way better than the last contest!! Ronan is
> a pure genius to have dog vs cat.
>
> I don't care about the other contestants at this
> point. Want to see if it'll be enemies to lovers.
>
> They'll never get together. They seem too
> mismatched anyway? Like he's clearly more
> confident than she is.

Every comment was like knives poking at her skin,
and Clem still couldn't stop looking, doom-scrolling
into oblivion. Eventually, she deleted her social apps
entirely and chucked her phone across the room onto
the opposite armchair in frustration. Jess hopped down
from the sofa in surprise and Kitty opened her eyes wide,
ears angled. Even Binx stirred, head raising, a grumpy
expression on his face.

'Sorry, kitties,' Clem mumbled.

She snatched up a kitten bun and bit into it. This was
one of the ones that miraculously hadn't burned, and
although it tasted fine, the texture was too claggy, not
soft and fluffy enough. Clem sighed.

A few minutes later, Emmie appeared in the doorway
of the Cat Lounge. She was wearing a pair of high-
waisted jeans and a white top, with an extremely baggy
hoodie that looked at least five sizes too big for her.

'Hey, Clem,' Emmie said, smiling warmly. She must have noticed Clem assessing the hoodie, because she looked down and tugged at it. 'It was raining earlier so Jared lent me his hoodie to come home in.'

'Ah, that's nice of him,' said Clem, distracted.

'Oooh, have you been experimenting?' said Emmie. She placed her backpack down next to the sofa, gave Jess's ears a scratch, and sat down beside Clem, leaning over to look at the bread.

'Practising for the next round of the contest,' Clem explained. 'Lucas was helping but . . .' She trailed off, realising what she'd said. Maybe she shouldn't have let that slip since they'd agreed to keep it a secret, but she'd still not heard anything from him and she couldn't seem to keep her thoughts in order.

'Lucas? The guy from the dog-friendly place? Muddy Paws?'

'Please don't tell anyone,' Clem urged her, swivelling on the sofa to face her. 'We had this agreement to help each other with our weak spots. But now I don't think it was such a good idea, and I don't know if he was being genuine. What people are saying . . .'

'I've seen some of it,' said Emmie gently. 'It might be best not to look, until the contest's over. It won't do you any good to read the comments.'

Clem knew this was true. But sometimes she felt like an asteroid orbiting the sun – the sun being her phone. She was so drawn to the thing, she sometimes thought the only way to be rid of that feeling would be to get an old-fashioned brick phone with no apps and no internet. Or to throw the phone into the sea.

'I know it's hard,' Emmie continued. 'I sometimes fixate on my art accounts, especially since they've grown. And with twenty positive comments, the ones that stick out are always the negative ones. Can I try one of the buns?'

Clem nodded. 'I threw away the ones that were too burnt to eat. Help yourself. They're too dense though.'

Emmie tore a roll from the cluster and took a bite. Clem couldn't read her expression.

'Not bad,' she said. 'They taste good. I see what you mean about them being dense. Hey, don't look so glum. I'm sure you'll sail through with flying colours once you nail it down.'

'Lucas's dad is in hospital,' Clem told her. It felt good to unburden herself, and Emmie had always been nice to her, so she knew she could trust her.

'What? Is it serious?'

'I don't know . . . He was here earlier helping me, and then he rushed off. I messaged to ask how things were and he hasn't replied.'

'He might be dealing with things. I'm sure he'll answer when he can.'

'He was giving me tips, but . . .'

Emmie continued to eat the rest of her bun. Kitty had moved from her spot on the rug to sit at Emmie's ankles. Her irises were ringed in black as if she were wearing eyeliner.

'You can't have bread, Kitty!' said Emmie, making a shooing motion with her hands. Kitty didn't move. 'It's not for you.'

'We kissed,' Clem blurted. 'Me and Lucas.'

It was too much to keep to herself. She'd wanted to address it with Lucas but he'd rushed off to hospital, understandably. Emmie almost dropped the last small piece of bread she was holding and Kitty raised her front paws expectantly, like a meerkat. When it was clear Emmie wasn't going to give her anything, she set them down again.

'When?' said Emmie, eating the last of her bread.

Clem briefly explained what had happened. 'I know it's not important right now, with his dad being unwell, but . . .'

'Go on?' Emmie encouraged her.

'With all these comments, and this dog-and-cat rivalry angle the contest is spinning . . . I feel like I got carried away. Like it wasn't a good idea to kiss him. And then this person I know turned up at the contest and it's compli-cated . . .' She explained about Genie and the video. It was trying, to repeat the same story she'd already told Lucas. But Emmie would see the video if she hadn't already. 'I don't know if Lucas was helping me for the right reasons,' she added. 'And I feel bad even saying it right now . . .'

By the time she'd done, Emmie was frowning, a little crease over the bridge of her nose. 'Do you think Genie shared that video around?'

Clem shrugged. 'She took it, so who else could it be? It did get around back then, so other people could have downloaded it too, but she turned up at the contest. It can't be a coincidence.'

'You could talk to her and find out? Maybe she wanted to see you and make amends?'

'I don't know . . .'

'It's your decision. I don't blame you if you don't want to. She betrayed your trust. As for Lucas . . .' Emmie paused, considering, and dusting off her hands. 'Did he say how he felt about things?'

'We didn't really have chance to talk about it properly. Earlier, he . . . he kind of implied I'm beautiful, and he mentioned the kiss, but he had to rush off . . .'

Emmie beamed at her. 'Sounds like he likes you! So why do you think he isn't being genuine?'

'Well, he's the competition, isn't he? And he *really* wants to win. He has solid enough reasons for wanting the prize money. Which I completely understand.' Clem took a breath, and let the words out in a rush: 'How am I supposed to trust him when he wants me to lose, though? I haven't known him for long . . .'

'Long enough to kiss him,' Emmie said slyly, nudging Clem with her shoulder.

'Ugh.' Clem covered her face with her hands – her cheeks were burning.

Emmie laughed. 'It's good to see you taking some initiative.'

Clem could barely fight the guilt that crept over her skin like ice particles. Lucas wanted to win the contest for the sake of his parents; she hadn't been able to take the *initiative*, as Emmie put it, to enter it herself. Sylvie had been the one to push the button in the end.

She shook her head, flopping against the sofa in defeat. 'I didn't enter the competition myself.' She avoided looking at Emmie as she spoke, her chin tucked into her chest. 'I filled in the form and got scared. Sylvie happened to come across the application and thought I'd forgotten to ask her to fill in her sections. So she typed them out, and pressed send.'

Silence fell, and still Clem couldn't look at Emmie, fearing her judgement. She instead traced a line in the leather sofa with the pad of her finger.

'Does that matter?' said Emmie eventually.

'What?' Clem jerked her chin up. 'What do you mean?'

Emmie's expression was soft. 'It doesn't matter if Sylvie sent it off, or you. You're in the competition now, and you're *doing* it regardless of any fears or doubts. You're doing a brilliant job. Don't beat yourself up about that.'

'Th-Thanks,' Clem spluttered. She wasn't entirely sure she was doing a brilliant job – but maybe Emmie was right. She'd done more than she'd given herself credit for. The problem was, she wasn't sure how she'd manage if things spiralled. If she made more mistakes, or if Genie – or Lucas, for that matter – did something to hurt her, would she revert back to the person she was? Being too afraid to leave the house, to be around people, to *do* anything?

'Do you like him? Lucas?' Emmie asked her.

'I do,' said Clem. She knew it was true – being bold enough to kiss him, to go with her instincts in spite of everything, proved it. But for now, she needed to push her instincts to one side. She wrung her hands in her lap. 'It's just . . . The speculation, the filming, what people are saying, and now Genie . . . and Lucas's dad being in hospital . . . I don't know . . .'

'Genie's in your past,' Emmie reassured her. 'Try not to pre-judge people in the present for that, Clem. Maybe you need to get to know Lucas better, and see how the contest unfolds. It'll probably be easier once the cameras are off you,' she added, 'and you don't have random strangers on the internet to deal with. That's probably making you even more sceptical about him.'

Clem nodded. That was what she'd thought too, and having it confirmed to her made her feel lighter, her chest less tight. 'Thanks, Emmie.'

'No problem,' said Emmie, slapping her hands on her knees as she got to her feet, startling the cats who were dotted around the room. 'How about an iced coffee?'

# Chapter 19

Clem wanted to call Lucas but she'd never done that before, and her palms became sticky whenever she thought about it. It was already a warm evening, the sun sinking and turning the living room of the cottage shades of terracotta. Clem was sitting on the rug on the floor, playing with Misha with a dangly toy: a stick with a tweeting bird on the end. She flicked the stick up, the bird sailing high, and Misha leaped into the air and performed a pirouette like a ballerina, making Clem laugh.

'I have no idea how you do that without breaking your back!' Clem marvelled, flicking it in the air again and watching Misha dive, ramrod straight, into the air. She caught the bird between her paws and pinned it to the rug, claws extended.

Clem glanced at her phone. Lucas still hadn't messaged her and she'd been sitting with this sickly, gut-wrenching anxiety that something might be wrong. Both her parents were in good health – albeit she didn't speak to her dad much, since he lived at the bottom of the country with his new partner and her children. She'd be awfully upset if either of them ended up hospitalised. She hoped Lucas's dad was okay.

She swirled the dangly toy around the rug and the wooden flooring, and Misha leaped forward, dangerously close to piercing Clem's bare legs with her claws as she caught it roughly.

Her phone buzzed on the coffee table. Clem moved so quickly, she banged her knee on the corner and hissed through her teeth. She dropped Misha's toy and grabbed the phone.

It was Lucas. She pulled open the message at once.

> Sorry I left suddenly. Wanted you to know all's okay.

She tapped out a reply.

> I thought something awful happened. Is your dad okay?

His response took a good five minutes to come through. Misha sat assessing Clem, her tail swishing as if demanding more play. Clem absently ran the toy in a loop around the rug, springing the cat into action and sending her charging around in a semi-circle. Finally, he replied.

> *Lucas:* Yes, he had a fall but he's not too badly hurt. Thanks for asking. We should probably talk
>
> *Clem:* I was going to say that too. I didn't want to bother you with your dad being in hospital
>
> *Lucas:* Yeah. Listen, that kiss, I know it took both of us. I kissed you back. But maybe I shouldn't have. I have a lot going on. I like you but I don't know if I'm ready for a relationship. I'm sorry. I should have said that before. I didn't mean to lead you on or anything

Clem's ears were roaring, and even though Misha was uttering little squeaks beside her, wanting her to flick the toy in the air again, she sat stock-still. A burning sensation was creeping over her skull and neck, hot and full of shame. She wanted the rug to swallow her up.

She'd planned to do as Emmie suggested: to tell him she didn't regret kissing him but maybe they should see how things were after the contest, because doing anything more right now would be too hard for her under the watchful eyes of internet strangers. Plus, she wanted to be sure she could trust him – though she hadn't planned to tell him that part. But here he was, closing the book on things for good. Not just postponing them. Ending them before they could start.

Her hands shaking, she typed out a reply, having to go back and correct typos three times. Then she deleted it, because she hated conflict and didn't want to sound confrontational. Lucas sent another message.

*Lucas:* I'm sorry. I think this hospital thing made things clear

 *Clem:* What do you mean?

 *Lucas:* My family have to come first. I have to look out for them. I'm really sorry, Clem

Tears sprang into her eyes. She forced out another message:

*Clem*: We shouldn't be teaming up. Bread, cake, whatever it is. We shouldn't help each other

 *Lucas:* Yeah

Clem chucked her phone onto the sofa.

She couldn't believe she'd been so stupid. Kissing him had been a huge mistake. They were competing – they weren't meant to be locking lips. There had been so many jokes about cat versus dog, about them being rivals. She was starting to think that was the best way to think about Lucas Bowen: as her rival, and nothing more. It would hurt much less.

*

Clem was in the main café room at Catpurrcino, staring down at another batch of failed kitten buns sitting on the counter. Emmie was standing beside her. The rolls didn't *look* bad, necessarily – they were shaped like cat heads, with tiny paws, as they should be, but they were smaller, less voluminous than they were meant to be. Clem huffed out a sigh, wedging her hands onto her hips.

It was early evening, and she'd stayed at Catpurrcino after closing time to practise the bread. Emmie had no plans tonight and had offered to come downstairs and observe, keep her company. It was only eight o'clock but Emmie was already dressed in a pair of fluffy toadstool slippers and a set of pink Princess Peach pyjamas. Almost all of the cats were sleeping in various spots around the room – most of them on cat towers, but Salem was curled on the window seat across the room, a black splodge with no visible face. Binx was giving them the side-eye from a nearby chair.

'They shouldn't be this small,' Clem complained, jabbing a finger in the direction of the kitten buns.

'Let's taste them,' Emmie suggested.

They each pulled off a kitten bun – the buns were designed to be tear-and-share – and popped it into their mouths, chewing slowly. Clem winced – still dense and claggy. She swallowed reluctantly, unhappy with the result.

'The same as before,' Emmie said, and she continued to chew.

Clem groaned. 'It's meant to be extremely soft, with a feathery texture – wispy.'

'So it's definitely too thick.'

'Yes. Lucas *has* to have lied to me. His advice was a load of rubbish.'

A creased line appeared on Emmie's brow, and she leaned her elbows on the countertop. 'You really think he did that? That he's purposefully sabotaging you?'

'Why else would it keep failing? I followed the recipe exactly, but tweaked it and took on board his suggestions.'

'You should try it without them. It might give you an answer.'

'I never got it right when I did it by myself, either, though. Something kept going wrong and I couldn't figure out why. Although . . .' Clem whipped out her phone. 'I could ask someone. I was googling it all the time before, trying to figure it out, but too many different recipes came up. I got mine from a book and it's really specific.'

'Who will you ask?' said Emmie.

Clem smirked and tapped at her phone. Her increased following had intimidated her before – but maybe she could use it for something she needed. 'The internet. Just in a slightly different way. There are loads more bakers following me now.'

She tapped out a post quickly – one that would disappear in twenty-four hours – talking about the recipe and what was going wrong. She set it up as a Q&A for people to leave answers.

'People might have suggestions,' Clem told Emmie, 'and I can also throw out Lucas's suggestions, to see if he was being genuine, or if he lied.'

The answers came in faster than she was expecting, the notifications popping up within five minutes, while she and Emmie were getting themselves a pot of tea. Some people were doing some extreme mathematics to try to help, though she thought that was going too far. She decided to implement the easiest suggestions first: using a stand-mixer instead of kneading by hand. And she'd go back to her original recipe, *without* the suggestions from Lucas.

'I'm going to try again,' she told Emmie.

'Right now? Can I eat these ones?' Emmie asked, with a grin, pointing at the kitten buns.

'Of course. But you can go back to your flat, you know – you don't have to hang around down here.'

'Why *wouldn't* I hang around when I get access to your leftovers?' said Emmie, tearing off a hunk of bread. 'I should have brought Jared too. There's no way I can save him any of these – it tastes too good. They'll be gone in minutes.'

Clem laughed. 'I'm glad it won't go to waste, even if the texture's off. I'll be in the kitchen.'

She left Emmie with the tear-and-share bread – confident she'd eat the entire thing herself – and retreated into the kitchen. Donning a cat-print apron, she looked around at the shiny silver surfaces, the shelving units, the industrial oven gleaming at her, as if winking, letting her in on a secret.

'Right,' she said, tying her apron string. 'Let's go again.'

Clem knew the recipe off by heart, but she pulled it up on her phone – she'd taken a photo of the page in the book where she'd found it – and scanned through it anyway. She had to be sure everything was perfect.

She made the tangzhong paste first, whisking together the flour and water in a pan before moving on to the heating stage. The paste never went wrong, even though it had to be at a specific temperature – she had a thermometer to keep tabs on that. When she was done with it, she left the paste to chill in the freezer and moved on to the dough.

This was where she had to be careful. She slowed down, double- and triple-checking the recipe as she warmed milk, melted butter, and added sugar and salt. Every step, every word of the instructions, followed meticulously, until she had a ball of dough to work with. She'd normally start hand-kneading now, on a floured surface, until the dough was smooth but slightly tacky. Instead, she went straight to the stand mixer.

'We'll see if you're right, Lucas,' she muttered, when she'd set it up and was watching it swirl around, mixing the dough. Part of her hoped Lucas *was* right, but she had a sinking feeling in her gut he hadn't told her the truth.

★

It was another few hours before Clem returned to the Cat Lounge, where she found Emmie with her legs up on the leather sofa, with a games console in her hands chiming happily. Lilian was curled in her lap, fast asleep, but she looked up when Clem stepped inside, sniffing the air, catching the scent of the sweet bread and baking Clem brought with her.

Clem had practically been *vibrating* in the kitchen as she shaped the dough balls, because she'd known something was different – the size had seemed more correct, even after she'd proved them, and once baked, they looked beautiful: light amber-gold, not burnt like last time. They were fully cooled now. She'd decorated them in a rush, because she'd been buzzing with the knowledge that Lucas was *wrong*. The sensation was still scoring her skin.

'Ready to taste-test?' she said to Emmie, voice quaking slightly. 'They've already come out better.'

Emmie sat up, and Lilian leaped away from her, hopping down onto the floor and stretching herself into a C-shape, tail high in the air.

'So that means . . .' Emmie said, swinging her legs over the side of the sofa. Lilian toddled away, jumping onto the armchair opposite instead, where she settled down to wash her paws and face.

'Yep,' Clem ground out, taking a seat beside Emmie, the leather sofa deflating beneath her. 'He was wrong. Here, let's try them. But I'm pretty sure they're good now.'

Clem set the new tray down next to the old one – Emmie had demolished most of it but a few buns were still left. 'To save room for the best,' Emmie told her, grinning. She tore off a bun from the new batch, and Clem followed her example.

'Cheers,' said Emmie, and they knocked their buns together like glasses of wine.

Together, they took a bite. It was instant – the texture was perfect. Soft, fluffy, a tender crumb. Cloud-like, exactly how it was meant to be. As she chewed, Clem pulled apart the rest of the bread to take a peek at the middle. Inside, it was gorgeously springy and soft. Jess appeared through the cat flap, as if sensing food was being doled out, and sat at their feet expectantly.

Emmie sighed happily. 'Oh my God, this is heavenly,' she said. Her happy expression faded as she looked up at Clem. 'But surely he didn't lie to you on purpose? He probably made a mistake. Got mixed up.'

Had he? Clem didn't know. He'd rushed off to the hospital shortly after. Was it possible he'd made a mistake, given the circumstances? Or was he trying to make her mess up? Was that why he'd offered to help her in the first place?

'I don't know,' she said slowly. 'He offered to help me way before his dad ended up in hospital. I know I sound awful. I know he's going through a bad time, but . . .'

'You don't sound awful,' said Emmie, polishing off the last of her bun and dusting off her fingers on her pyjamas. Jess was watching her every move. 'You had a bad experience with Genie, so I understand why you're suspicious.'

'You know . . .' said Clem in a small voice. Her throat was as thick as her early batch of bread as she thought of her recent exchange with Lucas. 'He told me recently he doesn't want a relationship.' She swallowed down the hard lump that was building inside her throat. 'Said his family come first. He doesn't want to get to know me better. Not anymore. And I told him we shouldn't bother helping each other.'

Emmie scootched closer to Clem on the sofa and put her arm around her. 'I'm sorry, Clem.'

'What should I do?' Clem asked her. 'I was going to follow your advice last time, to see what happened in the contest. See if there was something between me and Lucas, afterwards. But now . . .'

Emmie's tone turned fierce. 'You know what I think you should do? You should *win*.'

# Chapter 20

By the time the second round of the contest arrived in June, Lucas had easily spent every spare moment he had either in his kitchen at home – with Dwayne taste-testing his bread – or in Muddy Paws Café's kitchen. He'd struggled to settle on what to do for this round, and had eventually chosen an assorted basket, filled with different types of bread they offered at Muddy Paws Café: tomato and basil flatbread, sliced banana bread, crusty baguettes, toasties, English muffins. The basket would be a picnic basket – something to represent local dog walkers stopping in for some snacks to complement a sunny-day picnic by the lake. His dad had tried all of the bakes and given his gold seal of approval to every single one.

He hadn't spoken to Clem since he'd told her he needed to focus on his family. And yet he couldn't get her face out of his mind. While making his own bread, he could only think of how he'd offered to help, and let her down.

This morning, the bus was carrying the contestants through the snaking pathways of the Lakes; there was boundless, rippling water to their left, pockmarked with rainfall. It was a gloomy but warm summer's day, the lake itself a polished silver reflecting the clouds. It only made him think of kissing Clem under the umbrella, the weight of her lips reassuring, soft against his. The way his spine had trembled as though she'd been running her fingers over his skin. The surprise lingering on her mouth when he drew away.

'Er, hello, Lucas? What planet are you on?' Dwayne asked, waving his hand in front of Lucas's face.

'W-What?' Lucas turned to him, but kept his spine pressed against the seat. If he leaned too far forward, he'd see Clem, sitting by the window in the row opposite. He'd carefully avoided making eye contact with her so far, or even looking at her at all.

'Never mind,' said Dwayne. He shook his head. 'Make sure your head is in the game when we get there instead of in the clouds.'

It was no less grey outside when they arrived at the location and filed off the bus. Lucas hurried forward to get off before Clem did, but he couldn't avoid her when he reached the tent and their workstations, since they were positioned right beside one another. Rain was pitter-pattering on the tent's surface and stray leaves were swept up in the building breeze, sticking to one of the transparent sides. He couldn't help but shoot a look Clem's way as everyone waited, chattering.

She was talking to Sylvie quietly. And even though he'd been reminding himself of his reasoning all the way here for keeping away from her, he felt like he'd been struck in the solar plexus. She was wearing bright red lipstick, her hair skimming her shoulders, and a crisp white T-shirt decorated with a lazing cat. The words hanging beneath the cat read *nope*. Her jeans were high-waisted and baggy, the shirt tucked in. A thought zipped through his mind before he could catch it and discard it: that this woman would look stunning even if she were wrapped in a crinkled old sack.

Soon Ronan and the other judges were breezing into the tent, looking significantly windswept, hair askew. A cluster of staff darted around, fixing their hair and their make-up, wiping rain from Jonathan's glasses, before the filming could start. Ronan was dressed in a salmon-pink suit decorated with faint brown stripes, and a pale green tie; he looked like an unfashionable children's TV presenter. Viviana and Laurette were both immaculate as always, hair smooth and shiny, frizz-free. Viviana's smooth brown skin was dusted with gold highlight, making her look like a shimmering elf. The thought only reminded him of Clem, and how they'd joked about her failed lembas bread. Learning about her – her quirks and interests – had made him feel so . . . light.

'Hi, everyone! Nice to see you all, and welcome to round two!' Ronan bleated, once the cameras were rolling. 'Bread week! Now, you all know the rules . . .'

He launched into an explanation of what would happen next – mainly for the sake of the audience, since the gathered contestants knew already. The camera was fixed on him the whole time.

'We can't wait to see what you come up with! Good luck and get baking!' Ronan finished with a flourish, giving them a thumbs up.

There was the usual rush as everyone scrambled around their workstations, gathering equipment. Nerves whooshed inside Lucas like the leaves outside being churned up by the wind. *This is no different to a morning's work in the café,* he told himself.

*Except it could change everything for Mum and Dad,* said another little voice in the far reaches of his mind. *What will they do if you fail?*

But he couldn't think about that. Only about what came next. The process.

Ingredients stacked up on the workstation, he nodded at Dwayne, who returned the gesture, looking equally determined. They hardly needed to speak; they'd been over this dozens of times. They'd been like ballet dancers in the kitchen, winging around one another. Now, they launched into the routine, whirling around and mixing ingredients and prepping.

The first time his concentration broke – outside of being questioned by the judges for the sake of the camera – it was when a sharp burning smell reached his nostrils. When he looked up, Clem was snatching up a pan and removing it from the heat, waving Sylvie over with a panicked expression.

'We need to start over!' he heard her cry. 'I've burnt the tangzhong paste . . . But when we redo it, we'll have wasted time. We'll still have to wait for it to chill . . . We have to hurry up.'

Sylvie said something in response that Lucas didn't hear, patting her on the shoulder and swooping across to their workstation, her bun slightly askew. Clem disposed of the burnt mixture, her cheeks as bright as her lipstick – the camera was fully homed in on them, capturing the debacle. There was an itch in his feet – as if they wanted to move over and help her – but he held firm. Her lip was trembling.

*We're in competition,* he reminded himself. This wasn't a first date where he had to be on his best behaviour.

He nearly stumbled over his own feet, Dwayne grabbing him by the arm to steady him.

'Focus on this workstation,' Dwayne said quietly.

'Sorry,' Lucas mumbled. 'I'm on it.'

'Your parents,' Dwayne reminded him.

'I know.'

And so, he held them in his mind as he rolled and shaped dough and set things in the oven to bake, the smell of fresh bread and herbs and spices filling the tent in a mouth-watering concoction. He flinched when Clem dropped a dough ball on the floor, in the same area where she'd been walking, and it rolled around, coming to rest by his feet.

*Don't*, he told himself. *Don't help.*

The camera had followed everything, now positioned on him, a great shiny eyeball waiting to see what he'd do next. He was looking down at the dough ball leaning against his shoe; he couldn't prise his attention away from it. He wouldn't pick it up, wouldn't get involved. But when she knelt down to pick the ball up herself, and glanced up at him, his chest caught, as if there was something stuck in his ribcage.

Clem straightened up and hurried away with a mumbled, 'Sorry.' She declared to Sylvie that they'd have to throw it away – they couldn't bake it when it had been contaminated.

Things really weren't going well for her in this round. Was that his fault? He should be pleased his competition was performing poorly – but he wasn't. Instead, he was grappling with the desire to help.

He tried to ignore it, concentrating instead on dusting the work surface with flour, tipping out his dough, rolling it until it was the correct thickness. These English muffins needed to be *perfect*. Everything needed to be perfect. Dwayne prepared a baking tray as Lucas meticulously cut out eight perfectly shaped muffins, leaving them to prove.

It was a juggling act, working on five different types of bread at once. There was a knot in his chest, tightening as he and Dwayne skirted around one another at the workstation, bumping shoulders at one point.

Once everything was baked and laid out in front of them, the arrangement had to be perfect, too. Lucas set the basket at the end of the workstation – it was round, with a curved handle and a lid, and he placed a strip of red checked cloth inside delicately. It reminded him vaguely of something Red Riding Hood might carry. Good – if it looked whimsical, inviting, that could only be a plus point for the judges.

'Come on then,' Dwayne said, rubbing his hands together next to Lucas. 'What's going to look best? I'd maybe have the baguettes sticking out at the side, like this . . .' He demonstrated, placing them in the basket and leaning them on the sides. 'The English muffins can hold them up.'

'Flatbread and toasties on top,' Lucas suggested. 'They look the most inviting.'

They leaned over the basket, as if they were dressing a baby for a photo session, and stood back when they were done to assess. The team at the workstation in front were racing around to try to get everything finished on time, the woman's hair sticking up like she'd been electrocuted.

'Looks good,' said Dwayne, as Lucas adjusted a few of the flatbreads so the toppings were more visible.

When Ronan called time, Lucas, Dwayne, and the rest of the contestants lined up along the back of the tent to face the verdict of the judges. Lucas was acutely aware of the difference between his bake and Clem's as he placed his picnic basket full of bread down in front of him. He'd arranged it lovingly, the basket half open so the judges could see the assortment of breads sticking out, their scents wafting across the tent. But there was no denying that some of his bread had come out far smaller than it was meant to be – and the crumb structure of the sourdough in particular wasn't right, gaping tunnels running through the loaf. His jaw hardened. He wasn't happy with that but there was nothing he could do about it.

By contrast, Clem's bake looked stunning. The kitten buns were connected together – as share bread. They were a shade of dark amber, lighter on the edges, sets of cat paws jutting out from each bun, the faces perfectly decorated with little whiskers, noses, and eyes. Some of the eyes were curved to create a happy, smiling cat, others were sideways V's to show an expression of mischief. They had a glazed look, shining in spite of the gloomy day. To go along with the kittens, there was another, larger loaf of tiger bread, crusty and thick, and shaped to look like a giant mother cat, complete with whisker-like indents and thick, doughy paws.

Lucas swallowed. Her bake was perfect.

Clem's head was raised, her hands stuffed in the pockets of her jeans and her shoulders straight. Sylvie caught Lucas looking and smiled at him, mouthing *Good luck*. Hesitant, he sent her a smile of his own and a nod. Had Clem not told her anything about what had happened between them? He felt a flutter of appreciation. He knew he'd hurt her and she had every right to complain to others about it.

Like vultures, the judges began stalking their way up the table, observing the bakes, with Ronan at the head of the group, leading his flock. When he reached Lucas and Dwayne, he paused and adjusted his tie, inhaling deeply and flicking a dazzling smile at the camera.

'Ah, I love bread week!' he said, smacking his lips overly theatrically. 'The smell never gets old.' He inhaled deeply. 'What have we got here? Can you tell us what you've made, Lucas?'

'It's an assortment of breads we sell at Muddy Paws Café, made up in a picnic basket,' he explained. 'It represents the summer experience we offer. Dog walkers, hikers, travellers – if people aren't staying for coffee, they can take something away with them for a picnic by the lake.'

'Ah, excellent,' said Ronan, leaning closer and breathing in the scent of the bread.

'A wonderful concept,' Laurette offered. 'Although it does look like you've under-proved some of it.'

'Can we try a bit of everything?' said Jonathan.

'Go ahead.' Lucas gestured at the basket, and the judges dug in. He glanced at Dwayne, who gave him a nod, and Lucas began explaining to the judges what the different types of bread were inside the basket.

When everything had been nibbled on at least once, Ronan looked up, still clutching half a slice of banana bread. 'The taste is wonderful, especially the banana bread,' he decided. 'The flatbread especially is my favourite – the herbs and the garlic work well and the crust is perfectly crispy. Sadly, the sourdough is weak – Laurette is right, definitely under-prooved. The crumb has far too much tunnelling. Look at those gaping holes!'

'The texture is also quite . . .' Viviana paused, as if searching for the right word. She still held a piece of sourdough, like she didn't want to finish the rest of it. Lucas's stomach clenched. 'It's gummy,' she concluded. 'And the flavour is bland, which is a shame because your flatbread is so delicious.'

'The banana bread *is* delicious, though,' said Jonathan, going back for seconds. 'The banana flavour is well balanced – not too overwhelming. And I love the hints of cinnamon and the chopped walnuts. A great touch.'

Jonathan was peering into the basket again, as if searching for a visible mistake. 'Such a shame about the sourdough,' he concluded. 'The English muffins don't seem to have risen high enough, either. They've collapsed.'

Lucas didn't know what to say – he nodded mechanically, hoping the embarrassment wasn't showing. His hopes of getting through this round were slowly sinking. What the hell had he done wrong? Was his head not in the game, like Dwayne had said, because he'd been too focused on Clem? Or had he been too worried about his father after what happened at the hospital?

When the judges moved on to Clem standing beside him, more of his hope ebbed away, and he risked a look in her direction. She was holding back a smile, and Sylvie had hooked an arm through hers in support.

Ronan studied her bake with an unreadable look on his face. 'And can you tell me about your bread today, ladies?'

'The main loaf is a mother cat,' Clem explained. 'It's a fairly common recipe with my own spin on it, and we worked together on it. The kitten buns for sharing are Hokkaido milk bread – I used the tangzhong method for those. Both bakes represent our work with a cat shelter, and our care for all cats. Last winter we had an incident during a snowstorm where a pregnant stray cat was found. The cat ended up going to Sylvie with one of her kittens, and our delivery driver adopted one of the others. We had planned to have one more bread-kitten here, but . . . well . . . There was a minor mishap in the kitchen.'

'Ah, yes, we saw,' said Laurette, smiling in amusement.

'Well, in any case, it's a lovely theme and concept,' Ronan said. 'And it looks marvellous – such a wonderful presentation.'

The other judges nodded in agreement. Lucas glanced along the table. Everyone else had gone all out, too: there was an impressive, intricate star bread with chutney, and a collection of breads shaped like mush-rooms – although that one did look wonky, more like a sad, melting village.

Behind Clem, Sylvie was squeezing her hand tightly. Lucas looked away, focusing hard on the judges, rather than on Clem's face. Fear was chewing away at him. If he'd never kissed her back, never offered to help out in the first place . . . Why had he allowed her to distract him like this? What had he been thinking? He could end up kicked out of the competition and then what would his parents do? They could end up homeless and he knew he would blame himself for not keeping his head in the game.

The judges broke apart Clem's kitten buns first, sharing them around. They chewed thoughtfully.

'It's beautifully soft,' Ronan said.

'The sweetness is good too,' Laurette added, holding a tiny piece of milk bread between her delicate fingers. 'The texture is perfect – the tangzhong has worked so well to make everything tender and fluffy, as milk bread should be.'

'You must have worked hard to get this right,' said Viviana. 'The wispiness is gorgeous . . . It melts in your mouth.' She peered down at the share bread, where their pieces had been torn off. 'The way you've shaped and decorated these is beautiful too. I love the faces.'

'Perfectly in keeping with the theme,' Jonathan agreed.

The judges moved on to the main tiger loaf, slicing into it, the slices coming away with a *crunch-crunch* of the knife. They appeared extremely happy with this bread, too, smiling and nodding as they bit into it.

'Excellent,' Ronan commented. 'It's not often I'm speechless but I can't think of anything to say to you except praise.' He held out his hand to Clem, offering her a handshake.

Clem looked like she was going to cry, even though she was grinning widely. She blinked and reached out to shake Ronan's hand.

'Brilliant work, Clem,' said Jonathan, giving her a wink as the judges moved away from her.

Lucas's heart was hammering, and he was nauseous. The others seemed to pass with flying colours, too – except the bakers of the mushroom bread, who were from the little farm shop over in Kendal. They were on par with Lucas when it came to the coolness of the judges' comments. Viviana said the mushrooms looked like Halloween decorations, instead of being cosy and inviting as they were meant to be.

The judges went away to deliberate.

When they finally returned, and assembled at the top of the tent to reveal who would be leaving, Lucas's ribcage twisted uncomfortably, because he had a horrible feeling he knew who it was.

*I'm done*, he thought. *Completely done*. He hadn't been creative enough. A picnic basket? Why couldn't he have done something more intricate? And why had he let himself down with the sourdough and the muffins?

'Everyone did their best this week, and you should all be proud of yourselves and what you've accomplished,' said Ronan.

The camera panned across the contestants, collecting shots of expectant faces. Lucas's shoulders were tense; he was working hard to keep his nerves from being obvious to everyone.

'We've thought long and hard and come to a unanimous decision. We'll be sorry to let this pair go. They've been so imaginative and skilled with their creations, and we know everyone else loves them, too. They just had a bad week, unfortunately. And everyone else upped their game.'

Lucas closed his eyes. It was him.

# Chapter 21

'We're so sorry . . . Bundles of Bread. You'll be leaving us this time,' Ronan announced.

Lucas thought he'd heard wrong, at first. He wasn't leaving? The judges were stepping forward to commiserate with the bakers from Bundles of Bread, the farm shop, who moved out of the line to shake hands with Ronan and the others. So he definitely *had* heard correctly. A gleam of happiness alighted inside him – he was through. It wasn't over. Beside him, Sylvie gave Clem a massive hug before hurrying off to shake hands with those who would be leaving. Viviana was patting them on the shoulder, talking to them quietly.

'Mate, we did it!' Dwayne cried, slapping Lucas on the shoulders so hard he nearly sent him staggering forwards. 'That was a close one.'

Clem was nearby, and she gave Lucas a look he couldn't read. The smile she offered up looked . . . not right, like she was a marionette being forced to do it. The camera was fixed on the group of well-wishers for the time being, angled away from them.

'Congratulations,' said Clem, somewhat stiffly. Why did she sound so strange? She crossed her arms as she studied him, leaning against one of the workstations. 'I suppose you didn't get your wish after all.'

His wish? What did she mean? He'd wanted to win – that was his only wish. And she'd known that all along.

'What are you talking about?' he said, puzzled.

'You know exactly what I'm talking about.'

'I really don't . . . ?'

He was baffled by this, both his getting through and Clem's words. He'd clearly messed up – but someone had screwed up worse than him, and he'd scraped through by a hair. One of the bakers from Bundles of Bread was sniffling as Jonathan shook her hand vigorously. The judges were now moving on to congratulate those who had got through, a swirling group of people chattering animatedly.

'Clem, what are you talking about?' he asked her. Dwayne was hovering between them, looking equally confused.

'You know.' Her lip trembled. She bit down on it. 'I'm not saying it here, in front of the camera and everyone else. You know exactly what it is.'

The camera swung their way, like a laser scorching into his cheek. Their conversation died out. He didn't want to talk about this in front of the camera, and neither did she.

He shoved his hands into the pockets of his jeans, nodding at Ronan, who came over and clapped him on the shoulder, congratulating him for making it through. There was a faint smile playing on Lucas's lips and he wondered if anyone else could tell it was false – that he was putting on that persona he'd advised Clem to adopt on camera. It was an odd mix: the happiness that he'd got through, overshadowed by unease at what Clem had said to him. Maybe she was upset after he'd told her he wasn't looking for a relationship, that his family came first?

Lucas brushed the thoughts away like dust. He had simply been honest with her. It would have been worse to let things continue, wouldn't it?

Filming stopped, and Lucas let out a long sigh of relief.

'What was *that* all about?' Dwayne asked. He motioned to Clem, who had crossed the tent to join Sylvie, her back to them both.

'I haven't got a clue,' he said.

'Did you say something to her?'

'Not . . . not today. I mean, I told her recently I wasn't looking for anyone . . . right now . . . and I'm not interested,' he said.

'Ah, man,' said Dwayne, rubbing a hand across the top of his bald head. 'Why would you do that?'

'Because it's the truth.'

'Is it? Sure, maybe you weren't looking to date anyone. But that was before she came along. And I've seen the way you look at her. Reina the *dog* could probably see it. You like her, man. Accept it.'

★

Everyone filtered outside with their bakes, where the usual refreshments would be set up, alongside a small audience who would taste their creations for some extra footage. Clem kept fiddling with her hair, tucking the same strand behind her ear. The rain had long since stopped, warm sunlight breaking through the clouds and streaking across the tent's surface, but the grass was damp and squidgy beneath their feet. Clem's rising happiness deflated like a pierced balloon when she thought about facing up to Genie again. Maybe she wouldn't be

222

here in the audience today; maybe what happened last time put her off?

Unfortunately, Genie *was* there amongst the group outside the tent, sitting at one of the tables on the far right, beneath a large canopy that provided shade. Her highlighted hair was gleaming like it had been polished.

Clem crossed the grass, careful not to slip on the wet blades, and set some slices of her loaf and a kitten bun out on the table in front of Genie. The seat across from her was empty, and around them, the gathered crowd were being served other samples. The cameraman took some shots, and moved off to film some post-round interviews with the judges and the contestants from Bundles of Bread, who were hovering a little way away across the grass.

'Hi, Clem,' Genie said. Her voice was as silky as Clem remembered it – authoritative, confident, as if the lip gloss was smoothing out the words for her. She'd liked that confidence about Genie when they first met, how she'd dropped into a chair beside Clem in a seminar and said *sitting together is better than sitting alone, right?* That was the moment they'd become friends.

Unfortunately, Clem also clearly remembered when they had *stopped* being friends.

Genie was wearing a matching set of baggy beige joggers and a crop top; she'd always been effortlessly fashionable, even in basics. Her hair was sleek and straight, highlighted in shades of blonde and copper – her signature style. That much hadn't changed. But everything else had, including this aura between them. An unease dancing around them like the wind, whispering of the past.

223

Clem folded her arms as a gust of wind whistled around the canopy, easing some of the warmth. 'Why are you here?' she said, trying to keep her voice level. She didn't want Genie to know she was feeling edgy.

'I tried to add you, online,' Genie said, leaning forward. 'And to send a message. Did you—'

'I saw,' Clem cut across her. 'I don't have anything to say to you.'

To her surprise, Genie scowled, a flicker of something crossing her face that looked awfully like malice. 'I have plenty to say to you,' she ground out. 'Things I should have said back then.'

'It's been years,' Clem pointed out, restraining herself from saying *Genie*. Because using her name was too familiar, too personal. It didn't sound like Genie wanted to apologise, so what was going on? She couldn't believe Genie looked so cross, when *she'd* been the one to film that video, to tarnish their friendship.

Clem didn't understand and she was growing shaky, because she didn't want any more conflict. When it all happened, she'd thought there had been a misunderstanding. And even if there hadn't been, that Genie would realise her mistake and apologise for playing such a cruel joke on her. She'd given things a few days to settle down – her own emotions too. Only, her emotions never did quite settle because the video was spread around to other students, and people laughed at her in the corridors, taunted her in lectures. She was too afraid to apply for internships in conservation, in case anyone who was hiring had been at the event and recognised the girl in the silly costume, who came to a careers evening dressed as though it were all a joke.

And Genie never reached out, or stuck up for her. Days turned to weeks, to months, with Genie avoiding her whenever they crossed paths, sitting as far away from her as possible in lectures.

Clem developed so much anxiety from it, she dropped out of university. After she left, at the one-year mark, it stopped being a sharp, fresh pain. A lingering bruise that only hurt if you poked at it.

And Genie was here, poking.

'I know it's been years,' Genie said, leaning closer to her, 'which is why I can't believe you're still doing this. You're unbelievable.' She choked out a wry laugh.

'W-What?' said Clem, mystified, glancing over her shoulder to check that the camera hadn't come their way. 'I have no idea what you mean.'

'Of course you don't. Like you didn't recognise him straight away.' Genie rolled her eyes. She picked up the kitten bun, tore off a piece, and popped it into her mouth, sighing. 'Your baking's good. Shame you weren't as good a friend as you are a baker.'

Clem's reaction to that was to bristle like a hedgehog. The quaking in her knees was picking up; they were almost banging together. She hadn't done anything wrong. Why was Genie here, dragging up the past?

'I won't stand here and listen to you insult me. I'm leaving,' said Clem, turning to stride across the grass.

She was barely ten paces away when Genie snatched at her wrist. Clem turned; Genie was standing behind her, face as dark as thunderclouds. Her grip was vicelike, sharp and bony. Clem checked over her shoulder to make sure they weren't being scrutinised, but the cameras were still further away, filming the judges.

'You're hurting me,' said Clem, trying to tug her arm away, but Genie held on, only clinging to her harder. Her grip was cutting into Clem's arm, turning the skin red.

And then Lucas was somehow there, between them, a flash of dark hair and sandy cologne that caught in Clem's nostrils and made her dizzy. He grabbed Genie's arm, staring daggers at her. Lucas was taller than them both, peering down at Genie.

'Let go of her,' he ordered. His tone meant business, silky but firm.

At the sight of his face, Clem stilled – jaw set, determined, eyebrows furrowed. Defending her. Why was he doing that, when he was trying to make her *lose* in the contest? She couldn't help the prickle running over her neck, the rush of pride that he'd stuck up for *her*.

Genie's grip slackened. She freed Clem's arm, and Lucas released her, too.

'Are you okay?' Lucas asked Clem, reaching for her arm, checking it over, as if worried she'd been bruised. His thumb traced her olive skin where Genie's hand had been, the red mark left behind, and she shuddered in spite of the warm day and the sun settling on her hair. Why was he being so caring when he'd told Clem he wasn't interested in her?

It was only making her *more* interested in him.

'Why do you have to be so nice?' she muttered, half to herself.

'Oh, of course you only care about *her*,' Genie hissed. She crossed her arms.

Lucas turned back to her. 'What are you talking about, Georgina? I invited you here as a friend, not so you could intimidate Clem.'

226

'Do you even *remember* her?'

*Georgina?* Clem thought. 'Her name's Genie,' she said, confused.

'What?' said Lucas. 'Do you two know each other?'

'You were the only one who ever refused to call me Genie. I told you I wanted to use it in our last year of high school,' said Genie. 'I guess you always saw me as little Georgina from a few streets over. Thought Genie was a phase.'

'Will you *please* tell me what the hell is going on?' Lucas fired at Genie – or Georgina. Whatever her name was. Clem felt like she'd never known her at all, with her two names and her dark expression. 'Why did you grab her?' Lucas added.

Genie laughed, throwing back that mane of beautifully golden hair. 'I see Clem's been playing the innocent act again. I'm sure that's how she reeled you in, too. You don't remember, do you, when you were working at the student bistro?'

'That's a bit broad, Georgina, given I did that the whole time I was *at* university to make extra money. You're going to have to be more specific.'

'I used to come in the bistro to talk to you, when I could. Between lectures or if I had a break,' Genie clarified. 'And Clem . . .' She glared at Clem, talking about her like she wasn't here, which only made her hackles rise further. 'I told her there was someone I liked who worked in the bistro, how we grew up together and I'd always liked you. Next thing, I saw her flirting with you in the library.'

Aghast, Clem was rendered speechless for a minute. She *vaguely* remembered Genie having a crush on someone who worked at the student bistro, but Clem had never seen him before – she tended to avoid the bistro, as it got so crowded with students, and she preferred to hang out in the library or a quieter café elsewhere. Often, she'd rather drive home to her mum's cottage to sit with Misha than go in the bistro – it had always been over-stimulating, full of chatter and noise and chaos.

But *flirting* with Lucas? She hadn't met him then, so she didn't think she'd ever . . . She looked from one to the other, fitting everything together in her mind until it dropped into place like Tetris pieces sliding into perfect gaps.

She *had* met him before.

# Chapter 22

In the distance, Clem could hear one of the judges laughing as they were interviewed across the grass; it was almost a marker of how outlandish this Genie situation was.

'This is ridiculous,' said Lucas, scowling, and speaking before Clem had the chance. 'I'd never even *met* Clem then. You came here to cause trouble over a bunch of coincidences and random accusations?' He shook his head. 'I thought you'd got past all this—'

'Got *past* it? I told you how I felt about you—'

'And I told you, you're like a sister to me.' Lucas heaved a sigh, rubbing his forehead, looking apologetic now. 'Please, Georgina—'

'It's Genie,' she snapped.

Ironic, that she was criticising him for not using the name Genie when she was still calling him *Lukey*. 'Genie then,' he said. 'You can't keep doing this, otherwise we won't be able to—'

'What, you're going to threaten me now?'

'No,' he said gently, as if he were trying to handle a savage dog. 'I'm not threatening you. I wouldn't do that. But we can't stay friends if you're always going to try to win me over, to make me feel something that isn't there. It won't work.'

Even though his tone was calm, gentle, Genie looked like she'd been slapped across the cheeks, two red patches appearing high on her cheekbones. She sucked in a lung-ful of air, and stomped across the grass away from them, without a backward look.

Clem automatically made to go after her – because clearly there had been some misunderstanding, something she hadn't grasped years ago that was now shining like a spotlight. But Lucas's hand settled on her shoulder, and she stopped, feeling as though she'd missed a step going downstairs. His hand was as warm as the sunlight on the top of her head.

'Leave her be,' he advised. 'It's best she calms down for now.'

'But she has it all wrong.' Clem couldn't believe Genie was Georgina. The friend Lucas had told her about – the friend who had dared him to climb a tree, been distraught over his injured leg. 'I never knew it was you, in the library. I didn't know you were the one she liked from the bistro,' she went on.

'W-What?' Lucas sounded caught off guard.

'You said you'd never met me, but when she mentioned the library . . . I kind of remembered,' Clem admitted. 'We just didn't know each other's names. And it was a long time ago.'

She was monumentally embarrassed now, her insides doing a jig, because she couldn't fathom how this coincidence had happened. It almost made things feel . . . as though they were meant to happen this way, like she'd been meant to encounter Lucas again. Which was ridiculous because she didn't believe in fate or destiny, had never placed any stock in fortune telling.

'Are you sure?' he said.

'I couldn't find a book I needed, for an essay,' Clem continued. She looked at her feet, shoes poking into the spikes of grass, rather than at his face. 'I was searching the shelves. You had the last copy, and you returned it so I could have it. I was on a deadline.'

In spite of herself, her lips quirked at the memory. No wonder she hadn't remembered him, though – his hair had been cut extremely short, shaved slightly on one side, rather than the thick, dark messy hair he sported now. And he'd been completely clean-shaven, not a hint of the shadowy stubble decorating his jaw today. He'd looked tired that day, too, dark rings under his eyes, and told her he'd been up late watching movies.

Clem looked up. Lucas seemed to be thinking about it, his nose wrinkling as he delved into the past.

'Wait, that was *you*?' he said. 'No way, it can't have been. You had—'

'Blonde hair? Yeah, a phase I went through. Didn't want to fry it with bleach anymore, so I went back to my natural black. Dyed it before Genie filmed that video of me.' She tugged at a strand of her dark hair to demonstrate. 'It was longer then, too.'

He gazed at her with such intensity, it was like being placed under a microscope. It was a soft look, though, unlike the way he'd looked at Genie mere moments ago. She shuddered, clutching her bare arm.

Clem recalled other parts of the interaction in the library, too – how she'd been utterly captured by those green eyes, how she wanted an excuse to stay long after he'd given her the book. She'd asked what movies he'd been watching – sci-fi ones, for an essay – and they'd swapped favourites. When she explained she loved the Lord of the Rings trilogy, but had never seen the extended versions, he said they should watch it together sometime.

She'd thought about him for *months* after that day in the library, disappointed she'd never spotted him around campus afterwards so they could make good on his suggestion. He'd stuck out in her mind like he'd ignited some spark inside her.

'I kept hoping I'd run into you again but I didn't, then I graduated,' he admitted.

'Really?' she said slowly. She was equal parts frustrated and bubbling over with joy at this. Because he'd lied to her, hadn't he? Tried to sabotage her chances in *Whisked Away*, with false advice. And he'd said he wasn't interested in her, had to focus on his family. But would this change anything?

'Yeah . . .' He tailed off.

'I can't believe I never ran into you again,' she said. Admittedly, she had become something of a recluse after dropping out, at least until she got the job at Catpurrcino.

'I was up and down the country for a while,' he explained. 'Catering jobs with Dwayne. Festivals, live-action roleplay events.'

They stood on the grass in silence, warm summer sunlight bearing down on them, conversation drifting through the air from the judges, the audience, and the staff. Somehow, things were more layered now between Clem and Lucas, like the building of a cake – the edges of their relationship softening in ways she didn't want it to. And Clem felt awkward in a dizzying, delightful way, knowing he'd wanted to run into her again. But the unease was nearly burning a hole in her chest, too, it was so intense.

'I can't believe this . . .' she said. 'I can't believe it was you. I never would have thought this would happen . . .'

'It is pretty weird . . .'

The conversation lulled, punctuated by birdsong in the trees and the chatter of the audience, the clanking of spoons on plates. The sound brought Clem crashing back to reality, as if she'd taken a tumble in the grass. A short distance away, the small audience were still enjoying their bakes; some of them were being interviewed on camera. Clem's kitten buns were sitting abandoned on Genie's table, their glaze and their amber hue iridescent in the sun. The sight of them reminded her why she'd been so conflicted before. Had this changed anything? Did it matter that they'd met before? What she really wanted to know was whether he'd tried to sabotage her.

'I need to ask you something,' Clem whispered, conflicted. He'd defended her from Genie; that meant something to her. But she had to ask.

'Is this about what you said in the tent? About me getting my wish . . . ? What was that all about?' There were etchings of confusion on his brow.

'Did you lie to me?'

'W-What? Lie about what?'

She drew closer to him, lowering her voice in case anyone overheard; she didn't want him to be dragged over the coals on social media. Her voice trembled, something inside of her screaming at her to stop, because she hated arguments – and she'd already dealt with one confrontation today with Genie. But she had to say it. She might as well get all of the confrontation

233

out of the way in the same few hours, rather than have to revisit this again.

'You offered to help me out with the bread, the kitten buns. Did you lie to me about the method to try and wreck my bake?'

He stared at her, stunned, his expression unreadable. Then he laughed, shaking his head in disbelief. 'What? No, of course I didn't.'

Clem took a few steps away from him. Her fingers were trembling with anxiety but she clenched her fists, letting the annoyance rise up in its place. Better to be mad than anxious. 'Really? Because every time I tried your method, it ended up a mess. I finally fixed it on my own and it turned out perfectly. If I'd taken your advice, I probably would have been voted off. Did you want that?'

'You can't seriously think I'd be that conniving.' He was scowling now, the lines of his face taut, a tension in his cheekbones. 'I'm not like that,' he retorted. 'I helped you because you were struggling! I kissed you because I like you, and—'

'And why did Genie turn up here, in the audience?' Clem continued, in full flow and unable to stop. 'Did you bring her here on purpose?'

'You're being paranoid. I didn't know why she wanted to come here, until now. You heard me; you saw what happened.'

They were at an impasse and she didn't know what else to say. Genie had once wronged her and they'd been friends. How could she know if Lucas was telling the truth?

'We should find the others,' Lucas said stiffly. 'The bus'll be here soon.'

Clem didn't answer – her brain was busy doing cart-wheels over their interactions, trying to work out what to think.

★

Lucas had got through to the next round of *Whisked Away*. Still, he felt distinctly unmoored by what had happened after the filming – what Genie had said. What *Clem* had said. All the way home on the bus – which was so hot it was stifling, the windows thrown open not making any difference – it was like someone had shaken up a tub of marbles inside of him, tossing around everything he thought he knew. When he finally arrived at the house with Dwayne and shoved the key in the lock, the marbles were still rolling. Dwayne insisted they have a drink to celebrate getting through to the next round, and once Reina was settled happily on her scruffy blanket on the sofa, chewing a dog treat, they went into the kitchen and grabbed a couple of cold fruit ciders from the fridge.

It was still bright outside, warm light beaming through the glass of the back doors, splashing across the granite countertops and painting them in yellow. Dwayne cracked open his cider with a hiss, falling into a seat at the kitchen table.

The house was bright and airy, with lots of big windows, everything beautifully decorated with plush carpet and modern furnishings. It was a step up from Lucas's old flat, which he'd rented alone for a small fortune – yet had blown windows, ancient carpet, and swollen, scuffed cabinets in the kitchen. Dwayne had inherited this house – and a lump sum of money – when his father passed away. They'd opened Muddy Paws Café soon after, and alongside becoming his business partner, Lucas had ended up living here, renting a room from Dwayne. It worked out pretty well: there was plenty of space for both of them, and they'd already flat-shared at university, so they meshed well. It came in handy when they needed to talk business, too – they'd created a Muddy Paws office slash meeting room upstairs.

'Come on, out with it,' said Dwayne, taking a long glug of cold apple cider and smacking his lips in satisfaction. 'Why were you acting so weird on the way home? I saw you talking to Clem. What happened?'

Lucas looked at the condensation on his can of cider, dripping down the surface. He should be happy, buzzing. And he *was* glad he'd got through, of course he was. He couldn't process what he'd learned about Clem. And Genie, come to think of it.

He sighed, cracked open his drink, and told Dwayne all about it.

'Georgina's still hung up on you?' said Dwayne in disbelief. He snorted. 'Can't believe she's still calling herself Genie.'

'She used to say she thought it was trendy. I never thought she'd stick with it.' Leaning against the kitchen counter, Lucas drank some of his cider, the twang of fizzy fruit refreshing. 'I shouldn't have invited her to be in the audience.'

'Why did you?'

'She kept complaining she was bored and wanted to come. And I did say I'd catch up with her while she was here.'

'Pfft. Bored. She's here visiting her family, right? So, she should go do that.' Dwayne leaned back in his chair. 'She's not bored at all, mate. She's hoping you'll change your mind about her. She probably heard about the contest, saw the way you were with Clem, the comments.'

'Well, I know that now. I thought she was over all that – over *me*.'

'I don't think anyone truly gets over that,' Dwayne said. 'Not while they're friends with the person, at least. Did you really think it could work, being friends with her when she wants something more?'

Lucas's jaw tensed, and he clutched the can of cider so hard a dent appeared in the side.

Georgina had been in his life for such a long time. They'd grown up together. When his father first began experiencing pain, and things at home became difficult, she was there for him. He'd go round to her house to escape, or they'd call on their other friends and spend hours at the cinema seeing films back to back, wasting their pocket money in one go. He couldn't kick her out of his life, could he? After an entire childhood together?

'I thought it'd be a natural thing,' he admitted, moving across to the table and taking a seat opposite Dwayne. 'That when she moved away, she'd meet someone, or . . .'

'I don't think she has. Otherwise, why would she be here?' Dwayne gave him a knowing look over the top of his glass. 'What was it you said before? *Family comes first. Women aren't worth it.*' Dwayne snorted, taking a swig of cider, throwing his head back to drain the can. 'You should apply that to Georgina.'

'You know what I meant. Proper relationships.'

'Are you really going to stick with that? After what you just learned from Clem? Sounds like you liked her, in the past. That she's the one that got away.' He grinned.

It was more complicated than that, but one thing still held true in his mind. 'Family *does* come first,' he said eventually, frowning. 'Why *wouldn't* they? I have to help them.'

'You've been helping them since you were a kid.'

'They need me.'

'You can't fight everyone else's battles for them, mate,' Dwayne pointed out. He looked out through the glass of the patio doors, into the garden, where green trees were swaying in the summer breeze and the sky was a patch of fading blue. 'You also need to fight your own. D'you think they'd want you giving up opportunities for them? To give up someone you clearly had – *have* – a thing for?'

'I'm not,' he said lamely. But the words sounded weak and small.

Dwayne's words were poking at him. Each one was like a stab to the chest because he knew his friend was right. And even though he'd always told himself that the people he'd dated didn't understand – he had responsibilities, commitments, family to help out – deep down, he understood why they left and why he ended up alone. Because he could never commit to them enough to make them happy. He was too busy making sure his parents were okay.

Dwayne studied Lucas, his brown eyes almost sad. 'But the question is, how long are you going to keep putting off your life? Are you going to let Clem get away a second time?'

Lucas didn't have an answer, because it stabbed far deeper than anything else – so he drained his drink in one go and didn't reply. Reina padded in to join them, nudging at Lucas, so he scratched the top of her golden head until she wagged her tail.

'Aren't you going to talk to her?' Dwayne asked.

'We did talk.'

'Yeah, but you know what I mean.'

'She thinks I lied to her. And I *didn't*. I was trying to think on my feet because my dad was in the hospital, and I got things wrong. Now she thinks I'm trying to sabotage her.'

'Talk to her again. Tell her what you just told me, that you were stressed out and it was an accident. Tell her how you really feel.'

Lucas watched the trees being blown about by the wind, leaves green and bright, as he patted Reina's head. He didn't know if he wanted to open himself up to those feelings, not when he had his family to think about – and when Clem already thought he was a liar.

# Chapter 23

Clem couldn't help it. She'd been checking social media to see what people's reactions were to the recent round of *Whisked Away* – in part to distract herself from thoughts of Lucas, from the memory of that day at the library. Her mum was out at work, doing some family portraits at someone's home, and she had all day to herself. It was rainy and grey, so she'd spent it mostly cocooned on the sofa, with Misha curled on the ridges of her legs, fast asleep and breathing softly. Clem had eaten a full packet of cookies – the empty wrapping sat on the coffee table – partly driven by her guilt at accusing Lucas without proof and the niggling confusion about whether or not he was trustworthy.

In spite of the rain, it was warm, so she was dressed in a loose-fitting cotton dress. Misha wasn't helping much with her fur and the added warmth, but Clem didn't want to move her. She was stroking across her neck and spine as she slept, tracing the stripes.

Scrolling, scrolling, scrolling. Clem couldn't stop. Something had shifted in the comments; that was evident. Misha adjusted herself on her legs, until she was coiled on her ankles instead.

Lucas had gone from the darling of the show to the villain, and it was causing more and more theories to sprout about their relationship off-screen. Clem's mouth turned bone-dry as she read them and realised what they were discussing. As if things weren't already difficult enough, the audience had noticed her strained interaction with Lucas.

She swiped up to the video of the round, watching until she saw herself on the screen behind the others, mouthing congratulations to Lucas. The camera hadn't picked up what she said to him next – the focus was on the contestants from Bundles of Bread, who'd been voted off. But it was clear she'd said *something*. Clem knew exactly what she'd said. *I suppose you didn't get your wish after all.* In the clip, Lucas's face fell, his skin turning ashen and a crease marring his brow. She'd been upset with him, so her own expression simply looked sad.

> What's the matter with him?? He seemed to really care about her before, and now he's gone cold. It's weird. Did something happen between them?
>
> I can't believe he didn't help her this time!
>
> He must have some sort of strategy to win and she's part of it. He knows she's talented, probably thinks she's a threat. Maybe she realised that herself.

Lucas was really taking a beating in these comments. That last accusation made her throat pulse with emotion. Were they right? People thought she was talented, and that meant a lot. But were their suggestions about Lucas correct? She sighed, rubbing the back of her head, where an ache was starting.

Regardless of what the truth was, she didn't enjoy seeing him being dragged like this. He needed to win for the money to help his family, which she understood. For her, she wasn't sure it had really been about the money at all. She had a small amount tucked away already to use for moving out; any extra for starting her business would be a bonus. She could build on that by living here a while longer. Lucas was in a more dire situation.

But he'd seemed adamant that he wouldn't lie or trick her in order to win.

She wanted him to be telling the truth, because she wasn't sure what she'd do if she learned he'd been using her.

Three quick raps came on the door knocker, making her jump. Misha leaped up in surprise, rushing upstairs to hide. Clem sat up. Maybe her mum was expecting a package? She shoved her feet into her slippers and headed for the front door.

The last person she expected to see standing there on the step was Lucas. She froze, the door half open.

Now, that flutter stirred within, like a butterfly preparing to take flight. He was wearing a loose blue V-neck and dark jeans, and she was struck once again by the intensity of his green eyes and thick brows. She couldn't believe she'd forgotten about him, and that he'd been the guy she'd seen in the library.

'What are you doing here?' she asked. She didn't open the door fully. Half of her wanted to usher him inside and kiss him senseless – he looked so good in blue – and the other half wanted to send him away, the comments she'd read online repeating in her mind like a chant.

'Can we talk?' he said quietly.

'About what?' She wondered if he'd seen the comments flying around the internet too.

'I know you're upset with me. But I'd like to talk,' he reiterated.

She glanced over her shoulder at the empty cookie packaging and scattered crumbs on the coffee table, and *The Hobbit* playing on the TV. Conscious of the mess, she yanked the door open fully anyway.

He stepped inside, and she shut the door behind him. 'Thanks,' he said.

'Do you want something to drink?'

'No, it's okay. I won't stay long.' He hovered by the door awkwardly as Clem took a seat on the sofa nearby. He didn't sit down, so she turned to the side so she could see him better.

'I wanted to apologise,' he told her, 'for inviting Georgina to the contest to be in the audience. If I'd known you two were friends—'

'We're not friends anymore,' said Clem quickly.

'Right. But if I'd known what had happened – that she was the one who filmed that video of you – I never would have asked her.'

She nodded, unsure of what to say, shifting on the sofa awkwardly. Misha crept out from the stairs slowly, sniffing along the carpet and looking up at Lucas uncertainly. Apparently deciding he wasn't a threat, she padded inside and rolled over on the rug, rubbing herself against the material and stretching out her front paws.

'And I want you to know – I *didn't* sabotage you, Clem. I didn't lie,' he said firmly, holding eye contact. The intensity of his expression made her chest whoosh and she had to look away. 'That day, I'd just found out my dad was in hospital. I was trying to help you, but I was thinking quick, trying to remember tips I'd heard, so

I could leave, and make sure he was okay.' He took a long, deep breath. 'If you can't believe me on that . . .'

Hot shame crept over Clem's face, the guilt chewing away at her. Her mind had turned cluttered and messy – filled with social media comments, with Genie's actions in the past, with her own anxieties piling up like stacks of crumpled paper.

He was looking at his trainers now, not at her directly, and he looked . . . *hurt*. Sunshine was gleaming through the small, arched window above their front door, outlining him in yellow light, as if the world itself wanted to highlight him.

'I'm sorry for accusing you. I didn't know what to think,' she said, and rushed on desperately, trying to excuse herself even though she felt terrible now. 'I know you want to win.' She fumbled around in the dark for more reasons. 'I've not known you very long,' she finished uselessly. 'I'm really sorry.'

'I'm not that kind of person – I offered to help you and it was genuine,' he said, letting out another sigh. 'Although . . .'

'What?' The word tripped over itself, stumbled – her pulse spiking. He'd said he wasn't interested in her, but it was before they'd found out about their interaction in the library.

'It looks like you didn't need my help after all,' he explained, brushing his fingers through his dark hair and prompting her lips to part involuntarily. 'You figured it out, made those kitten buns a success. You really have a good chance of winning this, Clem.'

The air was sucked out of Clem's chest. The last thing she'd expected him to do was compliment her like this.

She wished he wouldn't be so nice about her – she hadn't even sent off the application herself. She didn't need this in the same way that he did, and it was eating her up. 'I . . . Lucas,' she fumbled. 'Listen . . .'

He shook his head. 'No, it's fine. We've only just started to get to know each other, and I'm sure you've been reading those comments online . . .'

'It's *not* fine,' she ground out, frustrated with herself. She had misjudged him, suspected he was going to hurt her like Genie had, and yet he didn't know the truth about how she got to this point in the contest. 'I didn't even enter *Whisked Away* myself!' The words came out in a big, breathless rush.

The silence was thick with her admission. Eventually, he said, 'What?'

'I started filling out the application and got scared. The only reason I'm here is because Sylvie saw my half-finished form and thought I'd forgotten to ask her to fill in her sections. She completed it and sent it off on the staff laptop.'

He didn't say anything.

'I'm so sorry. I shouldn't be here, but you and your family need this . . .'

'Don't pity us Clem,' said Lucas, and his eyes flashed. He gave her a stern look she'd never seen on him before, one that made her flush.

'I wasn't. I just . . .'

'Forget about it,' he said, waving her remark away. 'I'm not holding it against you. You got into the contest, didn't you? It doesn't matter how you got here. Your skill is what gets you through the rounds.'

Lucas had his hands stuffed in his pockets and was shifting on the balls of his feet, as if trying to decide whether to stay or leave. Did he really not care about how she'd come to be on *Whisked Away*, or was he trying to mask how he truly felt about it? She couldn't tell, and he looked reluctant to keep talking about it.

'Was there something else you wanted to talk about?' she asked hopefully. They still hadn't addressed whatever was building between them, in spite of everything going on. 'You said . . . you said you always hoped you'd run into me again someday, didn't you? After we first saw each other in the library?'

Lucas opened his mouth, closed it again. A lump rose in Clem's throat at his hesitation, and she fought it down, doing her best not to cry. This was her fault for misjudging him and messing things up. She couldn't expect things to go smoothly now, not least because she'd admitted Sylvie had entered the contest for her. Or maybe it had nothing to do with that, and everything to do with Genie.

'Now we really have run into each other again, but you're hesitating . . . I can see it. Is it because of Genie? She likes you,' said Clem, swallowing down the lump again, harder this time – it wouldn't stay gone. It was hard to speak around it.

'It's nothing to do with her,' said Lucas. 'I've already told her she's like a sister to me.'

'Then what? It sounds like we both liked each other. I definitely liked you and . . .' She sucked in a breath. 'Is it because we're competing, or because I messed up?'

He watched Misha roll around on the rug, pushing her stripes into the fabric – the only happy party in the room. Lucas looked conflicted, the frown on his face never shifting.

'No, it's nothing you did. Misunderstandings happen. It's just . . . I have to help my parents,' he said, sounding strained. 'I can't get distracted – by anything. And I think maybe this . . .' He gestured vaguely between them. 'I don't know, it's not the right time. I just wanted you to know I wouldn't lie to you.'

'Okay. Well, thanks for coming,' Clem told him, turning away, fighting against that lump in her throat again. Her vision became clouded with tears and she had to blink them away rapidly.

'I'm sorry. It's . . . it's too important. My parents need me.'

His words hung in the air before she replied. 'Do your best in the contest. Once it's done, we don't have to see each other again, if that's what you want.'

'I didn't say that,' he said, sounding utterly tortured. 'I need to focus right now. On the contest.'

'What about after the contest?'

'I . . . I don't know.'

She didn't look back to see his expression and she didn't reply, because she feared she would burst into tears in front of him if she did. Clem heard him tug open the door, his footsteps vanishing outside, the door closing with a thunk behind him.

★

The next day, after spending an ungodly amount of time on the sofa on Sunday being a sloth – and definitely not the cute kind – Clem went to work at Catpurrcino. The weather was sunny, and birds were singing out tunes in the trees and winging their way across eggshell-blue skies. The cherry tree was no longer in bloom outside Catpurrcino and Clem missed the sight of its vibrant pink petals scattered everywhere like sweets. Still, today seemed more positive, possibly because of the sunshine and the crying she'd done, as if she'd purged everything she'd been feeling lately. Maybe she could put Lucas behind her. It was for the best, she told herself. A small part of her resisted the thought, wondering what could have happened if things had been different.

Inside the main room, the café was fairly quiet, as it usually was on a Monday – an elderly couple were enjoying a pot of tea by the window. Most of the cats were sleeping, tucked away in alcoves around the café. Salem bounded over to her to be stroked when she crossed the room, and she smiled, bending down to tickle him behind the ears and along his silky black fur. The scent of brewed coffee hung in the air, tickling her nostrils.

Emmie was behind the counter, leaning against it, on her phone. Her hair was scooped up off her neck with a cat-shaped claw clip. She looked up when Clem pushed her way through the gate and smiled. 'Hey, Clem,' she said. 'Thought I'd check my own socials, as it's so quiet in here today.'

'How's it going?'

'Really good,' Emmie said, turning the screen round to show her a pink illustration of a strawberry shortcake with a cat's white head poking from the top. 'People like the illustrations of cats that look like cakes. I've been reposting them during the contest and I must have attracted some of the *Whisked Away* fans.'

'Glad to be of service,' said Clem.

She still remembered Emmie asking her last year if it would be okay to do this – merge Clem's cat-themed baking with her illustrating. Emmie's art had been taking off online since she'd launched a web shop with her boyfriend Jared's help and started filming art progress videos, but Clem was glad the contest was bringing her more attention as well. She deserved it. She'd been talking about dropping her hours to part-time, which was why Sylvie had hired Matt as a new barista, although he only worked a day or two at the moment.

'I should make you a – oh . . .' She trailed off, looking over Clem's shoulder as the door to the café opened.

Clem turned. A couple had entered the door – a tall, portly man with a rounded belly and a sheen of sweat on his head, who was walking with a stick. There was a shorter woman at his side, her face creased with concern as she struggled to open the latched gate for him.

Hurrying across to them, Clem said, 'Here, let me help you.' She tugged open the latched gate, so the man could hobble through. The woman, wearing a pink top and a pair of shorts, followed.

'Thank you so much,' said the woman.

They both looked . . . oddly familiar. The woman had green eyes, the colour of grass, with a delicate shape to her nose. And the man with her – even though his hair was completely grey, right down to each strand on his beard, it had the same messy and mussed-up quality as Lucas's, and his brows were equally thick. They had the same jawline, too.

'You must be Clem,' said the woman, touching her arm. 'I'm Meredith. This is Richie.'

'You know me . . . ?' Clem began.

'Of course!' Meredith's smile widened. 'We've been watching *Whisked Away*, and Lucas has told us all about you.'

# Chapter 24

'You're Lucas's mum and dad?' Clem said, to confirm her suspicions. Meredith had said *Lucas has told us all about you*. She had to repeat that in her head to process it. He'd told his parents about *her*. She wanted to ask what he'd said but the conversation was already moving forward and she didn't know how to backtrack.

'Aye,' said Richie, hobbling over to a table in a corner, and dropping into a chair with a laboured sigh. 'Bloody knees, they're a nightmare today. Ah, that's better.' He sank back into his seat. When he looked around, taking in the place, his expression changed, the frown of pain smoothing out into something more curious. 'There's a cat up there!' he cried, pointing up to a U-shaped shelf built into the wall, his voice as high-pitched as a child's. A long, brown tail was dangling over the edge. 'Look, Meredith!'

'I see it,' said Meredith, moving towards the table and smiling at him softly.

'You can order your drinks over there at the counter,' Clem explained, gesturing over to Emmie, who waved at them from her spot behind the counter. 'Drinks are unlimited when you've paid for some time here. Food is extra. But I'm sure our receptionist explained that already.'

'Thank you,' said Meredith. 'What would you like, Richie? Some cake?'

Richie craned himself forward, gritting his teeth as he did so, looking at the big chalkboard menu hanging over the counter, and the rows of doughnuts and slices of cake piled up in the glass cases.

'I'll have one of her famous cat doughnuts,' he replied. 'And a black coffee.'

'I'll be right back,' said Meredith, heading over to place their order with Emmie.

Clem hovered by the table, knowing she had to get to work, but finding her feet unable to move – she was curious about Lucas's parents. Lucas's father had actually visited; she was surprised Lucas wasn't with them. Maybe he wanted to avoid her, after everything.

Binx wandered over, his shoulders swaying from side to side and his tail high in the air, and hopped up onto the table in front of Richie, who laughed in delight. He'd only just walked through the door and his joy was infectious – she found herself mirroring his expression.

'Hello, who have we got here?' said Richie. He stroked along Binx's body, and when he reached his rear end, Binx curled his tail around his hand, lifting his head into the air and purring.

'That's Binx,' said Clem. 'Sylvie said she named him after a cat in a movie – *Hocus Pocus*? He likes to sit on laptops when people are working. I think he likes the warm fans. So he's always jumping onto tables.'

'There's no laptop here, little dude, but you're welcome to stay,' said Richie. As if he'd understood, Binx sat down, tail curled around himself, and allowed

Richie to keep petting him. Binx's eyes were fixed on the window, watching a bird loop past the trees, his pupils thinned.

'You've been giving my son a run for his money,' said Richie. Meredith returned to the table with a tray of food and drinks, and dropped into a chair close to him. He rubbed his hands together in glee and winced again, stretching out his fingers and placing them on his thighs instead. 'I can't wait to try one of your doughnuts – see if they're as good as—'

'Don't intimidate the poor girl,' Meredith warned him, shooting Clem a kind-eyed look.

'I'm glad you came,' said Clem honestly. 'Sylvie mentioned you might.'

'I always meant to bring Richie.' She hesitated, as if she were going to elaborate, but she didn't. 'I've been here before to see Sylvie, through my work at the cat shelter. You won't have seen me if you work in the kitchen.'

'I'm usually hidden away in there,' said Clem. 'Speaking of – I have to get to work now. Enjoy yourselves.'

Clem left them to it, stowing her bag and jacket in the staffroom and heading through to the kitchen, getting herself settled for the day. She pulled a cat-print apron and a black hairnet on.

Lucas was at the forefront of her mind. Did his parents mean she'd simply come up in passing, in conversation about the contest? Or had he said something more specific about her? The kiss sprang into her mind, the feel of his mouth soft against hers, mingling with the rain. The way his fingers had brushed hers in the library, years ago – she still remembered the shock it had sent through her system. She couldn't stop thinking about him as she mixed ingredients and spread out the mixture for her cat biscuits on baking trays. By the time they were baking in the oven, she'd decided to get in touch with him. She pulled off her apron and went into the staffroom.

Yanking her phone from her jacket pocket, she brought up his name, hesitating at the sight of his picture, that messy dark hair. Taking a steadying breath, she typed out a message.

> I saw your parents at the cat café. I'm glad they came. Your dad seemed happy.

After a brief hesitation, she added something extra:

> I won't go easy on you, so you better do your best to win.

Meeting his parents had softened her, and she really didn't want to show any ill will, even if nothing more would ever happen between them – so she added a smiling cat emoji to show that she was half joking.

He replied while she was making herself a cup of tea in the staffroom.

> They didn't tell me they were going. I'm glad.
> Thanks for telling me.

Bubbles appeared on the screen, indicating he was typing something else. The message popped up as she was stirring sugar into her tea.

253

You better do your best as well. Cats are meant
to land on their feet, so I'm sure you can handle
anything they throw at you, right?

He followed the message up with a series of dog emojis, and the playful rivalry in the message made her pulse quicken in ways she wished it wouldn't.

★

Clem had spent almost all of her free time at the cat café, prepping for the final round of the contest and practising her bake. It was a cake, and cakes were her forte. For this finale, *Whisked Away* wanted them to make a knockout cake worthy of a glossy magazine cover: a detailed diorama representing their business. So, Clem was planning on making a cake that looked like Catpurrcino, complete with the shopfront – the cats in the windows, of course – the beige and white awning, and the chalkboard sign they kept outside. She was adding the cherry blossom tree out front, positioned to the left of the building, in all its bright pink glory. It wasn't in bloom anymore, now summer was in full swing, but it was one of her favourite things about the café. She'd wanted to make the cake bright and happy, a reflection of the way people felt when they visited, and Sylvie's aim that the café be a place of refuge and comfort.

She was testing a different type of sponge – vanilla had been too bland when she tried that out, but strawberry sponge with a thick cream sounded perfect, and she'd decided to try putting fresh strawberries in there, too. She'd chosen to make it dairy-free and vegan; she wanted to make this diorama something that would include as many people as possible.

Clem had been looking online for inspiration, and how best to do it. She was sitting in the Cat Lounge with her laptop open on her knee. It was a bright and clear day, sunlight pooling across the leather sofa, and she was sitting in a patch of shade so she could see the laptop screen clearly. Lilian was perched on the seat next to her, dozing in the sunshine, which was warming up her patches of black, white, and orange fur.

Clem's phone buzzed on the arm of the sofa beside her – when she checked it, her mum's name was flashing up on the screen.

She took the call, still absent-mindedly scrolling through a cookery website about the best types of vegan cream. 'Hello?'

'Hi sweetie!' her mum trilled. 'Are you at Catpurrcino again?'

'Yep, still practising. Where are you?'

'I just left a photo shoot. Are you coming home soon?'

'I'll probably be here another hour or two,' she said. 'I want to test this strawberries and cream—'

'Say no more. How about you let me taste-test, if you don't mind some company?'

'Ha, okay. Phone me when you get here and I'll let you in.'

About thirty minutes later, her mum had arrived. Clem let her in via the back door, and took her through the narrow corridor, past the kitchen, and out into the main café room. Here, her mum paused to make a fuss

255

of the cats. Many of them were sleeping, dotted around the cat towers and shelves, but Eric strutted over when he caught wind of a newcomer, his bobbed tail wiggling in delight.

'Ah, hey, cutie!' her mum crooned, crouching down to give him a tickle under the chin. 'I feel sorry for Mish. She's been on her own all afternoon.' She crossed to one of the cat towers to give Duchess some attention, running her hands over her fur.

Clem felt a crescendo of guilt. 'I wanted to go home sooner but the vanilla sponge wasn't working the way I wanted it to, and I wanted to try something new.'

'Ah, she'll be fine though, she's probably slept the day away. You said strawberries and cream . . . ?'

'Come through here and I'll show you.'

She led her mum into the Cat Lounge, where Lilian was snoozing. She looked up when they stepped inside, her big green eyes shimmering in the sun and her dark pupils barely visible. Clem grabbed her laptop and gestured for her mum to sit down. Once she'd sunk onto the leather beside Lilian – who immediately ran away at the movement – Clem placed the laptop in front of her and clicked into her planning document.

'Here's what I'm thinking. All my ideas are in there.'

Her mum fell silent as she digested everything. Clem had pages of notes. She had images of cakes she'd saved for inspiration, notes on what she wanted the cake to look like, clippings from websites with tips on dairy-free and vegan cakes, photos of the cat café shopfront to make sure she got it right and didn't miss anything. She'd typed out a few sentences on what she wanted to say to the judges when she presented the diorama to them. She'd never done so much prepping before. But she wanted to go up against Lucas with everything she had.

'This is great, Clem,' said her mum. Jess strolled in and hopped up onto the sofa behind her, nuzzling her hair. Her mum reached round and stroked Jess's head; the big black-and-white cat erupted into a series of vibrating purrs.

Clem sighed. 'I heard on the weather that there's going to be a big summer heatwave. Hotter than usual. Right when the last round is happening. It'll be harder to concentrate in a hot tent full of ovens – during a heatwave. Where's the rubbish British summer when you need it?'

Her mum smiled. 'I heard about that. But I still think you're going to win.'

'You have to say that though. You're my mum. It's your job.'

For a long moment, her mum was silent, studying her, though she was still tickling Jess's furry cheek. 'I know you've been giving yourself a hard time, Clem,' her mum answered. 'About mistakes you've made, about not entering the contest yourself.'

Clem swallowed. She'd expressed some of these feelings to her mum over the course of the contest, so it wasn't like it was a secret between them. 'I know.'

'The thing is, you have *almost* everything you need already,' her mum continued.

'Do I?' said Clem, because she wasn't sure. She was never sure, always questioning and running over the what-ifs.

'You have the skills, the talent. You solved the problem with the kitten buns and didn't let that faze you. And you work hard. You know exactly what you want. You're only missing one tiny thing.'

'What am I missing?'

'Faith in yourself.' Her mum dropped her hand from Jess's fur, and instead pulled Clem towards her, squeezing an arm around her shoulder. 'You can do whatever you set your mind to, and handle whatever life throws your way.'

# Chapter 25

The day of the final round was *hot*, the country caught in the sticky grip of the promised heatwave. Even though he was as prepared as he could be, Lucas wasn't especially looking forward to being cooped up in a tent with a series of ovens switched on, adding to the heat. It was like nature itself was trying to make things more difficult for them all – turning the air stifling and oppressive. The coach that would take them to Wray Castle didn't have air-conditioning, and he was sweating before they stepped out into the car park, his T-shirt clinging to his skin.

He couldn't help but notice Clem – Dwayne had nudged him on the way here and jerked his head in her direction, as if to say *look at what you missed out on*. She was almost shining as she stepped out into the sun. She was dressed in a forties-style dress with a shirt-like collar, and a row of buttons up the front. It was decorated with a pattern of pastel-pink and pale-blue cats, and she'd paired it with white sandals. Her trademark red lipstick was in place, making her lips look as full as strawberries. Lucas had to fight the urge to go over and talk to her – to tell her she looked absolutely stunning. He was almost winded by regret, because aside from her being downright beautiful, he'd really sensed something more growing between them. Had he been wrong, to push her aside like that?

*Focus on the contest*, he told himself. Focusing on that was the only way he could win.

Across the stretch of grass to the side of Wray Castle, the tent was a brilliant white beacon. The *Whisked Away* team had gone all out for this final round. The area for the mini-audience had been expanded – it now encircled a good portion of the tent, allowing for a grassy space in between, like a stage, where they would announce and film the winner. The trophies for the winners had been erected on a platform with an archway bursting with brightly coloured flowers rounding it off. Unlike the other rounds of the contest, which went out to audiences after they were filmed, this final round would be live, every mistake available for scrutiny instantly.

The heat bearing down on them was oppressive, making beads of sweat spring up along his neck. He could almost see the air shimmering. His nerves weren't helping matters. The cameras filmed them making their entrance into the tent, and he had to keep mopping his skin with tissues in between shots.

'What a day for it,' Dwayne grumbled, as they trooped to the back of the tent. It was no cooler in here – in fact, the tent encased the heat, trapping it inside. He shot Lucas a grin and held up his hand, crossing his fingers tightly. 'Hey, pray that the others are making ice-cream cake.'

Lucas snorted. 'They had enough warning – the heat-wave's been all over the weather. Plenty of time to change their minds.'

'We can hope . . .'

There were only three pairings left – Catpurrcino, Muddy Paws Café, and a popular cake shop called Life with Sprinkles. Lucas doubted their reduced numbers would do much to limit the body heat in the tent. It was already so hot in here and would only worsen when the ovens were on full blast.

They took their places at the workstations, where *Whisked Away* had provided them with bottles of water to keep them hydrated during the heatwave. Lucas was sweating in places he didn't even know it was possible to sweat.

He glanced across at Clem. She looked calm, collected, which took him slightly aback. In the other rounds she'd often been visibly nervous. A smile played at his mouth. He wasn't sure if she'd simply got used to the contest now, or if she'd steeled something inside of herself for this final.

The judges had assembled at the head of the tent, lined up in a neat row. Ronan's curls had turned frizzy, and even Viviana and Laurette looked more dishevelled than usual – Laurette had unbuttoned the top two buttons of her shirt dress to keep cool and Viviana kept fanning her face with her hand.

The filming began. The camera crew looked sweaty, their caps pushed up slightly to give their hair some breathing room. They were all wearing loose-fitting shorts with their *Whisked Away* T-shirts.

'Alright, bakers!' called Ronan, clapping his hands. As always, he was dressed to rival Clem, this time wearing a pale yellow suit with a garish patterned shirt and tie. His curly brown hair was extra poufy today, layered with the frizz. 'We hope you're ready for this knockout final, where we'll get to see what wonderful cake dioramas you've come up with to represent your businesses!' He looked around at them eagerly, hands still clasped together, as if he were addressing a class of schoolchildren. 'Now, I imagine it's going to be a little challenging today, with the heat . . .' He fanned his face, mock-theatrically, in the direction of the camera. 'But we're sure you'll manage!'

'I hope nobody had any ice-cream in their diorama plans. That could be a challenge . . .' Jonathan added, with a sparkly grin.

Dwayne nudged Lucas and they swapped a smirk at the fact he'd echoed Dwayne's earlier sentiments.

'We wish you all the very best of luck,' Laurette said, 'and we can't wait to see what you do.'

'Let's get baking!' said Ronan, with a flourish. Lucas didn't know how he could be so cheerful while wearing a full suit in this heat.

The usual clattering and clamouring ensued as everyone scrambled for their tools and ingredients. Lucas was boiling and light-headed before the ovens had turned on; he didn't feel prepared enough for this. He opened a water bottle and took a long swig. Shouldn't they have installed a fan, or something? It was as if he were about to sit a school exam, and even though he'd been studying for hours, none of the information seemed to have registered in his brain.

He took a deep, fortifying breath. No, he could do this. He thought of his dad, gritting his teeth, looking sombre but not complaining, and the lines of worry etched into his mum's features. Those images kicked him into gear, and he tried to ignore the camera roving around the room, fixating on each of them – but of course he had to answer questions from one of the judges as usual, which came as soon as he was sieving icing sugar for his fondant. It was Laurette, her hair tucked behind her ears to keep it out of her face. She was sporting a sheen of sweat over her top lip, and her make-up was slightly cracked in places.

262

'What's your plan today, Lucas? Can you tell us a little about your diorama?' Laurette asked him, leaning over his workstation.

'I'm making a vanilla and chocolate sponge cake,' he said, 'with chocolate ganache – a mix of white and dark chocolate, and double cream. It'll be a fairly tall cake to represent the whole Muddy Paws building.'

She gave a low whistle. 'That sounds impressive.'

'I hope so,' he said, measuring out the rest of the ingredients for his fondant.

Dwayne helped him carefully combine them, and melt the mixture on a low heat – which was excruciating in the existing heat of the tent. Dwayne would watch over that while he got started on the sponge, and sieve it into the icing sugar.

When the fondant was finally looking like *fondant* and had been rolled out – which he exhaled in relief at – he put it aside for an hour and set to work on the sponges and the ganache. All the while, he avoided looking over at Clem's workstation, even when he could hear her being interviewed, when he caught the lilting tones of her voice. He couldn't afford to get distracted this time, not like in those earlier rounds.

When the sponges came out of the oven and the ganache was ready, he spread thick coatings of chocolate ganache on top, building the sponge layers as he went, until he had something resembling a thick stack of pancakes. He used some wide straws to hold everything in place, cutting off the tops with precision, before adding a cake drum, and more layers of sponge and chocolate.

His attention strayed to Clem, even though he'd been trying to avoid her. Her bright red lips were pinched together in concentration and she was working with modelling chocolate, shaping a tree, with a bowl full of marshmallows and something else white and shredded sitting beside her that looked like coconut. Was she building the cherry tree, for outside the café? A sharp spike of worry shot through him – her design was going to look beautiful. How could he compete?

'Don't pay the others any mind,' Dwayne advised him.

Lucas was putting the final touches to the top of the cake tower, rounding it off and smoothing out the ganache. 'I know.'

He worked on some of the decorations until the fondant was ready to go. When Dwayne helped him carefully fold the white fondant over the cake, it looked like a little ghost, dressed up for Halloween. But it was a pain in the backside to smooth into place.

'No, that's not right,' Lucas said through gritted teeth. It was too misshapen. 'Pull that up . . . Hang on . . .'

'It can't have any weird lumps,' Dwayne added, as they tried again.

In the end, it *did* look slightly lumpy, but pulling it away again at this stage would only do more harm than good. Lucas tried to smooth it out as best he could using a plastic cake smoother, but this was probably as good as it was going to get.

Making the rest of the diorama was equally difficult: painstakingly measuring out the windows and doors for the café front, creating the little windows out of icing and sticking them down with water, making the front steps. Every piece of royal icing felt like it was torturing him. Everything had to be so precise, so intricate. He binned several iced decorations that failed miserably, and had to hold in a stream of swear words as the camera passed him by and filmed clips of his suffering. He was so sweaty, he kept having to splash water on his face and wash his hands. The cobblestone path was a nightmare to create for the cake, too, since it had to look natural, but his first few attempts looked like a young child trying to draw circles.

He had originally planned to make a miniature version of Reina, to dance around the front of the café, but he decided against that. Making a collection of trees with wafer-paper leaves was a struggle enough and he was running out of time.

When he was done with everything, it was like he'd run a marathon; his clothes were certainly sweaty enough to mark him out as an athlete. There was a tension head-ache forming on his skull, his neck ached from leaning over royal icing, and his fingers were pinched with effort.

He'd given it his all. Now to see what the judges thought. He drank more water, and splashed some on his face and neck to cool himself down.

'Okay, everyone, time's up!' Ronan called, clapping his hands to get their attention as the camera swung to face him. 'Please stop baking!'

Lucas's shoulders sank, because of course he could see Clem's creation sitting on the corner of her workstation – he'd avoided looking at it while he focused on his own cake, because he knew it'd make his confidence waver.

He'd been right.

It was glorious. Catpurrcino was hyper-realistic, even though the cake-building was quite small and far less tall than his own, the windows perfectly iced and decorated, the awning neatly coloured, the cherry tree a pink cluster of marshmallows and what appeared to be shredded coconut. She'd managed to add cat silhouettes into the windows, artistically painted on. The brickwork exterior was full of tidy, straight lines, and she'd made a chalkboard sign for the front and painted the café logo onto it – a cat sticking its head up from inside a cup of coffee.

He stood no chance against her.

Leaning around her slightly, he rose up onto his feet to check out what the other contestant had done: a representation of their cake shop, bright pink and full of character, with a recreation of their work van parked outside too – but it was not quite as intricate as Clem's.

'As you know, this round is going to be slightly different. We'll be judging your cakes outside in front of a much bigger audience than usual, to make the final extra splashy,' Ronan informed them. 'Please bring your bakes outside, where we'll chat to you about your individual dioramas. We'll then send you into the tent while we confer, do some taste-testing, and share your cakes with our audience. From there we'll announce our winner!'

They all headed outside into the hot sunshine with their bakes, Lucas clutching his carefully to be sure he didn't drop it. An oblong table was set up, draped in a cloth, where they could set their bakes down, and they lined up in the grass behind it. The heat of the sun was scorching Lucas's scalp, warming his hair, and he hoped they'd get this over with quickly so they could move off into the shade.

The audience was seated so they could watch from their semi-circle position – a series of faces, both old and young, some craning their necks to get a better look at the cakes on display. They were shaded under a canopy and

Lucas spotted his mum and dad in the crowd, his mum dressed in a pretty lemon-patterned sundress and white sandals, and his dad in a green button-neck shirt and dark jogging bottoms. He noticed his dad had a slight wince curving his mouth, imperceptible to anyone who hadn't spent a lot of time with him. He must be in pain, but trying not to show it.

But he'd come. They'd brought Reina too – Lucas hadn't wanted to leave her at home on such a nice day – and she was behaving herself, curled at his mum's feet with a chunk of beef jerky.

To his annoyance, Georgina was there too, a few rows behind them, sunglasses pushing her honeyed hair back. He worked hard to keep the frown off his face, because the camera kept sweeping around. But why was she here? He'd told her not to come; it was best if she stayed away. She'd better not cause any trouble.

They listened to the cake shop owner explain the nature of their business and what they'd been aiming to do with their pink diorama. The camera moved on to Clem, whose hands were grasping the sides of her skirt tightly.

'Can you tell us about your diorama of Catpurrcino, Clem, and how you've done it?' asked Ronan.

'Sure . . . so it's Catpurrcino in the springtime, with the cherry tree in full bloom.' She pointed at the tree she'd constructed, and her voice got stronger the more she spoke. 'The tree is made of modelling chocolate, and I used marshmallows rolled in shredded coconut for the blossoms,' she explained. 'The pathways out front are made with Rice Krispies and coconut. The cake itself is vanilla with a strawberry and cream filling.'

'And what were you hoping to represent about your business?' Laurette enquired.

The audience were listening with rapt attention, as was Lucas. The only sound was birdsong, somewhere in the trees, and a rustling breeze that cooled his scalp.

'Well . . . New beginnings and renewal. One of the main aims Sylvie has with Catpurrcino is to make people feel like they're comforted from the pressures of everyday life. A place where you can forget your troubles for a while. Hopefully, when you step out of Catpurrcino, you feel renewed. Ready to take on whatever life can throw at you next. But more than that . . .' She wavered before straightening her spine and continuing. 'It's been like that for me, too. Working there has given me so much confidence and it's because of the café I've been able to develop so much as a baker. I don't know if I would have done that without Sylvie, and everyone else at the café.'

There was a beat of silence where everyone absorbed this. Lucas's insides had frosted over, despite the heatwave, and he shifted his feet in the grass. How could he possibly match up? Muddy Paws Café as a business venture meant a lot to both him and Dwayne – it was something they'd both wanted to achieve – but there wasn't a deep, personal meaning like Clem's. They'd both floundered after university, talked about opening a café together, and put their hospitality experience to good use to do something they enjoyed. It didn't go much deeper than that.

'It's clear the café means a lot to you,' Ronan said, and the judges either side of him nodded, 'and that's definitely come through in your wonderful presentation. The cats you've added to the windows are a gorgeous touch.'

'It's beautiful, and we're looking forward to seeing what it tastes like!' said Viviana.

'Thank you,' said Clem, glancing down.

'And now for your rival, the dogs!' Ronan laughed, and the gathered audience joined in. As if on cue, Reina, who had been chomping on her beef jerky, looked up, barked and wagged her tail furiously, her fur shining like gold in the sunlight.

'Could we get a shot of the dog?' Ronan asked the cameraman. 'That'd be so perfect . . .'

There was a pause while the camera captured some shots of Reina. When the attention of both the camera and the onlookers returned to Lucas, he still had no idea what he was going to say to match up to Clem's speech.

'And how about your cake, Lucas?' Ronan asked him. 'Can you tell us what you've baked, and what it means to you?'

*What it means to you.* His neck was hot. This cake meant something to him not because of Muddy Paws Café, but because he wanted to help his family, his dad. He glanced at his father, who was watching Lucas closely. He gave him a tight smile through his pain, and his mum reached over and clasped his hand. He was enduring so much to be here for Lucas.

Something inside Lucas clenched, too.

'It's a vanilla sponge, with chocolate ganache – a mix of milk chocolate, dark chocolate, and double cream,' he explained. 'I used fondant and royal icing to decorate things like the windows and doors and the other small details.'

'It's certainly detailed!' said Viviana, moving closer to it to get a better look.

'As for the meaning . . .' Lucas began.

He hesitated. Their story wasn't his to tell. Not with a whole audience watching and an entire internet full of chattering *Whisked Away* fans waiting to speculate and gossip. That had already happened with Clem and he wasn't sure he could let it happen to his father too. His father was a proud man. He'd never come back from that. It was hard enough to get him to open up to medical professionals and he hated talking about his pain.

Taking a breath, Lucas made his decision.

'When I left university with a film degree, I wanted to work in filmmaking. But it was a difficult career to get off the ground. I ended up working a lot of catering events with Dwayne.' The two of them swapped a smile. 'Dwayne studied business – we met at uni. Anyway, we worked events all over the country. Weddings. Parties. Corporate. LARPing – you know, live action roleplay? Those were some of the most fun since we got to dress up like pirates and rogues.' Some of the audience members laughed, and frantic whispers broke out among those who probably hadn't heard of LARPing and wanted to know what it was. Ronan had to shush them.

Lucas smiled faintly before carrying on: 'All that hard work – we thought, there has to be something more we can do with this. After a while we wanted to go home and be more settled, and we decided to open Muddy Paws Café, a dog-friendly café.'

'I see. So, this cake is a representation of the hard work it took to build up the business, not long out of university? Your entrepreneurial mindset. I like it,' said Ronan, who was nodding. 'I started Ronan's Real Bakes not long after graduating, too.'

'Not an easy feat, to build up a business from scratch – we know what that's like!' Jonathan added. 'We can't wait to taste it!'

'Thanks,' said Lucas. His brain was stuttering like a failing engine. Did that mean his explanation wasn't completely terrible? Maybe he still stood a chance?

'Okay, everyone! Contestants, please head into the tent while the judges confer. We'll call you out when we're ready and we'll announce the results!'

Lucas turned to follow the others into the tent. As he did so, he spied Georgina, no longer sitting in the audience but walking across the grass to the left of the tent, her glossy hair gleaming in the sun.

No one else was paying her any attention, the audience chatting now, and the judges gathering together nearby to dish out the bakes for taste-testing. Where was she going?

Georgina vanished around the back of the tent, out of sight.

# Chapter 26

Inside the tent, it was still horribly warm and Clem's hair was sticking to her forehead. They'd been in here for five minutes already, just the three of them – the 'supporting' half of each pair had been asked to wait outside – and the silence was infused with awkwardness. Clem didn't know what to say to Lucas and she wished she were outside with her mum, who was in the audience, instead. Thankfully, the other contestant, Dinah, was rather chatty, complimenting them both on their bakes and their work. They were standing right at the rear of the tent near the long workstation containing the tea- and coffee-making facilities, and various snacks. Clem grabbed a few grapes to try to settle her stomach, which didn't actually do anything other than make her feel mildly sick. As Dinah carried on her part of the conversation with gusto, Clem thought she smelt something odd, like burning.

'Do you smell that?' she said, breathing it in again.

'Did someone leave an oven on?' said Dinah. She wandered over to some of the workstations near the front to check. 'Doesn't look like it. Where's that smell coming from?'

Clem looked around the tent, and gasped. Flames were licking at the bottom of the tent near the corner of the long workstation, and they were building, climbing higher. They might look small now – but not for long.

'The tent's on fire!' she cried. 'We should leave before it spreads. Quickly!'

Dinah didn't need telling twice – she nodded and rushed from the tent, probably to alert the others. But Lucas had hesitated halfway across the tent, glancing around, which made Clem stop in her tracks too, automatically, several feet behind him. She could already feel hotness spreading through her, intensifying the warmth of the heatwave, and panic rose up inside her.

'What are you—'

'Isn't there a fire extinguisher in—'

They didn't get to finish their conversation. The flames moved so rapidly, bursting across shelving units and cupboards containing ingredients and bags of flour and sugar, some of the ingredients exploding, making Clem cry out in fright. The fire quickly darted across to workstations, setting them alight with towers of bright orange flame that ate through the wood and chewed through everything in their path.

Clem's route to Lucas was blocked by the roaring, blazing spikes, and the tent was fast filling with heavy, dark smoke. Distantly, somewhere outside the tent, she thought she heard Reina barking.

'Clem!' Lucas shouted, the sound punctuated by coughs. 'Clem, are you—'

More mini explosions were triggered as the fire tore across the other workstations, ripping into ingredients. Clem shrieked in terror, staggering backwards away from the flames as thick smoke made her eyes stream and her lungs burn. She glanced up, coughing – the canvas ceiling was *melting*, leaking down like watery chocolate. The workstation behind her was on fire too.

The panic within her was chanting that she was in danger. It was blisteringly hot, with these scorching flames and the already boiling summer heat. They had to get out of here before the tent ended up collapsing on top of them. But it was hard to think straight; she was so afraid and her skin was so hot. It was like every path out was blocked by roaring flame.

She couldn't constrain her coughs and they ripped out of her, searing her chest. The panic spiralled along with them. She tried to find a way to get to Lucas, and the exit. Reina's barking persisted faintly. She had the horrible, wild thought that she'd never see Reina, or the outside of this tent, again. Her mum, Misha, her colleagues at the cat café, Lucas . . .

'Clem . . . I'm coming to you . . . get . . .'

She couldn't hear the rest of his words around his coughs and through the cacophony of the fire.

'No!' she choked out. Even though she was fearful, she knew he couldn't put himself in danger for her – he had to get out, otherwise they'd *both* end up hurt.

Logic had abandoned her, shoved aside to make room for her fears. She couldn't stop coughing. She couldn't breathe and it was awful – if she passed out in here, what would happen? She had a wild vision of herself collapsing right here on the spot, of the tent's melted ceiling and everything else crashing down on top of her, squashing the last of the air from her chest. They would pull her from this tent but she wouldn't be breathing when they did. Most of her irrational fears didn't come to pass, and that could sometimes be a comfort, but this time her anxieties felt well and truly real. All her catastrophising made possible in this moment.

'Clem! Stay . . . Okay? Stay low! Move . . . fast!'

Lucas's voice pierced her thoughts.

'Stay low!' he growled.

Clem crouched down, as low to the ground as she could get. She couldn't even take a deep breath to steady herself, but Lucas's words had prompted some rational thoughts. They filtered through her terror. Guidance on what to do. She lifted up the bottom of her dress and covered her mouth with it to stem how much smoke she was breathing in. *Have to get out have to get out have to . . .*

Squinting, Clem glanced left and right. The space to the left of the workstations was so far untouched by flames, and she hurried through the thick smog. There was a banging, smashing sound as she drew closer, and fresh panic spliced her. Was it more debris?

'Clem! I've . . . in my way . . .' Lucas's voice grew clearer as she quickened her way towards him, her eyes watering still, and his tall silhouette emerged from the smoke.

He was kicking aside debris – toppled cupboards and drawers and shelving units – swinging his foot violently. His shirt was pulled up over his nose as he bashed things aside, exposing his abdomen.

He was clearing a path for them.

Lucas looked up, saw her, motioned for her to come to him. Clem raced forwards and had never been so happy to have another person's arms encase her. She gave a strangled sob.

He drew her in, tugged her downwards, and pulled her towards the exit, both of them crouched low, trying to evade the worst of the smoke.

275

'It's okay!' he said, voice rough. 'Keep low, nearly there . . .'

They kept left, flames on the right still blazing and lashing, but he'd made an opening by kicking some of the shelving units aside – the exit and the sun becoming visible, a cube of light up ahead. They were going to make it!

Lucas pulled her towards it, and they burst out into the daylight, Clem coughing and spluttering and dropping her skirt down.

At once, other hands were on her, on Lucas, yanking them away from the tent. Clem was dazed by the rush of motion, by the bright wash of sunlight after so much black smoke. She couldn't speak; she could barely think. Every fibre of her being was shaking. Her collarbone felt like it was trembling beneath her skin. Lucas held her close to him, arm scooped around her shoulders to steady her.

'They're out!' someone shouted. 'Take them up the road with the others, near the castle entrance! It's spreading in the direction of the field and surrounding trees!'

Clem's vision was blurry – from the sun or the smoke she'd moved through, she wasn't sure which – and she couldn't make out who was speaking. The heat out here was disorientating, as if she should still be surrounded by flames. She was light-headed, the world tipping – from the smoke or the anxiety, she didn't know. But Lucas kept his arms around her as they were guided up the road, away from the ruined tent.

★

It wasn't the grand finale Lucas had been expecting. It had left him shaken. A stone was lodged permanently in his gut. He'd seen Georgina disappear around the rear of the tent before the blaze started. Had she caused this fire on purpose? As soon as the thought entered his mind, he rebuffed it, guilt making his skin prickle. Surely not. He was being stupid – Georgina wouldn't want to ruin this for him, even if he didn't return her feelings. And she'd never do something so reckless and dangerous; she wasn't that immature. It had probably been caused by something catching ablaze in the heat.

Georgina was nowhere to be seen when he craned his neck to look out over the crowds. Fire and ambulance crews were flocking around the area, and paramedics raced to him and Clem, who hadn't stopped shaking since they left the tent. He kept his fingertips gripped around her shoulders, afraid she might buckle if he let her go.

His parents charged over, too, his mum enveloping him in a hug, in tears, his dad trailing after her more slowly, looking ashen and grabbing Lucas's shoulder tightly. Another woman launched herself at Clem, flinging her arms around her – her mum, he guessed. They only moved away when the paramedics gently told them that Clem and Lucas needed to be checked over.

The fire was being brought under control so it didn't spread to the neighbouring woodland and trees. After they'd been looked at, Lucas and Clem were sent to hospital at once to treat their smoke inhalation, both of their parents following in their own cars.

Their airways were checked, and tight-fitting masks fitted over both their faces. Inside the ambulance, both of them were set up with IVs. The mask on Lucas's face was making him feel hot again, pressing into his skin, but the oxygen being pumped into him was a relief, and he sagged into the sensation. When he squeezed Clem's hand – because she still looked petrified, and as grey as stone – she didn't let go. He could feel her hand quaking and he looped his fingers through hers.

Even as they were transported from ambulance to hospital for more tests, and they were separated, he couldn't stop thinking about Clem's panic-stricken face, the smoke engulfing her like the thick, heady breaths of a monster, her shaking. The whole tent could have come down on top of her. She could have died.

He never would have seen her again.

Had that been Georgina's plan all along? It made him sick thinking about it. She still couldn't let him go, after all this time, but would she resort to *this*?

On the way out of hospital – he'd tried to find Clem but she'd messaged him to say her mum had picked her up – he fished his phone from his jeans and tapped out a message.

*I saw you go behind the tent, Georgina,* he wrote. *We need to talk.*

She saw the message but didn't reply. His suspicions prickled at him like ivy. Did she really have something to do with this? Considering the possibility made the prickling sensation increase until he felt hot and itchy.

Why had he fought so hard to keep away from Clem? He could have fought for *both* – his family and for her. He'd been so convinced that any relationship outside of the one with his family was a distraction, he'd ignored how he really felt about her. And if something had happened to her, he would have sorely regretted that forever.

His previous concerns had drifted away like a wisp of smoke, because he'd realised what he should have known all along. That if you cared about someone, it was worth holding on to. Life was too short. Perhaps in maintaining his friendship with Georgina, he'd been holding on to the wrong things.

★

The day after the fire, Lucas was at home, coffee brewing in the pot in the kitchen, and filling the house with the scent of rich, aromatic beans. In the chaos following the fire, no winner had been announced on the grass yesterday as planned. The online world was abuzz with talk about the blazing tent and what had caused it – how whoever was responsible should be brought to justice and punished. They were also demanding to know who had won.

Lucas's feelings on winning had churned in the aftermath of the fire. He poured steaming, hot coffee into a mug and splashed in some milk and sugar. He didn't know how he felt. His burning drive to win had gone, replaced by numbness. Maybe that was simply what had happened to him in the tent. Either way, he couldn't control the outcome and he was tired now, tired of pushing. And he was sick of this cough already, brought on by breathing in so much smoke – he hadn't slept well, even though the hospital said he needed plenty of rest. He kept waking up to cough repeatedly, his chest painful and tight.

A tap sounded on the front door. Tentative.

Hope soared, because for a moment he thought it was Clem. But he'd asked Georgina to come here.

Reina started barking and bounded into the hallway; he heard her claws clacking on the wooden floor. He left the coffee machine gurgling and went to open the door. Reina danced around his heels, bushy tail swinging, pink tongue on display.

'Down, girl,' he said, stifling another series of coughs as she tried to leap upwards and nearly toppled him over. 'Calm down.'

With Reina somewhat subdued, circling him in the hall, he opened the door.

Georgina stood on the doorstep, looking distinctly less polished and shiny than usual. Her hair was scraped up into a messy ponytail, with lumps sticking up along the side of her head, and her denim dress was creased. There were purplish circles under her eyes; she mustn't have slept. The only items she carried were her phone and car keys.

'Dwayne's not here, is he?' she checked. Her voice was strained, stretched out with panic.

Lucas held Reina by the collar to stop her from tackling Georgina. '*No*, girl,' he chided her, the emphasis on the word making him cough again. 'And no, he's at work like I said he would be,' he added, voice a little scratchy. 'All day.'

They had agreed Lucas would be on sick leave until he recovered – he'd spoken to his doctor this morning, who had also said that was a good idea. If he took good care of himself and there were no additional complications, he could be working at Muddy Paws Café in a week or two. Clem was also on leave from work – she'd messaged him the previous evening – though she apparently felt guilty about leaving Catpurrcino with a limited supply of baked goods.

'Come in,' said Lucas tightly, stepping aside. When Georgina stepped into the hall, he shut the door behind her and led the way into the kitchen. Reina danced alongside them, her tail wagging vigorously in excitement.

It was less bright in here, the sky outside having switched from luminous yesterday to clouded over and grey, the humid air and stickiness hinting at a thunderstorm to come. Thick, dark clouds were journeying across the sky.

'Coffee?' he said, gesturing to the machine, coffee still filtering through into the jug.

'Okay . . . thanks,' said Georgina.

When he started clattering around, she jumped, like a rabbit spooked by a car. He remembered how she liked her coffee. Milky, sweet – but not real sugar, it had to be sweetener. Behind him, she was twisting her car keys in her hand, jangling them. He glanced back. Reina came over to sniff at them, intrigued, and she patted the dog on the head.

'It was an accident,' she blurted.

Lucas almost upended the coffee mug he'd poured liquid into and grabbed the top to steady it, nearly splashing the scalding liquid on his hand. '*What?*' he said, turning to face her again, agape. 'So it *was* you! Georgina – I mean, Genie, have you got any idea what—'

'It really was a mistake!' she shrilled, tearful. She clutched her car keys tightly, knuckles whitening. Reina whined and licked at her hands. 'I went for a cigarette, figured I could be quick while the judges deliberated—'

'So what? You flicked a *lit* cigarette into dry grass? In the middle of a heatwave? Are you *stupid?*'

Her silence said it all. That was exactly what she'd done. He laughed in utter disbelief, although it wasn't funny. Reina was cocking her head, looking between them, sensing something amiss between the humans.

'Have you told anyone it was you?' he demanded. He had abandoned her coffee now, forgotten on the countertop. He coughed, rubbing his chest to ease the ache.

'No, I—'

'You *should*—'

'Lucas, I could get in serious trouble! I didn't mean to cause it!' she cried. 'As if my life isn't a mess enough, struggling for money in London, screwing up my chance with you—'

'Listen,' he interrupted her, voice hoarse, either from the coughing or the stress. 'This has to stop. I told you I wasn't interested. I thought you understood, thought you'd move on and find someone in London. But now you've come here and you've been picking at things from the past. Punishing Clem for it.'

Georgina frowned. 'I told her I liked someone who worked in the bistro, said I'd liked that person for years. She knew it was you and she talked to you anyway—'

'How do you *know*? Did she admit to that, or is this all something you made up to justify behaving like a child?'

Once again, she was quiet, because she had no argument. Lucas took a few deep breaths, trying not to cough. Reina scuffed her way over to his side, nosing at his hand, and he rubbed the side of her head.

'It was you, wasn't it?' he realised suddenly. 'Sharing around the video of Clem, from university? To try to make her look stupid? Why did you film it in the first place? Why would you do that to her? It was cruel.'

'I told you! I told her I liked someone from the bistro and she—'

'Someone? But you never mentioned me by name? She never knew it was the same guy she met in the library?'

Georgina pinched her mouth together, and he had his answer.

'You know what?' Lucas said. 'You need to grow up. I thought London would have matured you but you're still acting like a spoilt little girl, like we're in high school or something. We're *twenty-nine*. I don't need this rubbish.'

'W-What do you mean?' she replied, blinking away the emotion. 'We've been friends since we were kids, Lukey—'

'Don't call me that. We're done.'

'Done . . . ?'

'Yes, done. You can finish up this coffee if you want, then I want you to leave.' He strode to the fridge to retrieve the milk, splashing it into her cup with minimal effort, adding the sweetener. It hurt to say all this, like a knife to the chest to go with the other stabbing pains from the smoke inhalation. But he should have said it a long time ago. 'We can't be in each other's lives anymore.'

'Lukey, please—'

'Don't,' he said sharply.

Something in his tone, his face, must have made it crystal clear he was serious. Because he was. He'd held on to their friendship because it had been so long-lasting – she'd been at his side when he was a child, all the way into adulthood, and he'd thought that was something you shouldn't throw away. Now, he thought he had been buying into the sunk-cost fallacy, reluctant to let go because she'd always been a fixture in his life, something he'd always expected to be there. When she

283

moved away, he had hoped things would peter out gradually – eventually. That should have been his sign that the friendship was over. He couldn't be friends with someone who didn't respect his boundaries. No meant no; he was never going to change his mind. He was never going to love her in the way she wanted him to. He didn't know how else he could make her understand.

Despite this resolve, he felt bad – tears streamed freely down her face now, dripping off her chin. He rummaged in a cupboard for a packet of tissues, ripping it open and offering her one.

'Thanks,' she sniffed, dabbing at her face. Reina was at her side again, sitting this time, poking at her leg with her wet nose.

'Have some coffee and sit with Reina a little while – she'll make you feel better,' he said, more gently now. 'Then go.'

With a nod, she moved forward, reaching for the coffee mug with shaking fingers. Something unspoken hung between them – the fire, what she'd done. He didn't know if she'd tell anyone; he thought it was the right thing to do. The mature thing to do. To take responsibility for her actions. She'd never been any good at that.

'I hope you do the right thing,' he told her, before retreating from the kitchen.

\*

When he came downstairs half an hour later, Georgina had gone and Reina was curled in her dog bed over by the back door, her nose tucked between her paws. She looked up, tail wagging loosely when she spotted Lucas, before settling down to snooze.

His phone buzzed against the countertop – he'd left it on the side earlier. He coughed, rubbing his chest, picked it up and swiped to see a message from Clem on the screen.

> Did you see your email? From the judges?

He frowned down at the message, a slight pain in his chest. An email from the judges, already? Had they emailed with the announcement about who had won? He switched over to his emails and skimmed through the contents.

It wasn't an announcement. It was an invitation. He read through it, and replied to Clem.

> *Lucas:* Just seen it. I didn't expect them to want to film us again
>
> *Clem:* I did. Everyone wants it and it's the only way to end the show in a way that makes everyone happy, audience included. If they don't film it, they won't have anything to show
>
> *Lucas:* Even with how much shit they're in now, with the fire? So many people are mad
>
> *Clem:* I know
>
> *Clem:* We should hopefully know more about what caused it soon. I feel sorry for the judges. The filming's a low-key thing at least. Will you go?

Lucas made himself another coffee and sipped it, letting out a sigh – he'd hit on that perfect blend of the right amount of coffee and milk. A series of coughs followed. They were both still recovering, but filming was scheduled a few weeks from now, so they should be feeling better by then. He drummed his fingertips on the counter and his phone buzzed again in his hand.

Clem: I think we should go. We should see it through, since we came this far, and went through all this

He hadn't seen her after that day at the hospital, although he'd messaged her to see if she was okay after the blood tests and the lung checks and everything else. They'd both been advised to watch their breathing, told they might still have a cough and shortness of breath, possibly some pain, as things healed. He tapped out a reply.

Lucas: I'll go if you promise to get plenty of rest and sleep. And if you get any of those weird symptoms they told us about at the hospital, get checked out okay?

Clem: Of course I will. Same goes for you too

Lucas: Sure. Are you okay?

Clem: I think so

Lucas: You seemed pretty shook up. I was worried

Clem: I was

The display simply read *typing* . . . but Clem must have decided not to send whatever she was typing, because it vanished. Five minutes later, another message came through.

> *Clem:* Are you feeling okay today?
>
> *Lucas:* I'm doing fine. Coffee heals all, right?

She sent him an animated GIF of a cat swimming inside a coffee cup.

He decided not to tell her about Georgina. It wasn't that he was protecting her – it was more he didn't want to hurt Clem. If Georgina made the right choice, Clem would find out. And if she didn't, Lucas didn't know what he'd do – go to the police? Could he? If he was questioned about the fire, he couldn't lie and cover for her, he knew that much.

> *Lucas:* We should talk too. In person
>
> *Clem:* I think so as well
>
> *Lucas:* Are you free in the next couple of days?

Once again, the screen showed her as *typing* . . . It vanished as quickly as it had appeared. He waited, drinking his coffee, draining half the mug before she answered.

> *Clem:* I think we should meet after the filming when we're better.

Disappointment flip-flopped in Lucas's stomach. He'd hoped to see her sooner – to his surprise, the thought of going a couple of weeks without seeing her made things seem a little less bright, as if there wasn't anything in particular to look forward to. But he didn't want to be pushy, not when they both needed to recover. She was right – they'd been through a lot.

> *Lucas:* Okay, sure
> *Clem:* Good. May the best dog (or cat) win ☺

# Chapter 27

The day was bright when Clem arrived at the hotel and spa to find out the results with Sylvie. It wasn't quite as hot as the day of the fire, but still extremely warm. As they walked toward the entrance – the same path where she'd run into Lucas months ago before the auditions – she drew in a long, fulfilling breath of clean summer air. Her chest was feeling much better now, and she was glad to finally have stopped coughing, but there was a lingering feeling of unease that followed her around, like she hadn't quite shaken off the events of the fire. She hadn't been sleeping too well.

The sky was a pale blue canvas smeared with lines of white chalk, and a passing aeroplane tracked a long, ridged streak through it. It was warm, and she'd chosen a plain light summer dress. Cat-themed accessories glinted in the sunshine on her wrists and around her neck. Sylvie, too, had accessorised with little cats for good luck – her bun was poked through with a glittery cat hairclip, and her flat shoes were stamped with two happy red cat faces.

She smiled at Clem as they approached the reception, stepping into the cool, air-conditioned space. 'Remember,' she said, 'I'm proud of you whether we win or not. Okay?'

Clem smiled in return. 'I know.'

They were directed to the same big hall where auditions had been held, cooled and freshened by the air-con. There were no workstations set up here today – only the stage and podium. The *Whisked Away* crew had, of course, brought the trophies for the winner and second and third place, shining atop a table on the stage.

The judges were already here, milling about with the camera crew off the stage and having their make-up touched up. Viviana was having her face powdered and Jonathan was tapping away on his phone, talking to Laurette.

'Ah, you're here!' Ronan called to them. A woman was fixing his curls. He smiled and shooed her away good-naturedly. When he turned to Sylvie and Clem, Clem thought his smile looked strained, and under the layers of make-up, there were grey-tinted bags beneath his eyes. 'I hope you're feeling okay?' he said to Clem.

'I'm alright, thanks,' she replied. 'No real harm done.'

'It was horrible, what happened. It *shouldn't* have happened. I can't apologise to you enough . . .' He scratched the back of his head. Even his clothing was less sunny and polished. He was wearing a grey suit, and the only hint of colour was the baby-pink tie.

'It wasn't your fault,' said Clem. She knew how he felt – he looked as bad as she'd been in the aftermath.

He was about to respond, but footsteps padded into the hall behind Clem and Sylvie. Lucas, Dwayne and Dinah and her partner had arrived. Clem turned; she hadn't seen Lucas since the day they'd been taken to hospital. She'd mainly been at home resting with Misha.

To her relief, he looked okay – more than okay. He looked handsome. There was colour in his cheeks, as if his paleness had been tinted slightly red by the sun, and his hair was brushed behind his ears, spiking out below his earlobes. He wore a dark navy tee with dark jeans. She wanted to run at him, wrap her arms around him and never let go, sprinkle kisses over his jaw. Had it only been a short time since they'd seen each other? He'd saved her life. How could she ever thank him?

The judges asked them to line up in front of the stage, on white X's marked on the carpet with tape. It was a much less grand affair than what would have happened if the fire hadn't occurred. There was no live audience, no family members watching with anticipation. Maybe Ronan thought it best to keep things understated? Even though the *Whisked Away* fans wanted the results, many blamed the contest for what had happened and Clem imagined a splashier finale wouldn't go down well, or do much for his reputation.

When the cameras were rolling and the judges were side by side on the stage, Ronan glanced around, smiling. It didn't reach his eyes.

'Welcome!' he called. 'I'm so glad you're all here, and that Clem and Lucas in particular are healthy and doing well.' He cleared his throat. 'As you know, a full investigation is being conducted into what happened at the tent – and we hope whoever is responsible *will* be held accountable.' He continued for a few minutes about how the safety of his contestants was paramount, and *Whisked Away* took this very seriously. 'But let's move on to what everyone's been waiting for – the winner! We won't draw this out any longer for everybody.'

Despite his words, he allowed the pause to linger before carrying on. 'Dinah, your cakes have always been so artistic, and wonderfully flavoured. The judges were so impressed by your use of colour to re-create your cake shop – such vibrant pinks! – and how you managed to make a miniature version of your van.'

'The detailing was wonderful,' Viviana interjected.

'That being said, we thought the cake itself was a little too dry this time,' Ronan went on, 'and could have benefitted from more moistness. We'll be awarding you third place.'

Dinah nodded, her shoulders slightly slumped. The judges clapped, inviting her and her partner up onto the stage to collect the third-place trophy, which was small enough to fit into one hand. They also presented her partner with a gift basket stuffed full of treats, wrapped in a big plastic bow, shining and red.

'Some of your favourite baked goodies and ingredients,' Jonathan told them, winking. 'Thanks for all your hard work!'

After Dinah and her partner had accepted the prize, some of the crew took them off to the side of the room to watch the rest of the announcement. Clem's throat was pulsating and her ears were roaring with noise, as if she'd held up a shell to her ear to listen to the ocean. She glanced at Lucas, whose hands were stuffed into his jean pockets. His jawline looked stiff but, otherwise, his expression gave nothing away. Dwayne looked calm too, his arms folded over his broad chest.

Instead of feeling excited at the prospect of winning, Clem only felt a mild unease. Because *why* did she want to win? She'd told herself she needed the money, to move out. That hadn't been true. She'd been making excuses for herself for so long because she'd been afraid. And she'd always had everything she needed; her mum had been right. She'd just needed some extra confidence, and to understand that she would be able to cope with whatever life had in store for her, even if she didn't always feel that way.

'Lucas, your recreation of Muddy Paws Café was so intricate. We could see how your skills have grown over the course of this competition – how hard you worked. Especially on the level of detail on the building.'

'And the cake was well and truly delicious,' Laurette said, her arms folded over her chest. 'We always knew cakes weren't your strong suit – you said so on your application – but you accomplished so much with that cake. You have a lot to be proud of.'

'This was *such* a close one for us,' said Ronan, and Viviana and Laurette nodded either side of him. 'Probably the closest ever, in the history of *Whisked Away*.' He gave a long, dramatic pause. 'It's just Clem's was that little bit more polished and accomplished and we loved the representation of Catpurrcino a little more . . . so we'll be awarding you second place. Well done, Muddy Paws!'

The roaring ocean in her ears was screaming, and even though she'd felt uneasy about it, a rush of excitement that she'd *won* – that she'd got this far – nearly knocked her off her feet. When she turned to Lucas, there was no real change in his demeanour, and he walked up onto the stage to accept his trophy with Dwayne following in his wake. He took the trophy, the bright stage lights shining down on him, and Dwayne accepted the gift basket, shaking hands with Ronan and the other judges. Lucas was smiling but his mouth was barely lifting at the corners. He was gripping the trophy too hard, so tight she could see the lines of his knuckles. He hurried down from the stage, urged to one side by the staff.

'Which means . . . we have our winner! Congratulations, Catpurrcino!'

The judges were clapping, calling for her to come up to the stage with Sylvie. She stumbled forward, the camera capturing her every move, and she couldn't stop smiling, so wide it hurt her cheeks, though she knew Lucas was watching. Because she'd proved to herself that she could do this. She *had* done it, in spite of all the mistakes and her fears and self-doubts. She hadn't had the guts to enter this competition herself because she'd been so afraid, but here she was. Someone – the *Whisked Away* team, probably – poured confetti over her, pink like the cherry tree outside Catpurrcino in the spring, like the one she'd made out of marshmallows and coconut.

The first-place trophy was the biggest; she needed two hands to hold it, and they gave Sylvie the gift basket. The judges were patting her, uttering congratulations. She thanked them, the whole moment feeling like a delirious blur.

And then Lucas was there beside her. The smile she wore froze on her face, and the lens of the camera sought them out when the *Whisked Away* team realised what was going on. Clem's mouth was dry now, her palms slick. She hoped she wouldn't drop the trophy on her own toes, and hitched it up higher, tightening her grip.

What was Lucas going to say? She knew how much he'd wanted this, but she felt so validated. She couldn't *not* be happy with what she'd accomplished. But at the same time, her stomach churned with worry for him, tarnishing the moment.

He didn't say anything at first. He beamed at her and placed a hand on her shoulder, squeezing, and the warmth of his touch radiated through her. Up here on the stage, he was silhouetted by light, his dark hair and brows a stark contrast.

'Clem,' he said thickly. 'Congratulations – I knew you could do it. That diorama was a work of art. And we have a winner in the cat versus dog battle.'

Even though pride surged within her at his words, Clem could see the disappointment in his slightly sloped shoulders. A lock of dark hair hung over his forehead. She wanted to reach out and smooth it down, to tell him that it was going to be okay – they would find a way to help his family. But she couldn't. The trophy was still in her hands, and Sylvie was speaking again, to Dwayne this time, who had joined Lucas on stage. The judges approached them all once more in an excited whirl of comments.

When the cameras finally stopped rolling, they kept talking, telling her what an opportunity this was going to be for her and her baking career, in spite of the fire, how their past winners had gone on to do wonderful things. Cookbooks and newspaper columns and TV appearances. She nodded and chatted back, unable to believe that they were talking about her, that they had such high hopes for what she could achieve next.

'So, Clem, what are you going to do with your win-nings?' asked Jonathan eagerly. 'Any big ideas?'

She couldn't respond. She stared through them, over their shoulders, at Lucas, who simply smiled and offered her a thumbs up.

★

Clem had finally escaped the judges and the crew. She hadn't wanted to leave so quickly and to seem rude and they'd wanted to film an interview with her, which had taken multiple takes because she couldn't stop stutter-ing and trembling. They'd all pressed business cards into her hand afterwards. Somewhere amongst it all, Lucas had vanished. When they finally broke free of the hall and into the fresh air, she still couldn't spot him any-where, and she could barely focus on Sylvie's enthusias-tic words in her ear.

'Clem, you should be *so* incredibly proud of yourself,' Sylvie was saying, her joy laced through every word. The words came quickly, as if she couldn't keep up with her own enthusiasm. 'I knew you could do this – all of us at Catpurrcino did! You're so talented and I think this is just the start. There'll be so many more opportunities for you from this . . . Clem?'

'Oh . . . what?' Clem hadn't fully processed the last few sentences and was still searching the area and the distant car park, half on her tiptoes.

'Are you okay?'

'Yes, I'm great!' said Clem, not voicing what she was really thinking. How would Lucas be feeling, knowing he couldn't help his parents now? Would he feel he'd let them down? She knew that if she were in his place, she'd be riddled with worry about what to do next. 'I . . . I don't see Lucas anywhere. Did you see where he went?'

'Ah. No, I didn't.'

When Clem finally dropped onto flat feet again and looked at Sylvie, the older woman's eyes were glittering, as if Clem had let her in on a secret.

'What?' said Clem.

'You can't think about anything but him, can you?' Sylvie said. Before Clem could respond, she added, 'Why don't you go and look for him? We drove here separately anyway.'

'Do you mind?'

'Of course not. I need to get to Catpurrcino.' Sylvie gave Clem a quick hug, squeezing her tightly. 'Well done, Clem.'

Surprised, Clem squeezed her back. 'Thank you,' she said, smiling into Sylvie's shoulder.

Sylvie headed across to the gravel car park and Clem watched her drive down the track, away from the hotel and back to Catpurrcino. Clem stood next to the water running alongside the main path – the place where Reina had nearly upended her the first time she came here. Lucas had agreed to speak with her when filming ended, but he wasn't here. A summer breeze fluttered through the trees, cooling her skin. She tapped out a message to him, holding her hand around her phone to shield it from the harsh glare of the sun.

Where are you?

She waited a minute and he replied:

> Down the gravel track, through the gate for the country walk. I went to get Reina from the farmhouse, walking her. Come meet me?

Clem shoved her phone away and hurried down the path, to the end of the gravel track and the wooden gate that marked the entrance to the hotel. To the right, another country path forked off, leading into the trees, their leaves spreading out to create a canopy overhead. A sign pointed the way onto the path and a popular walking route. She peered down the narrow path – and spotted Lucas, Reina trotting at his heels, sniffing around the grass and the dirt with her tail hanging low.

She raced towards him. 'Lucas!'

He looked over his shoulder, saw her coming and waited for her to catch up. When she reached him, she was slightly out of breath. Reina was delighted to have another person in her presence, her tail beating a furious, yellowy swirl through the air as she sniffed around Clem's feet and nuzzled her hands.

'Hey,' said Clem, stroking Reina's nose and glancing up at Lucas. 'I was looking for you.'

'Sorry,' he said. 'I needed some fresh air, so I thought I'd take Reina for a quick walk while you were talking with the judges.'

'Are you good to talk? I could join you?' she said hopefully.

'Sure.' He looked crestfallen, the light gone from his eyes, even though he was clearly trying to sound upbeat.

'We don't have to talk about anything specific right now,' she said quickly. 'I know how disappointed you must be.'

'I am. But I don't want you to feel bad for me. I'm happy for you, Clem, really, I am. You're incredibly talented. I never doubted you'd do well.'

'You're happy for me? Even though . . .' Clem bit her lip to keep it from trembling, fearing what he might say in response. 'I didn't enter *Whisked Away* myself?'

'You're still hung up on that?' he said. 'I told you, that doesn't matter, Clem. You won because you're talented. Who cares how the application ended up in the judges' hands?'

The relief made her knees weak. He hadn't been masking anything before; he really didn't care that she'd ended up at the auditions because of a twist of fate.

She reached for his hand, threading her fingers through his, so grateful to have met such an understanding person. His eyes were faraway. 'Things will be okay, you know. I don't need this money. I can help.'

His attention shifted from the bright field to their left, illuminated by the sun, to her face, and he shook his head. 'I'd never take anything from you. You earned that money, fair and square, and you deserve it.'

'I want you to take it,' she insisted, 'even if you only take some of it. For your dad.'

'I won't take your money, Clem. I was probably silly to bank on this contest as a solution, anyway. It wasn't practical. I need to figure out something else.'

'The money doesn't matter to me, Lucas. But your father's health . . . that's important.'

He didn't respond. And she knew he'd never say yes to this – accept it willingly. Because he was good and kind and had respect for her. She couldn't believe she'd ever suspected him of sabotaging her chances in the competition. Here he was, being graceful and supportive after losing.

'Lucas, please,' she breathed, but she knew he wouldn't.

He placed his other hand down over hers. 'It's yours, Clem.'

Specks of pollen danced across the fields; Reina was wandering the path, nose pressed to the edges, snuffling the myriad scents. A loose leaf blew between them, cartwheeling away. It was so beautiful out here but he looked so dejected and she couldn't stand it.

She reached up, tracing his cheek with the tips of her fingers. He didn't stop her. He looked down at her, dark hair contrasting with the bright summer landscape, sadness in the curve of his mouth that she wanted to take away. Should she? Had something changed now? She remembered the way he'd kicked aside debris to free them from the tent, so fierce. How he clung to her hand in the hospital, kept texting her to check she was okay. The way he looked at her, like she was precious.

'I never thanked you properly for saving my life,' she whispered.

Clem pressed her lips to his, softly, an invitation. Would he accept?

He did. He melted into it, hands rising up to wrap around her waist, kissing her. His hands on her, as warm as the sun, gentle, safe, tugging her closer. Something unspooled inside her, a tension she didn't know she was holding, her hands shifting to his shoulders. The rigidity seemed to have fallen away from him and she was glad when he deepened the kiss, pushing his lips harder against hers, fingers firm against her back as if seeking something there. Her head spun, whirring like the pollen in the air, the movements of his mouth making her senseless, thoughtless.

They broke away slowly, breathlessly, her lips aching like they missed him. The hint of a smile was on his mouth now.

'That's better,' she whispered, hooking her arms around his neck, on slight tiptoe. 'I don't like seeing you like this.'

'I'll have to save your life more often if this is how you thank me,' he said, nudging her nose with his.

There had to be something else she could do to help him.

She thought of what the judges had said, about opportunity coming from this competition, and how everyone had been rooting for her and Lucas to get together.

Before, she'd seen that as a threat and something to be afraid of, because she didn't want so much attention. But there were people out there who had been rooting for them. People who still did.

Maybe there *was* something she could do.

For now, though, she just wanted to kiss him again. So she did.

★

Lucas had spent several days researching quick loans he could take out. He'd decided it was best to apply for one to help his parents with some of their more immediate concerns, like the rent struggles, and they'd figure out the rest later. His mum wouldn't like it if he told her where the money came from so he'd simply tell her he'd been paid a tiny sum for coming in second place. She wouldn't want to take it, so he'd send it direct to her bank account. He didn't want her to end up in credit card debt.

He'd just finished filling out an online application for a loan when his phone buzzed. He grabbed it and stood up to stretch; he'd been sitting at the desk upstairs for ages, and there was a crick in his neck.

It was his mum.

> *Mum:* I'm going to take your dad to the cat café tomorrow. Will you come? We'd both like to see you
>
> *Lucas:* Okay, let me know when

Lucas stretched out his arms and dropped them to his sides, glancing out of the window at the beams of sunlight stretching through the trees. He did need to talk to Clem properly, like he'd promised. About them, and what came next. And he'd been cooped up for almost a week, figuring things out.

He still didn't know what the next step would be, but these loans were a start. It would help them get through the coming months and he'd work on the rest.

# Chapter 28

When Lucas arrived at Catpurrcino the following day, the car park was already half full and he recognised his mum's blue car over in the corner, with the astronaut keychain dangling from the rear-view mirror, the metal parts catching the light. He clambered out, and wandered round the front of the café to reception, where he found Clem waiting for him inside, by the big poster of the cat café's rules.

'Hi!' she said, beaming at him.

Her smile was radiant and she was wearing that red lipstick that made her look even more beautiful. She had on a white shirt and a pair of black shorts; there were cat hairclips holding up half of her hair.

'Your mum and dad are already here,' she said. 'I insisted on paying for all three of you, so you can have as many drinks as you want. Come through.'

'You didn't have to do that,' he said, and she waved his words aside. 'Thank you.'

He experienced a twinge of guilt, and followed her through the door and the latched gate leading into the main café. He'd messaged her last night to suggest maybe they could talk while he was here.

The main room of the café was at capacity, with customers seated at the tables drinking iced coffees and fruity milkshakes overflowing with cream and sprinkles. It was bright, sunshine lighting up the room through the wide-set windows. A woman with a laptop was laughing as a grey cat with shiny green eyes tried to clamber onto her keyboard – she gently shooed it out of the way and the cat flopped down on a nearby chair for some ear scratches. Another cat, a calico, surveyed the room from atop a tower, looking regal and tall, blinking lazily down at everyone.

Clem led Lucas to a table in the corner by the window. His dad was seated in a comfortable-looking armchair, waving a feathery bird toy for a cat, a longhair with orange and brown fur who was swatting its paws into the air, trying to catch it. Lucas's mum was seated opposite. Both already had drinks: a black coffee for his dad and a creamy latte dusted with cocoa powder for his mum.

'Lucas! Here, sit down,' said his mum, pulling out the chair beside her.

'We can chat in a minute,' said Clem. She glanced over her shoulder at the counter, where a young man with wavy brown hair was working at the coffee machines, behind a row of glass cake displays. 'Can I get you a drink?' Clem added. 'Snack?'

'I'll take a flat white,' he said. And, given she'd paid for him to be here, he tugged some cash out of his wallet and added, 'And a few of your biscuits, I don't mind which. Surprise me.'

'We'll have a few more of those, too,' said his mum, smiling up at Clem. 'They're so good, I can't resist.'

'Sure.' Clem grinned and headed over to the counter.

Lucas assessed his dad, who was still wiggling the toy for the cat. The feline pounced at it and missed, skittering away on the flooring, making his dad laugh. Sometimes you couldn't tell when he was having a terrible pain day, versus when he wasn't, because he tended to push on through without complaining. Other days it was clear – if he couldn't leave the house to go for a walk, or do much around the house, everyone would know the pain was significant. Today, he'd made it outside, but that didn't mean he wasn't hurting.

'Are you okay, Dad?' Lucas asked.

'I'm fine,' he answered, waving the cat toy in the air again. The cat made a leap for it, performing a rather impressive pirouette.

'What did you want to talk to me about?' Lucas said, turning to his mum.

'Ah, probably best to wait till Clem comes back,' said his mum, sipping from her mug and smiling over the rim.

'Clem?' he repeated, dumbfounded. He needed to talk to her afterwards – but that was between them. Why did his parents want to talk to her as well?

'Ah, your mother's been cagey with me all day,' his dad grumbled. He reached forward for his coffee and Lucas caught the wince, the slight flicker of pain in his face. He covered it up quickly, like creased paper being smoothed out. 'She won't tell me a thing except she brought me here for a surprise.' His dad lifted his pair of white, caterpillar-like eyebrows.

'A surprise?' Lucas shot his mum a questioning look.

'All in good time!' she replied cryptically.

Clem arrived with his flat white and some sugar sachets, and passed around the cat-shaped biscuits. While everyone was busily munching away on colourful, crumbly cat faces, Clem pulled up another chair and took a seat, her dark hair glossy in the sunlight.

'What's this about?' said his dad.

'Probably best if you do the honours, Clem,' said his mum. She was watching the cat – it had knocked the toy from his dad's hand and caught it between its paws, rolling around with it locked between a set of claws.

'Okay.' Clem took a deep breath, finishing the last of her biscuit and dusting crumbs and icing from her hands. She looked from Lucas to his father. 'Mr Bowen, I don't know if you realise what Lucas's aim has been throughout this competition . . . why he wanted that prize money.'

'I had my suspicions – we both did,' said his father, drawing his coffee cup to his mouth. 'But I never would have taken money from him. We'll sort ourselves out and—'

'You won't need to,' Clem interrupted. Beside her, Lucas's mother was beaming, her hands clasped close to her chest.

'What do you mean?' said Lucas.

'I've been talking to your mum,' Clem explained, 'and I told her I wanted to help. We set up a fundraiser together – with you as the beneficiary, Mr Bowen,' she added. His father lowered his cup slowly. On the floor, the cat gave a long mewl, wanting more play, and batted the toy under the table. Lucas was speechless. 'You might not have won the competition or the prize money, Lucas,' Clem continued, 'but thousands of people have been rooting for us for weeks during *Whisked Away*. And when we set up the fundraiser, the donations quickly came pouring in from all over the world. I donated some of my winnings as well. I knew you wouldn't accept that from me directly.'

'But . . . Dad won't . . .' Lucas spluttered.

He turned to his father. Where he'd expected resistance and stubbornness, he didn't find any. His father's mouth was hanging open.

'I hope you'll accept it, my love,' said Lucas's mum quietly, leaning across the table and reaching for his hand, which was still clasped around his coffee cup. 'I know you don't like asking for help, accepting it, but when you see . . . Well, it's not enough for us to permanently resolve our housing situation, but we could get you seen by a specialist much more quickly, get some private treatment started. Could you show him, Clem?'

Clem nodded. She pulled her phone out of the pocket of her shorts, and tapped away at the screen for a few minutes before handing it to Lucas's father.

He nearly knocked over his coffee – Lucas grabbed it and set it straight, to save it splashing over the table. The cat, startled by the sudden noise, leaped up onto the window seat nearby and out of reach. Slowly, his father handed the phone to Clem, his thumbs unsteady.

'There's something else,' Clem said. She glanced at Lucas's mother, a cheeky glint in her eye. 'I kept this as a surprise for you, too, Meredith – because I didn't want to tell you before I told Lucas . . .'

'Told me what?' he said. What else could there be? He already felt winded with the sheer scale of what she'd done for him, his throat feeling thick. He drank a glug of coffee to force the lump down.

'I've been in talks with a publisher – and an agent,' Clem explained, her hands moving wildly as she spoke. There was a happy flush to her cheeks. 'The publisher approached me after the contest about a book deal . . .' She drew in a sharp breath. 'They asked me about doing a cat-themed baking book . . . But I had a better idea, and they loved it so much they put more money on the table. I told them to hold off on contacting you until I could tell you myself, in person . . .'

'A baking book?' Lucas repeated. His mind was repeating the phrase *they put more money on the table* in disbelief.

His mother clapped her hands over her mouth. One of the cats, who had been washing itself nearby on a chair, lifted its head, ears tipped back.

'Oh, Clem!' his mum cried. 'You didn't tell me any of this!'

'I didn't want to say anything until I could speak to Lucas,' Clem explained. 'The idea I put forward was a dog- *and* cat-themed baking book. One that we both contribute to, perhaps with bakes from the contest. They said it was a fantastic idea and they could see it selling really well because of how popular we were on *Whisked Away*. Did you know they had their highest audience numbers ever? Anyway, the publisher says we make . . . What was the phrase they used?' She glanced down at her phone, jabbing at the screen again. '*Dreamy PR*. Here, look at the advance offer they'd make for both of us.' Clem slid the phone across the table towards Lucas until it pinged against his coffee mug.

Lucas looked at the screen and had to swallow again, hard. But the lump didn't go away. His share would be enough for a deposit on a small house if he and his mum combined their incomes and applied together. He knew that – he'd spent enough time obsessing over finances to try to figure out a way to help them over recent weeks and months.

Clem had worked some kind of magic here. She could have accepted a deal for herself, without him, but she'd thought of a way to invite him along, to help him and his family.

'Clem,' he said hoarsely. His mother and father leaned over to look at the email too, and both of them gasped at the numbers.

He wanted to say thank you, but the words didn't feel strong enough to describe what he was feeling. While he fumbled for something more appropriate, his mother jumped to her feet, rounded the table and gave Clem a tearful hug. Clem patted her on the shoulder, smiling, until she drew away and took her seat again.

'For the fundraiser, all you need to do is agree, Mr Bowen, and we can get the funds sent straight to your bank account,' Clem said, all business. 'For the book deal, well, the ball is in your court, Lucas. Will you team up with me?'

The only other options Lucas had been able to come up with involved getting either himself in debt, or his parents getting themselves in debt. And after they'd struggled so much already, that had never seemed like the ideal solution. He couldn't believe she'd done this for them. She'd handed him the perfect solution. And he suddenly felt stupid for making himself stay away from such an incredible woman.

'Clem, of course I will,' he said. He stood up, and because thank you still didn't feel like enough, he leaned across his coffee mug and kissed her.

She tensed, as if surprised he'd done so in front of his parents and the rest of the café, but he didn't care. She kissed him back, and he broke away, dropping into his seat.

'Alright, we didn't need to see that,' his dad said gruffly, and his mum laughed and swatted him on the shoulder.

'Dad,' Lucas prompted. He didn't say anything else, hoping the pleading in his tone was enough – he didn't want to see them struggling anymore. They didn't deserve to.

'Okay,' said his father quietly, and he leaned into the armchair, as if relieving himself of the weight of many, many months and years. Lucas couldn't remember the last time he'd seen him on the brink of tears, but his chin was trembling. 'Okay. Thank you so much, Clem.'

★

The cherry blossom tree outside Catpurrcino no longer sported its beautiful pink flowers, but the delicate leaves were a luminous green now that seemed extra vibrant in the afternoon sun. Lucas was standing outside the café with Clem, to the left of the front entrance, and the foliage shushed over their heads as if calling for quiet. His parents still sat in the window of Catpurrcino, both talking animatedly – wide smiles on their faces. His mum laughed and wiped doughnut jam from his father's cheek with a tissue – they must have ordered more of Clem's treats – and his father laughed right back. When was the last time he'd seen them so happy?

'I don't know how to thank you,' he told Clem, turning to her.

'You don't have to thank me,' she said. 'It was the right thing to do.'

He reached for her hand, pushing his fingers through hers, gripping on tight. Her palms were warm. 'I can't

310

thank you enough. Seriously. And that baking book idea? Genius.'

'Well, it was partly your idea. You joked about a dog-versus-cat comic book. I adapted it to fit a baking book.'

'I'm surprised you remember that!'

She gripped his hand, taking a step closer, until he could smell the strawberry scent on her hair, making him want to reach out and brush it from her face.

'What will you do with your chunk of the advance?' he said. 'Didn't you say you needed to move out of your mum's? And you wanted to start a baking business?'

'I did . . . I do,' she said, nodding, and looking up at the sun bearing down through the trees. Tiny pinpricks of sunshine dappled her face, like flecks of the universe. 'If I'm honest, I'd been saving money anyway. I contribute at home but I've saved up quite a bit.' She inhaled, letting out a deep sigh. 'I kept telling myself it wasn't enough yet. That I wasn't ready. But that was fear and anxiety talking. I think I learned I should . . . have more faith in myself. I did something that scared me, entering *Whisked Away*, and it didn't turn out so badly, did it?'

He smiled softly. 'I agree.'

'I guess I'd forgotten to remind myself that I can handle things.' Clem moved another fraction of a step closer. Close enough to touch. A jolt burst through him, the whisper of her breath on his face.

'Of course you can. Look at everything you've done. And back there? Talking like a true businesswoman?' His lips quirked. 'You'll be amazing. You *are* amazing.' He reached out and tucked a strand of black hair behind her ear, fingertips trailing over the C-shaped curve. 'Everything is okay now, with my family. Thanks to you.'

'Then . . .' She looked unsure and vulnerable. 'What about . . . What about us? I know you said you weren't ready for a relationship before, but that kiss, at the hotel, and in the café . . .' She hitched in a breath, as if she were on pins, waiting for his choice.

He'd thought relationships were a distraction from what mattered, something that would drown you, if you weren't careful. It wasn't true, not when it came to her. With her, he wanted to dive in head-first, submerge himself and never come up for air. *She* mattered to him. And he needed to make that clear to her.

'I guess, like you, it was the fear talking,' he said. 'I want to be with you, Clem. And I'm tired of holding myself back.'

He kissed her – fiercely.

She seemed surprised at first, unmoving, but her arms snaked up around him and she kissed him, pressing herself into him, fingertips skimming his shoulders and pulling him in. She tasted of sugar and icing, and he locked his hands around her waist, hooking his fingers into the belt loops of her shorts. Her mouth moved against his as if they were made to be joined, in tandem, sweet and warm. It made his head spin, made him feel like he'd rushed forward into a sun-kissed sea, shimmering with promise.

When they broke apart, he was breathless – and she was, too. She looked at him, stunned, and held a hand to her face and broke into laughter.

'What?' he said, grinning.

'You have lipstick all over your face. Like a clown.'

'Oh. So do you. Well . . . I can't *possibly* go into Catpurrcino looking like that.' He reeled her in by the belt loops, making her squeal with delight as she pressed up against him.

'Well . . . that *was* the end of my morning shift. So I guess I have to leave, too.' She mock-pouted, the smeared lipstick making it look more adorable. He squeezed her waist.

'Whatever will we do?' he asked.

'I can think of a few things,' she said, and he laughed again.

'I like this side of you,' he told her.

'There are lots of sides of me you don't know yet . . .'

'I'm looking forward to getting to know them,' he said, planting a kiss on her mouth and lingering there.

She slipped her hand into his. The leaves over their heads rustled in a passing breeze, murmuring about the future.

# Epilogue

Sunlight filled the living room as Clem led Lucas inside the cottage she was renting. Reina was dancing along at his heels, her thick golden tail wagging. She'd been so lucky to find this place, and had enough of a deposit and some savings left over to be certain she could cover the rent, even if there was an emergency. They'd also signed the deal for the baking book, so they'd received their advances, and her mind was at ease when it came to affording this place. The walls were cream and white, the main window tall, and she'd hung a set of silky pale gold curtains that shimmered slightly in the light. With some of her prize money from *Whisked Away*, she'd splurged on a lovely plush sofa, scattered with decorative cushions, one of them fox-shaped. She'd also managed to buy a beautiful oak bookshelf from someone online, now filled with some of her favourites – and her baking inspiration scrapbook.

'It's come along in here,' said Lucas, as he took a seat on the sofa and attempted to coax Reina into a state of calm. '*Sit*, girl.' Reina obeyed, plonking herself down beside his legs, tail still swinging from side to side on the wooden flooring.

'Thanks,' said Clem, sitting next to him and snuggling into his side – one of her favourite activities. 'Sorry for the mess,' she added. 'Planning chaos.' Her laptop was wedged on the coffee table and a collection of papers were strewn on the floor and on one arm of the sofa. 'It's a little overwhelming.'

On top of their baking book, there was demand for her baking, too, people reaching out to ask if she could make cakes for weddings and birthdays, or for school events. She'd agreed with Sylvie that she'd reduce her hours, so she could focus on her side projects and building up her own business, although this did mean she'd no longer be alone in the kitchen at the cat café. Sylvie would be bringing on a second person to make up for her reduced hours and Clem needed to teach them some of her recipes.

Lucas squeezed Clem to his side, brushing aside her hair so he could kiss her forehead. Reina nosed his hand, eager to be in on the affection, and he patted her head.

'Remember what an amazing, talented person you are, and that you deserve this,' said Lucas. 'And you'll be alright. I'll be with you the whole way.'

'Aww. Thanks.'

'And if you're ever *not* alright, I've got you.'

'Good,' she said. Clem sighed happily, and Misha strolled into the room to see who the visitor was, her stripy tail high in the air. When she spotted Reina, she sidled across to the dog, sniffing around her paws. Reina kept still – respectfully still, as Lucas had taught her – until Misha sat down. Reina sniffed the top of her head, and Misha nuzzled into it like she would if Clem had scratched her behind the ears.

'I'm so glad they get along. Good girl,' Lucas said, stroking Reina vigorously between her floppy ears. She lifted her head, enjoying the attention.

'You've got her well trained. What did you want to tell me?' Clem asked. He'd messaged her to ask to see her, though they hadn't had plans to meet today – although he'd reassured her it was nothing bad. He apparently had good news to share and she suspected she knew what that might be.

He glanced at Clem and smiled. 'My dad has a diagnosis.'

'He does?'

'Finally, yeah. Rheumatoid arthritis, and they think it was fairly young-onset, which is why he's been struggling for so long. Dad used to put it down to stress or overexertion at work. Then they thought he had fibromyalgia and gave him painkillers.' He shook his head. 'That fall, the dizziness? Down to the RA. We could have been waiting for an answer to this forever, if it weren't for you.'

'I'm glad you have an answer now.'

'He's on new medication for the joint inflammation, different painkillers. Seeing a podiatrist for his feet.' He smoothed Clem's hair down, tracing the lines of her face. 'We obviously can't cure it, but we can manage it better now we know. He keeps calling you his guardian angel.'

She touched his arm. 'I'm glad your family approve of me.'

'I have something else to tell you . . .' He hesitated. Misha leaped up onto the sofa, and he rubbed beneath her chin. Reina watched with shiny brown eyes.

'What is it?' Clem frowned – Lucas's tone suggested this next part wasn't good news.

'You know the fire?'

'Yes? Did they find out how it happened?'

Lucas heaved out a big sigh. 'I didn't want to tell you before. I wanted her to do the right thing.' He explained that Georgina had been smoking behind the tent, that she'd flicked the cigarette butt into the dry grass. He'd confronted her about it because he'd seen her go behind the tent before the fire started. And he'd urged her to come clean.

By the time he was finished, Clem was scowling, a significant shadow cast over her day. 'She did it on purpose? I can't believe her! That's completely—'

'I thought so, at first,' Lucas went on. The words were tight, as if he regretted the accusation now. 'Apparently, there was an oil spill in the grass behind the tent. It came from the generator. Whoever Ronan and the *Whisked Away* crew hired to do the electrics for the contest, they seriously messed up. He might be suing them.'

'How do you know that?'

'Georgina messaged me. She came forward about the cigarette because I told her she should do the right thing.'

Clem exhaled a long breath. 'But she didn't do it on purpose?'

He shook his head. 'No. I feel bad, for thinking it in the first place. It was an unfortunate combination of the oil and the cigarette.'

Clem nodded. 'I never knew she liked you, all that time, you know. She was so cagey about the guy in the bistro, the same one she'd grown up with. Didn't give me any details. Like she wanted to keep you for herself.'

'She did.' He tugged Clem closer, pulling her onto his lap, and she squeaked, giggling as he held on to her waist. Reina pushed her snout towards them, but Lucas told her to lie down, and she obeyed, looking dismayed.

317

'Too bad for her – someone else has me wrapped around her little finger instead. I already told her – it's best we go our separate ways.'

'Are you sure you want to cut her off completely?' Clem asked tentatively, adjusting her position in his lap, hands clasped around his neck. 'You grew up together,' she added. She knew it must be painful to break away from a person who had punctuated so much of your life.

'Yeah,' he said. 'Should have done it a long time ago. As long as we're in each other's lives, she'll never move on from me – and she'll keep trying to pull me towards her. She's going back to London.'

In a way, Clem felt bad for her old friend. At the same time, she thought this was for the best. Over a mere misunderstanding, Genie had caused so much hurt. Moving on from that was the best thing for everyone. Even if Clem wanted to, she didn't think she could mend things with Georgina now, and it would be too awkward now she was seeing Lucas. But perhaps she would ask Lucas for her number, to wish her luck and thank her for doing the right thing.

'Anyway, forget that,' said Lucas, a gruff edge to his voice. He nuzzled into Clem's neck, kissing along the ridges of her throat until he reached her jawline, and making her shudder. '*You* are my focus now.'

'Good,' she said, and allowed him to pepper kisses along her collarbone, 'because I'm all yours.'

# Acknowledgements

I wouldn't be where I am with my writing without my incredible agent, Thérèse Coen, who has been supporting me for such a long time. Thanks to you, readers all over the world get to experience my stories, which is a dream come true. Thanks also to Una McKeown and the rest of the Susanna Lea Associates team for all their help with foreign rights so my stories can travel far and wide. And a big batch of Clem's best cat cookies to all the international publishers who have shown such enthusiasm for Catpurrcino. I had no idea my little cat café would strike such a chord around the world, but I'm so glad it did.

To Cara Chimirri, my editor. Writing a follow-up book was especially daunting, and your enthusiasm and excitement for *Cake Off* meant a lot to me. Thank you for all the insightful editorial ideas, and for being so supportive. To the rest of the Hodder & Stoughton team, thanks so much for coming up with the perfect title for Clem and Lucas's story and making gorgeous little cat-sized books for real-life felines to enjoy.

To Kelley McMorris, I'm in awe of your talent, and so lucky you're bringing Catpurrcino to life with such gorgeous book covers – including a cherry blossom cover of dreams! And a dozen cat doughnuts each to Lucy

Brownhill for the audiobook recordings, and to Helena Newton for copyediting.

As always, I'm so appreciative of the other writers who have been so encouraging to me during my writing journey, both the new faces and the old: Isabella Hunter, Dave McCreery, Molly Aitken, Ian Peek, Dandy Smith, Amita Parikh, Bryony Leah, Karen Legge, and of course Donna Ashcroft and M.A. Kuzniar, who wrote such glowing endorsements of my work. Huge thanks to the 2024 debut group for being such a lovely sounding board before my cat café books were released. In particular, to Eliza Chan, who met with me over coffee and helped me feel more emotionally prepared for being traditionally published, as well as ferrying me around to booksellers. And to Jack Strange, for the mutual support and giving me and Catpurrcino a boost. To all the writers, readers, and freelance editor friends who showed such excitement for the cat café and my traditional publishing journey – your enthusiasm has meant so much to me!

To my incredible husband, Neil, you inspire me to write good men into my books. Thank you for always soothing my worries and making me laugh. Here's to another fifteen years. Many cuddles to our furry felines, past and present, who have no idea that my random keyboard-tapping buys them treats (or that they've inspired me to write cat-themed books). To the rest of my family, I love you all to the moon and back. I don't know what I'd do without such an amazing support system.

Perhaps unsurprisingly, this book was partly inspired by *The Great British Bake Off*. Clem's kitten bun recipe was very loosely based on a bake detailed in *Baking with Kim-Joy*, written by a *Bake Off* finalist.

Final thanks to you, dear readers – for reading my work, tagging me in your lovely reviews and photos, and messaging me to tell me you loved one of my books. I'm so grateful you chose to take a seat at Catpurrcino.

When an unexpected blizzard traps Emmie and Jared in the Catpurrcino café on Christmas Eve, will Jared open up and let Emmie into his heart?

Don't miss the first book in the series,
*Snowed In at the Cat Café*